Town in a Maple Madness

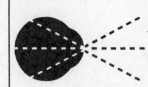

This Large Print Book carries the
Seal of Approval of N.A.V.H.

TOWN IN A
MAPLE MADNESS

B. B. HAYWOOD

WHEELER PUBLISHING

A part of Gale, Cengage Learning

Farmington Hills, Mich • San Francisco • New York • Waterville, Maine
Meriden, Conn • Mason, Ohio • Chicago

GALE
CENGAGE Learning®

LIBRARY OF CONGRESS CATALOGING-IN-PUBLICATION DATA

Names: Haywood, B. B., author.
Title: Town in a maple madness / by B. B. Haywood.
Description: Large print edition. | Waterville, Maine : Wheeler Publishing, 2017. |
    Series: A Candy Holliday murder mystery | Series: Wheeler Publishing large print
    cozy mystery
Identifiers: LCCN 2017009361| ISBN 9781410499400 (softcover) | ISBN 1410499405
    (softcover)
Subjects: LCSH: Holliday, Candy (Fictitious character)—Fiction. |
    Murder—Investigation—Fiction. | Large type books. | GSAFD: Mystery fiction.
Classification: LCC PS3608.A9874 T696 2017 | DDC 813/.6—dc23
LC record available at https://lccn.loc.gov/2017009361

Published in 2017 by arrangement with The Berkley Publishing Group, an imprint of Penguin Publishing Group, a division of Penguin Random House LLC

Printed in Mexico
1 2 3 4 5 6 7 21 20 19 18 17

For James and Matthew,
and for Rick

AUTHOR'S NOTE

It has been an incredible twelve-year journey writing the Candy Holliday Murder Mystery novels. Thanks to all who helped along the way, and with this edition in particular, especially Leis, Jenn, Allison, and Lily at Penguin, all editors extraordinaire; Danielle, Bethany, Katherine, Roxanne, and everyone in the editorial, PR, marketing, design, and production departments at Berkley Prime Crime; the immensely talented Teresa Fasolino for the incredible cover artwork for all the books in the series, and this one in particular, which perfectly captures the essence of the novel; the indispensable Mary A. Cook, whose proofreading skills, eagle eye, story suggestions, musical tastes (thanks to her husband, Joel), and deep knowledge of mystery novels have helped make these better books; Kae and Jon for their help from the start; George and Ruby; Barbara Boltz, the other B. B.; Todd Merrill at Merrill Blueberry Farms in Ellsworth, Maine, for answering numerous questions early on; officers at the Cape Elizabeth (Maine) Police Department, for a tour of a small-town police station; Sheila Connolly for her supportive words; Ellie and Lenora for their continued friendship; Brian Drost for a key character; and R. R. for listening to lengthy ramblings and story ideas. As always, warm wishes for Mat, James, and Noah. And, finally, many, many thanks to the fans, readers, and bloggers who have supported the series from the beginning.

PROLOGUE

He turned his back at the wrong time.

It was the last mistake he would ever make.

His vision flared white-hot as fire exploded in the small of his back and up through his insides. It spread along his arms, his fingers, and the backs of his legs like lightning. His arms stretched out and his entire torso arched forward as if hit by an electric shock, for that is how it felt to him. He shuddered as his breath left him in a grunt. His eyes bugged out, red fireworklike streaks slashing across his vision.

He stumbled forward a step or two, gasping for air, and fell to his knees. Pain shot through his kneecaps and up his thighs as his teeth clattered together. Red-tinged spittle flew from his mouth into the moist riverside air, and he thought he might have bitten his tongue, or suffered a heart attack.

Or perhaps it was something worse. Much worse.

He tried to reach around with one hand to find out what had happened behind him, but he couldn't get his arm to move in that direction, for some reason.

He knew what it was, though — or rather, guessed what it was, since he couldn't turn his head to look back over his shoulder to tell for certain. He'd known of the blade — he'd seen it, even coveted it himself, as others had, since it had a unique history. But he never suspected it would wind up in his back. There were signals all around, but in his arrogance he'd ignored them. He thought he had the upper hand. He thought he had the situation well under control. He thought they'd *agreed* on the whole thing. He never expected any type of retaliation.

My bad, he thought.

It didn't seem real. He'd come up with the plan, put it into action. But the situation had spun out of his control. He'd miscalculated, with lethal consequences. The realization sent a shock wave of panic through him.

He felt a hard push in the center of his back, as if someone had put a foot there and shoved. He was slung forward onto his stomach, his face dropping to the ground.

He hit it with such force that he lost consciousness for a few seconds, or maybe longer, for when he woke he found that his hands and feet were tightly bound together. There was a gag in his mouth. He had a hard time breathing and could barely open his eyes.

Everything after that happened in a haze. He could feel himself being rolled into the net, felt it being wrapped tightly around him. Then he was rolled toward the water. He could hear it lapping against the damp bank. It was downhill, so it was easy to push him in that direction. Pinpoints of light — possibly stars in the sky, possibly reflections on the water, possibly something else — rotated in circles across his corneas. He knew what was happening, and struggled against the net, tried to move his arms and legs. But he was too tightly bound. Escape was impossible.

He entered the water and was set adrift. The river engulfed him, swallowed him whole, pulling him down and into its deep flow. It was so cold it shocked him all over again, making his body stiffen and numbing his brain and muscles and the pain that still coursed through him. As the water folded over him, he squeezed his eyes shut, making gold- and lavender-colored sparkles swirl across the insides of his eyelids. He felt the water rise up his nose and burrow deep into his ears. He dared not take in a breath.

He was facing downward and tried to roll himself around so he could get his mouth and nose above the surface of the water, but the power of the river's grasp was too much for him. It mercilessly dragged him along, and he had little strength left to fight against it, for his lifeblood was flowing out of him, weakening him.

Good thing there aren't any sharks around, he thought, *or I'd be a goner.*

But he knew he was a goner anyway, though he struggled as much as he could right up until the final seconds. Death came violently at first, his body jerking a few times, but right before the darkness took him, there was a moment of peace. A wonderful, blissful moment of peace.

He knew the whole story. He knew it would not end here.

There was still much to be told. The true ending was yet to be written.

But, to his regret and dismay, he knew his part in the story was done. It ended here, deep in the dark, cold waters of the English River, flowing down toward the sea, drifting in a direction that would eventually take

him right past the small coastal village of
Cape Willington, Maine.

13

CANDY'S COMMUNITY CORNER
by Candy Holliday
Special Correspondent

Get Ready for March Madness

So much to talk about, so much going on, and so little space, so I'll be quick!

This year promises to be one of the busiest ever for our little coastal village of Cape Willington. In addition to all of the regular annual community events for which our town is so widely known — including the Lobster Stew Cook-off in May, the Strawberry Fair in June, the Blueberry Festival in July, and the Pumpkin Bash in October — we're adding a new early-spring event called Maple Madness Weekend! It takes place this coming Saturday and Sunday, March 25th and 26th, and it's being held in conjunction with the annual Maine Maple Sunday statewide celebration, which has been going on for years.

Highlights of the weekend will include tours of the town's two sugar shacks — one out at Crawford's Berry Farm, operated by Neil Crawford (with enthusiastic support

14

from his shaggy dog, Random), and the other at the world-famous Sugar Hill Farm, run by Hutch and Ginny Milbright. They'll have their sugar shacks fired up and boiling sap all weekend, so be sure to bring the entire family and stop by for an up-close demonstration of how sugar maple sap becomes maple syrup. You also can pick up bottles of freshly made maple syrup out at the Crawford farm, so be sure to stop in. (I'll be there, so come by the table and say hi!)

But that's just the beginning of the weekend's festivities. For the first time ever, the town will play host to a trendy "pop-up" temporary restaurant — in this case, fittingly, a family-friendly pancake house, located in the brand spanking new English River Community Center, down at River Walk Plaza (formerly known as Warehouse Row, of course). As you've no doubt heard, that area of town is currently undergoing a renovation, thanks in part to a grant from the Pruitt Family Foundation, which is funding the town's new River Walk project (more on that in the next issue).

The Maple Madness Weekend will also include a Maple Marshmallow Roast and Community Bonfire on Saturday night in Town Park, with plenty of food booths, activities, and live music, and a Maple Scavenger Hunt on Sunday afternoon. Plus, you can enjoy specially prepared maple dishes and foods all weekend at the village's many fine and casual dining establishments (see below). We're expecting a big crowd for this one, and the whole town is pitching in to help out. No tickets are required; just dress warmly and have fun!

Out Like a Lamb?

We all know how unpredictable March weather can be here in Down East Maine. It certainly came in like a lion, with plenty of bluster, but I think (hope?) that we're in the lion *cub* part of March now. (Winter has to end sometime — am I right, people?) At least it's warmer during the day, which is good for humans and good for the maple trees, as it gets the sap (and the blood) flowing. We hear it's been a pretty good year so far for our local maple syrup producers, so let's continue to support them. And keep your fingers crossed for good weather this weekend!

Here's Mud in your Tires

I'm sure I don't have to remind you, but it's M-U-D season here on the cape. So watch out when you're driving on those long dirt driveways, lanes, and back roads, which can easily turn into rivers of muck at this time of year. The other day I was chatting with local landscaper Mick Rilke, and he reminded me of the three most important things you need to keep in mind to successfully navigate the cape's muddy roads at this time of year. Mick should know, so here they are:

1. In snow, drive slow; in mud, drive as fast as you can.
2. Stay in the ruts when possible — unless you're going sideways, in which case . . .
3. Hitch up the horses.

Thanks for the pointers, Mick! But seriously, folks, be careful out there. Early spring can easily fool you, as all true Mainers know, so don't be its latest victim!

A Fabulous Weekend for Foodies

Okay, back to the food. Restaurants all around town will be cooking up special dishes for this weekend's celebration. Here's a tasty sampling. (Warning: Extreme hunger may occur while reading!)

For starters, our good friends at the Black Forest Bakery, Herr Georg and "Frau"

Maggie Wolfsburger, will be whipping up some supremely scrumptious Chocolate Maple Brownies. I've sampled them, and they're heavenly. You have to stop by and try a few!

Dolores Kilborne at Duffy's Main Street Diner tells me they'll be going all out with Maple Glazed Sausages. Made from their own secret recipe, the sausages will be hand grilled on maple sticks over a roasting flame. You know there will be a long line around the block for those! That'll give the guys at the public works department something to talk about!

Over at the Rusty Moose Tavern, they'll be serving up Maple Burgers all weekend, accompanied by a side of Maple Glazed Onion Rings. Of course, there's always good company at the tavern (and plenty of salty stories) to enjoy with your burger, rings, and beer.

Melody's Cafe will serve up freshly baked Maple Banana Bread and Maple Drop Cookies, made with generous amounts of maple syrup. Melody has outdone herself once again! And Phil, the manager over at Village Pizza, tells me he's putting together a special Maple and Bacon Flatbread Pizza. Maple syrup and bacon together on a pizza? Absolutely brilliant!

While it's too early in the season to open up the Ice Cream Shack, Lyra Graveton informs me that she'll be manning (or wom-anning?) a booth at the marshmallow roast, where she'll serve up scoops of Maple S'more Ice Cream. For the record, that's maple ice cream with marshmallow and chocolate swirls in a graham cracker cone. Did I mention brilliant? Yum!

On a tonier note, the Lightkeeper's Inn will be pulling out all the stops this weekend with a full Maple Feast, complete with Maple Glazed Ham coated with maple-roasted nuts and a drizzle of maple syrup. It will be served with Maple Mashed Potatoes, Maple Glazed Carrots, and Maple Biscuits. That's truly a maple feast!

Also, at the marshmallow roast and throughout the weekend, vendors in Town Park and along Ocean Avenue will be sell-ing maple cinnamon buns, maple granola bars, maple-glazed doughnuts, and much more.

In addition, the Pruitt Public Library will host a special showing of maple-themed paintings by local artists all week. And at a Saturday morning workshop held at the Lightkeeper's Inn, Chef Colin Trevor Jones will show you how to make your own maple cream candies! So plan for a very sweet (and very sticky!) weekend of noshing!

The Bosworth Report

Closed for the season. (Judicious is in hibernation; he should reappear by early May. We'll keep you posted on any sightings, which are extremely rare at this time of year.)

ONE

"I think," said Hutch Milbright in a low, confidential tone, "that somebody's been stealing my sap."

"Your sap?" Candy Holliday flicked her cornflower blue eyes toward him and tilted her head inquisitively. "What, you mean from your maple trees?"

"That's it exactly." Hutch jabbed a thick, callused farmer's finger in the air for emphasis and leaned in so close she could smell the onion bagel he'd had for lunch on his breath. He was a man in his late fifties, burly and dark haired, with a florid face and a scruffy beard. He wore overalls and had a toothpick dangling loosely from one corner of his mouth. He tossed the toothpick around with his tongue periodically as he talked.

"I got this sugar bush — that's this cluster of sugar maple trees, you know — out on the back side of the southwest ridge, over by the Crawford place." He waved a hand in a general westerly direction. "You know the area I'm talking about. Some pretty good producers. Valuable little grove. Anyway, I was out there this morning with the tank wagon to collect the sap from those trees, and the whole bunch of 'em got multiple taps in them. Four or even five in some trees. I couldn't believe it! As you probably know, you can do up to three taps in some of the bigger trees, but never four or five. Personally, I never do more than two taps per tree, but there they were, all these trees with four or five taps in them. And these are big taps too." He held up a thick thumb and forefinger, a fair distance apart. "Regular taps are five-sixteenths of an inch, maybe seven-sixteenths, tops. But these are nearly an inch. Triple the regular width. I got some photos on my phone to prove it. Looks like a professional job. Someone who knew what they were doing. Practically milked the trees dry."

Hutch paused a moment to let that thought sink in. His mouth grew tight, and he squinted at her. "Some of them might not survive."

Candy wasn't sure if he meant the trees or the sap thieves, but guessed it was the former — or possibly both. "But why would anyone want to do that?" She'd heard of people stealing sap from sugar maple trees on land that didn't belong to them — she'd read an article about it in the Portland Sunday paper a few years back — but never thought it would happen in their sleepy little village.

Then again, you never really knew what your fellow villagers were up to, did you? She'd learned that lesson a number of times, in often surprising ways, over the past few years. Some in this coastal community could be quite devious and secretive, and at times, even murderous.

"It must be for the money, is all we can think of," said Hutch's wife, Ginny. She was a sensible, rustic-looking woman, in faded jeans, a dark-colored hooded sweatshirt, and big mud-stained boots. Wispy strands of uncombed brown hair framed her flat, weathered face. She had a working person's hands, with large knuckles and unpolished nails, and watchful eyes. She stood a little stiffly in a small circle with her husband and Candy, shuffling her feet nervously as the three of them spoke.

They were just outside the Milbrights' sugar shack, which was not in operation today. Candy had been here on other days when it was going full blast, though, and she recalled catching the aroma of the sweet-smelling steam that emanated from the building's cupola and swirled into the air around them. She missed it today.

"You can make a lot of money with stolen sap," Hutch was saying, and he nodded his head for emphasis. "But I don't have to tell *you* what maple syrup is going for these days, do I?"

Indeed, he didn't. Candy often helped with the maple sugaring operation at Crawford's Berry Farm, run by her good friend Neil Crawford. She'd been out there several times over the past week, helping him collect and boil sap from his own trees. It was something she'd been doing for the past few years. She didn't get paid for the work, but she got a few free gallons of maple syrup out of the deal, enough to last the year, with some left over to give away to friends. Considering maple syrup retailed for forty to sixty dollars a gallon or more at the grocery store, it was decent payment for her efforts. Plus, Neil helped out at her own farm, Blueberry Acres, whenever he was needed, so her efforts were reciprocated. And she just enjoyed doing it, since the flowing sap in the sugar maples was among the first signs that winter was almost over and spring was on its way.

24

But her thoughts weren't on spring right now. They were on illegally tapped maple sugar trees. And sugar shacks.

Besides the Milbrights, Neil owned the only other maple sugar shack on the cape.

She knew what they were implying.

"You think Neil had something to do with this?"

"Well, he's the only other person around with an operation to turn sap into syrup, isn't he?" Ginny pointed out.

"Makes sense he might want to increase his profits at the expense of someone else, especially a competitor with a farm so close to his," added Hutch, and he nodded toward his wife. "That's why we decided to talk to you first, before we went to the police."

"The police?" This caught Candy off guard. "But Neil would never do anything like that. He has plenty of sap of his own. Besides, maple sugaring is just a seasonal activity for him. He makes his real money from the strawberry fields."

"Nevertheless, everyone can use a little extra bump in their bank account these days, can't they? Whoever tapped those trees will get at least a few batches out of it — and it's close to the end of the season, so it's the premium stuff." Hutch grimaced, as if it pained him to have to spell it out for her. "I'm sure there's a simple explanation, Candy. Maybe he thought those trees were on his own land. Maybe he just got turned around in the woods somehow. Or maybe he'd been smoking something funny when he tapped those trees. Makes no difference to me. He just needs to stop it, and stay on his own land. So you need to have a talk with him."

"We don't want no trouble," Ginny added with a sour expression. Her arms were crossed loosely in front of her. "We just want it to end. We won't even ask for restitution. If it stops, we'll just let it go, no hard feelings."

"That's right. No hard feelings," Hutch echoed, though he seemed uncertain as he said it.

"We've had a few things go wrong around here lately," Ginny revealed, with a shift of her eyes. "We can't afford to lose that money. It's been a rough time for us, and, well . . ."

"We don't need to add to it with whatever shenanigans Neil Crawford might be up to," Hutch finished for her.

"Shenanigans? But . . . but . . ." Candy sputtered for a moment, uncertain of how to respond. "I'm sure he didn't have anything to do with those trees."

26

"Maybe not, but he's the most obvious suspect, isn't he?" asked Ginny. Her gaze had narrowed and her jaw was firmly set as she waited for a response.

Candy hesitated to admit that the other woman was probably correct in her assumption — if what they were saying about the tapped trees was true. But Candy still had a hard time believing Neil Crawford was involved with this in any way. It must be a mistake of some sort.

Still, the Milbrights had a reputation for causing a ruckus around town whenever things didn't go their way. Especially Hutch, who could become quite cantankerous when he got worked up about something. And it was common knowledge that Ginny knew how to rile him up, egg him on, though always behind the scenes, rarely in public. He was the outfront person; she was the brain behind the scenes.

They could be an unpredictable couple. They had lots of ties around town. It would be a mistake to let this get out of hand.

Against her better judgment, Candy nodded toward Hutch's pocket. "You said you have photos?"

It took him a few moments to react, but with a nod and a "Yeah, yeah," he pulled out his phone and started punching at the screen. He cursed at it a couple of times, and Ginny tried to talk him through the process of bringing up the photo app. "I hate these newfangled things," he grumbled a time or two, but finally he figured it out and held out the phone toward Candy.

There were perhaps half a dozen images. She flicked through them quickly. Hutch must have had an unsteady hand and a questionable photographer's eye, because most of the images were blurry or badly lit or off-center. But one or two showed what appeared to be large, freshly drilled holes in the tree trunks. A few had makeshift plastic or stainless steel spiles — hollow pegs a couple of inches long, similar to a spigot or spout — still tapped into them, but most were just raw, gaping holes in the tree bark. The collection buckets, whatever form they'd taken, were gone.

She scrolled back through the pictures, taking a closer look at each image. "What about footprints?" she asked, her attention still focused on the phone's screen.

"Footprints?"

She glanced up at Hutch. "Yeah, did you look around to see if you could find any sort of clue as to who might have done this?"

Hutch shrugged. "I didn't think to do that," he said.

Candy nodded and handed the phone back to him. "Anyone with a drill and some hardware from Gumm's Hardware Store could have tapped those trees," she said. "You don't even need anything from there. You could just use PVC plastic tubing for something like that. And plastic milk containers for collection buckets. It's some high school kids, probably, as a prank. Or maybe someone who just wanted to make a small batch of syrup."

"You might be right," Hutch said as he slipped the phone back into his pocket, "but there's something else. Late yesterday afternoon, while I was out working on the northwest side, I caught sight of a red vehicle out through the trees. It must have been on that dirt access road that runs along the conservation land at the back of the property. Not many people use that road, you know. It's pretty muddy right now, since the thaw's under way. Easy to get stuck out there with nobody around. That's why it caught my attention. Who could be driving back there at this time of year? I wondered." His gaze focused in tightly on her. "I seem to recall your boyfriend drives a red car, right?"

"Neil? He's not my boyfriend, but . . ."

Abruptly she stopped.

29

Hutch was right. Neil drove an old red Saab station wagon.

Candy paused a moment, glancing from one Milbright to the other as she tried to focus her thoughts. "But why me?" she asked finally. "Why get me involved? Why don't you just talk to Neil yourselves?"

"Well, for several reasons — one being, like I said, he's your boyfriend."

Candy took a quick breath and was about to protest again, but Hutch held up a hand and pressed on before she could respond. "But that's not the only reason. It's also because you're our local problem and mystery solver, aren't you?" He gave her an assured smile that told her he'd already thought this through. "We've been talking about it, Ginny and me, about what to do, and you have experience in these areas — chasing down the clues, flushing out the culprit, that sort of thing. You can get to the bottom of this fast. Besides, I'd get too confrontational if I talked to him myself. Just my nature. I'm not trying to make any enemies."

"We're good people," Ginny assured her. "We don't want to cause no trouble. I'm sure you understand that, Candy. We just want these taps to stop."

"Gin's right. We just want it to stop —

30

before it gets out of hand, and I go over there myself and introduce him to the business end of my fist," Hutch concluded.

He made the last statement in such an easygoing manner that Candy wasn't sure if he meant it or not. But his smile had disappeared, and there was a faintly menacing look in his eyes.

Probably best not to take a chance. Best not to let this thing escalate more than it already had.

Still, the last thing she wanted was to get involved in a local dispute over tapped trees. That was a definite puddle of mud. Easy to get stuck in something like that. She had too much else to do.

Candy had been in the kitchen at Blueberry Acres, rinsing off the breakfast dishes earlier that morning, when Ginny had called. Candy had hoped to quickly finish her chores, dash out of the house, run a few errands, maybe even stop at the local garden center before heading into town for a community event at the riverfront. But her plans had been put on hold when she got the call from Ginny, who asked if she could stop by Sugar Hill Farm as soon as possible to talk about something important. "Something *very* important," Ginny had emphasized over the phone, her voice edged with concern. "You could say it's an urgent matter. When can you get over here?"

Candy had hesitated. She knew how the Milbrights could talk. It might be difficult to extricate herself from a conversation with them once it started. Besides, what could they possibly want to talk to her about? She'd spent the better part of an afternoon with them just a couple of weeks ago, interviewing them for an article she'd been writing for the town's weekly newspaper, the *Cape Crier,* and discussing their plans for Maple Madness Weekend, which started tomorrow, on Saturday morning. But she'd finished and submitted the article a week ago. It was already published, running in the paper's current edition. She'd also mentioned them in her column this week, as a friendly gesture to give them some extra publicity. But the paper had gone to press. It was out on the streets today — too late to add or change anything. There didn't seem to be much point in talking to them right now.

Standing in her kitchen, hands still damp from doing the dishes, Candy had weighed her response, considering the pros and cons, but in the end, curiosity got the better of her. Ginny had said it was urgent, so Candy decided to give the other woman the benefit of the doubt.

Just to keep the peace. And to find out what was going on.

"I'll be there in twenty minutes," she had told Ginny.

Once she'd arrived at their place, the Milbrights had been personable enough, at first. But as the three of them walked from the driveway out past the barn to the sugar shack around back, the small talk had slipped away, and Ginny's tone had turned more serious as she told Candy how hard they'd worked to get the place ready for the upcoming weekend's festivities, and how much time they'd put into collecting and boiling sap over the past few days, and stacking firewood, only to have *this* happen. That's when Hutch had told her about the tapped trees.

Now they were both watching her, waiting for some sort of response. She had to tell them something. They didn't look like they were about to let her off the hook.

"Is all of this really *that* serious?" she asked finally, still trying to find a way to wiggle out of the middle of a potentially sticky situation.

"There's a sap thief running around Cape Willington," Hutch said, his hardened expression an indication that he was unwilling to give ground. "That's pretty serious, especially if it gets in the way of this weekend's events — or escalates, if you know what I mean."

Candy sighed. She knew what he meant. She also knew she didn't have much of a choice.

"All right," she told them, making no attempt to hide the reluctance in her voice. "I'll see what I can find out."

"Today," Hutch said. "We can't let this thing drag on."

"It's got to be nipped in the bud," Ginny added crisply.

"Right. Nipped in the bud." Candy nodded, looked from face to face, and sighed. "Okay. Today."

Two

As she drove away from their farm, Candy wasn't quite sure what to make of her encounter with Hutch and Ginny Milbright. What they'd told her had been unexpected, to say the least, and puzzling. She couldn't stop thinking about some shadowy tree tapper who might be lurking in the woods around Cape Willington, causing trouble with a cordless drill, a hammer, and some plastic buckets.

Possibly someone who drove a red vehicle, glimpsed through the trees by Hutch, out on a muddy back road behind the Milbrights' property.

Candy had never been on that particular road, but she'd been on others like it, numerous times. They had a long dirt lane out at Blueberry Acres they had to contend with, and Neil had one at his place as well. Dirt roads like theirs were ubiquitous in New England. They were as common as

35

maple trees and stone walls. In fact, there were probably more unpaved roads on the cape than paved ones. They crisscrossed the landscape like veins in a leaf. A lot of them led out to isolated farmhouses or fields, to secret spots on the coastline, or along conservation land, or around ponds and along streams, or simply connected the major paved roads to one another. Some were single lane, others were double — and all of them could become rivers of mud and muck at this time of year.

Candy and her father, Henry "Doc" Holliday, took good care of their lane at Blueberry Acres. They'd raised it slightly where they could to improve drainage and minimize the mud, and Neil did the same. But a dirt road was a dirt road. At times it could become impassable, no matter what you did to it, especially during fast thaws in the spring, when the days were warming but the nights were still cold. She knew, as all locals did, to avoid dirt roads as much as possible at this time of year, and travel on them only when you absolutely had to.

So why would Neil have been driving on that back road late yesterday afternoon? Why would *anyone,* she thought, drive on that road at this time of year? Where did it lead? she wondered. Where did it originate, and where did it terminate?

She had no real reason to doubt the truth of Hutch's story. Judging by the photos on his phone, the taps looked authentic — and fresh, if she was any judge of these sorts of things. But if that was true, if the illegal taps did exist, who could have put them there?

Certainly not Neil. She didn't have to think twice before she ruled him out — despite the fact that he drove a red car. It just wasn't something he would do. It was too out of character for him. He was one of the most honest and generous people she knew — though she could understand why the Milbrights were suspicious of him. The two farms were, after all, competitors of a sort. She'd heard grumbles before from the Milbrights, who thought Neil was siphoning off some of their potential profits by running his own sugar shack just a few miles from theirs.

But if not Neil, then who? Who would be so desperate to steal someone else's sap? And for what purpose? Was money the real motivation — or was there some other reason behind the taps?

It could have been done by someone completely random, she thought — a vagrant, a transient, or, as she'd told the Milbrights, just some teenage kids out on a lark.

But what it if had been something more? Something deliberate? An act committed with some specific purpose in mind?

As she drove toward town, her gaze swept the surrounding landscape. She half expected the alleged sap thief to step out of the woods lining the road right in front of her, conveniently carrying a bucket of sap. Caught red-handed — or sticky-handed. It would, at the very least, be a quick resolution to this new mystery. But, of course, as she drove on, that didn't happen.

She sighed. She was already letting her imagination run away with her — never a good thing, especially in these circumstances. But she felt conflicted, uncertain of what to do.

At least, she thought with a swell of hope as she stared out the windshield, the weather was improving. The past week or two had been cold, damp, and overcast, but the day was clearing and the air was drying out, thanks to a southerly wind. Billowy, fast-moving clouds swept across the sky in front of her, paralleling the coast. She had the side window cracked open, and the air blowing into the cabin felt almost balmy, though it was barely above forty degrees. The snow was mostly gone, except for lingering patches way back in the woods, and the ground was warming, giving off that unmistakable fresh scent of early spring.

All in all, typical for late March, and not a bad day at all.

Ideal, in fact, for the community event she was headed to this morning. It was taking place at the old warehouse, dock, and boat-building complex along the English River, a run-down collection of creaky, century-old buildings commonly known as Warehouse Row, close to Cape Willington's downtown business district. The village leaders were unveiling a new facility today, dubbed the English River Community Center, just in time for the upcoming weekend's festivities. It was located in an old reclaimed and remodeled warehouse, and was part of a larger community project called River Walk, an extension of the already existing Ocean Walk, a winding bench- and flower-lined gravel pathway that began at the lighthouse and meandered southward along the ocean-front to the Lobster Shack, a popular tour-ist destination. In addition to the just-completed community center renovation, long-term plans called for new shops, restaurants, and art galleries in the ware-house and marina area, which had been rechristened River Walk Plaza. It was an at-tempt to revitalize that area of the village,

and was one of the most buzzed-about top-
ics of the year.

Candy didn't want to miss the community
center's big reveal, which was scheduled to
take place at eleven, just a short time from
now.

Things were happening in town. A big
crowd was expected for the unveiling. She'd
planned to meet her friend Maggie
Wolfsburger there. She knew she should
head in that direction.

But she was torn.

She couldn't get the illegal tree tapper out
of her mind. For one thing, the timing
seemed so odd, just days before a
community-wide maple-related event this
weekend. And the location of the taps didn't
make sense. Everyone in town knew about
Hutch Milbright's reputation for having a
short fuse and going after those he thought
had wronged him or Ginny. Why would
someone risk tapping trees on his land,
knowing what he was capable of? If you're
going to tap trees illegally, why not do it
someplace else, on a farm where the owner
wasn't quite so unpredictable — at Neil's
place, for instance? If someone had tapped
his trees, he might not have even noticed, or
cared much if he did. His commercial
operation was much more low-key than the

Milbrights', who relied a lot on maple syrup sales for their annual income.

So why would someone purposely steal their sap and rile them up like that?

The more she thought about it, the more something smelled fishy to her.

As she came to a stop at an intersection with the southern branch of the Coastal Loop, she checked her watch. Ten twenty. Forty minutes until the unveiling of the new community center down at the warehouses. Not too far away. No more than ten minutes from here.

She had thirty minutes to spare. Enough time to make a quick stop, if she hurried.

She looked first one direction, then the other, before turning the steering wheel to the right, away from town, and toward Crawford's Berry Farm.

Might as well nip this thing in the bud as quickly as she could.

THREE

That was the plan, at least. But when she pulled into the unpaved parking area in front of the house at Crawford's Berry Farm, climbed out of the Jeep, and looked around, she realized her hope for a quick resolution was in jeopardy, as there was no one around to talk to.

Neil Crawford was nowhere to be seen. Neither was his big shaggy dog, Random, who certainly would have greeted her with enthusiasm if he'd been in the general vicinity.

Their absence wasn't unusual, especially at this time of year. They were often off in the woods beyond the far edge of the strawberry fields, collecting sap, gathering the last of the season's firewood, or just out chasing squirrels and cracking off the remaining ice crusts along the banks of meandering streams and from around big wet boulders.

It was probably something like that, Candy mused as she walked toward the farmhouse. She climbed onto the porch and rapped on the front door, but wasn't surprised when no one answered. Neil wasn't the type of guy to hang around the house on a day like this, with the weather improving. He'd be out somewhere on the property, taking care of one project or another. There was always work to be done around a farm, no matter the time of year.

Hands tucked into the front pockets of her yellow fleece jacket, which she'd left mostly unzipped today, Candy climbed down off the porch and walked around the side of the house. Her gaze promptly swung left, toward the maple sugaring shack at one side of the fields.

The sugar shack had one specific purpose — to turn the sap of sugar maple trees into syrup. A small, wood-framed, rustic building half tucked into the woods, it looked as if it had been on this land for a century or more, like something from a Rockwell painting or a Currier and Ives print. But Neil had helped build it himself, only a few decades earlier, along with his father, older brother, and other members of the Crawford family not too long after they bought the place, when Neil was in high school. They'd

43

been upgrading the sugar shack ever since, and Neil had continued the practice after his father's unexpected death a few years earlier. The shack housed an evaporator as well as various large pots and pans, skimmers and scoopers, worktables and shelving, a place to stack buckets, an area for filtering and bottling the sap, pot holders, ladles, a few chairs, and the general detritus that gathers around a work area.

It didn't look like it was in operation today. The door was closed, and no curls of smoke sprouted from the upper cupola at the center of the building. So Neil wasn't in there boiling sap right now. He might be out collecting it, though. The tractor and the sap-collecting cart it pulled, usually parked along one side of the sugar shack, were gone, she noticed.

Her gaze shifted out across the stubby strawberry fields toward the far tree line. So Neil and Random were out in the woods somewhere, probably collecting sap. She studied the landscape, searching for any signs of them. She had a vague idea where Neil's tapped sugar maple trees were located, but there were several clusters of them in various directions. It would take her an hour or more to search for Neil and Random in those woods — something she

44

didn't have time for right now.

Instead, she pulled out her phone and tried to call Neil. But as she suspected, he didn't pick up. He rarely carried his phone with him when he was working in the fields or walking back in the woods, leaving it on the counter in the kitchen or on a windowsill in the living room to buzz happily away, unanswered. She waited for it to ring a few times and ended the call without leaving a message.

She held her breath for several moments and listened intently, hoping to catch the low rattling hum of the tractor's motor, or just the vibrations of it echoing through the woods. She thought she heard a distant rumble a time or two, carried on the wind, and maybe even a few barks, but it was hard to determine from which direction the sounds had come. The wind seemed to keep shifting around, mixing everything up. And, she thought, it could just be the typical sounds of nature. It was hard to tell.

On a last-ditch effort she held up a hand to her mouth, called out to them loudly several times, and turned an ear toward the woods. But there was no response. The sounds she'd heard earlier were gone. If Neil and Random were out there, they were moving away from her, deeper into the woods. They could be gone for a while.

She considered leaving a note but decided to just call Neil later on. He was usually back at his house around lunch-time. She'd give him a buzz then, or maybe swing by again sometime in the afternoon.

As she walked back toward her Jeep, she passed Neil's red Saab wagon, parked near the barn, and couldn't help pausing to take a quick look at it. It was, after all, implicated in an alleged theft. It bore checking out. But she didn't want to seem like she was snooping. She was just being thorough, she told herself. And she was curious. She might find something that would prove the Milbrights wrong — or, at least, hopefully not right.

The wagon was essentially Neil's work vehicle, just as Candy's Jeep was for her. On quick inspection, glancing through the windows, she found that it was filled with all the expected items — bags of sand, tire chains and snow shovels, jackets and snow boots, and various crates and boxes of stuff. And tools of all kinds. But no drill, as far as she could see. That, at least, gave her a moment of relief.

She checked outside the vehicle, around the wheel wells and down on the undercarriage, but saw no excessive splatters or dried dirt patterns that might indicate Neil had driven recently on the muddy road behind the Milbrights' place. Nothing that was out of the norm. Like her, he drove on dirt or muddy roads all the time. He often took the Saab back into the strawberry fields. There was no real way to determine whether he'd been on that back road yesterday, and she saw nothing specific to indicate that he indeed had.

Again, a brief feeling of relief. At least there was nothing obvious to connect Neil to the activity of which he'd been accused.

In fact, now that she thought about it, she wondered if she'd have been able to broach the subject with Neil even if he was here. The whole thing suddenly seemed far-fetched — the idea that Neil would have tapped the Milbrights' maple trees, for whatever reason. There must be some other explanation. Or it was just some sort of mistake.

Still, she knew she couldn't completely dismiss the Milbrights' concerns — not right now, at least, not until she learned more. If what they'd told her was true, and she was convinced Neil had nothing to do with it, then *someone else* must have tapped those trees — someone who possibly drove a red vehicle. Someone who might have been out on that road yesterday. Someone who might know what was going on.

She'd been gazing absently out toward the fields and woods, but at this last thought she turned back toward Neil's Saab wagon. It was an old vehicle. The red paint job had faded quite a bit over the years. There was some rust around the wheel wells. It wasn't the type of car that stood out in a crowd, or in a forest. That was for sure. It probably hadn't been washed in years. Would it even be noticeable out on a back dirt road, seen through the trees? More than likely, it would blend into the landscape like a deer.

So, if she assumed that it hadn't been Neil in his Saab, then who could it have been?

Who else around town drove a red vehicle?

It was an intriguing question, and got her mind working in a different direction.

Right off the top of her head, she could think of several people who fit the bill.

Mick Rilke, a local landscaper, for one. She'd talked to him just a couple of weeks ago, when he'd given her pointers for driving on muddy roads. He'd made her laugh. When they'd talked, he'd been in his red snowplow truck, which he drove during the winter season. As a landscaper, he'd certainly know something about tapping trees.

Anita Weller, a teacher at the village's

elementary school, drove a red Volkswagen Beetle, Candy remembered, and Paige Booker, who worked at Hatch's Garden Center, darted around in a small red hatchback. Paige had always been helpful and knowledgeable, and respectful of plants. Not the type of person to illegally tap maple trees — though she'd probably have some knowledge about those sorts of things, just like Mick did.

And there were others who could be involved, Candy thought. Wanda Boyle, managing editor of the *Cape Crier,* drove a big SUV, which was maroon in color but could be mistaken for a red vehicle. With its big tires and big engine, it could easily navigate that muddy back road. And local gift shop owner Malcolm Stevens Randolph tooled around town in a small red sports car — when the weather was decent, which it hadn't been recently. He tended to keep his vehicle spotless. She couldn't imagine him driving on anything but a paved road, unless absolutely necessary.

There were undoubtedly others, but those were all she could recall at the moment. As she turned and started toward her Jeep, she went back over the list in her mind.

Mick Rilke. An interesting character — and definitely a possible suspect. He was a big man and a hard worker who always got the job done and treated people fairly, but he also could be gruff at times, and overly boisterous at others. During her limited encounters with him, though, she'd always found him to be quite personable and humorous.

Mick, she knew, owned two trucks. During late spring, throughout the summer, and into the fall, he usually drove his gray landscaping truck, which was a fixture around town. But when the weather grew colder, he switched to his seasonal job, plowing snow for homeowners and private businesses. For that, he used an old red pickup he'd bought a few years back. By changing vehicles, he didn't have to detach the plow and restock his truck for his summer job as the weather warmed, and do the opposite in the fall.

A snowplow truck like Mick's, she thought, was often equipped with chains, though those were installed mostly during blizzards and ice storms. She doubted he currently had the chains on. But, like Wanda, he easily could have navigated the muddy road behind the Milbrights' place in his truck.

Could he have tapped those trees? It was certainly a possibility. He probably had all

50

the right equipment, though you didn't need much more than a drill, a hammer, a few stainless steel or plastic spiles, and a bunch of buckets. He was usually all over town. He could have ventured onto that back road, and onto the Milbrights' property, at just about any time, and no one would have ever known or seen him.

But for what purpose? Mick could be a little over the top at times, but she'd never thought of him as a troublemaker. Why would he go onto someone else's land and tap their maple trees?

It was a question she could ask about any of the others around town who drove red vehicles, all of whom seemed increasingly unlikely to have anything to do with this alleged theft. Wanda Boyle, for instance, was not the type of person to go hiking through the woods, though she camped out occasionally with her family. Anita Weller? Paige Booker? Malcolm in his little red sports car?

Candy shook her head. She couldn't picture any of them back in the woods, illegally tapping trees.

She'd reached the Jeep and was just about to jump into the driver's seat when her cell phone buzzed in her back pocket. She pulled it out and checked the screen.

It was a call from Maggie Wolfsburger, her best friend. Formerly known as Maggie Tremont, she'd married Herr Georg Wolfsburger, proprietor of the Black Forest Bakery, in a memorable ceremony out at Blueberry Acres last year. Now many around town had taken to calling her Frau Maggie, though Candy still called her friend by the abbreviated nickname she'd used for years.

"Hey, Mags, what's up?" Candy asked.

Maggie sounded oddly breathless. "I'm so glad I got hold of you. Where are you? I don't see you around. Are you here? You're missing it!"

Maggie, she knew, was at the new community center, where they were supposed to meet. Candy glanced at her watch. Ten forty-five. The event was scheduled for eleven. She still had time.

"Missing what? The ceremony hasn't started yet, has it?" Using her other hand, she pulled car keys out of her front pocket and, climbing into the vehicle, inserted a key into the ignition and started the engine.

"No, that's not it." Maggie paused, her voice trailing off as she was momentarily distracted by someone who had shouted nearby. Candy heard the shout through the phone.

52

"What's going on there?" she asked as she pulled the driver's side door closed, snapped her seat belt into place, and pulled the gearshift lever into drive. She feathered the gas pedal and swung the Jeep around in a wide arc.

"It's chaos here," Maggie said, her attention back on the conversation. "You won't believe it."

"Why? What won't I believe?"

"I know it sounds crazy, after all we've been through in this town, but it's happened again," Maggie said, and in a rush of words, she added, "It's Mick Rilke. That landscaper guy? He's the one this time. At least, that's what they're saying."

Candy felt an odd tingle at the back of her neck. She held the phone a little more tightly to her ear. "Who's *they*? The one what? And what are they saying about him?"

"Well, he's gone."

"Gone where?"

"Gone. You know. Permanently." Maggie stammered around as if searching for another word. Then, bluntly, she said, "He's dead. Apparently something happened to him."

"What?" Candy slowed the Jeep as her stomach lurched. "Say that again. What happened?"

"Mick Rilke is dead," Maggie repeated. "At least, that's what I've heard. I don't know for sure. They just found his body. It was floating in the river. It went past the docks and someone spotted it right before it went out to sea. Like I said, crazy, right?"

"Crazy, indeed," Candy said. She felt suddenly lightheaded, but she gunned the engine anyway. "Hang on, I'm on my way. I'll be there in ten minutes."

FOUR

The landscape whizzed past the side windows as she tried to comprehend what she'd just heard.

Mick Rilke? Really?

Was it possible? Was it true? The whole idea seemed, at the very least, utterly unbelievable, even surrealistic.

Just moments earlier she'd been thinking about him, considering him a suspect in the alleged sap theft. Now, according to Maggie, his body had been found floating in the English River.

What had happened to him? How had he wound up in the river? Had he drowned somehow? Or had he already been dead when he entered the water?

Candy didn't want to let herself jump to *that* conclusion just quite yet. But Maggie was right. It *was* crazy.

Was his death accidental? Or was it something . . . worse?

She hoped that, whatever had happened to him, it *had* been accidental, though she knew that might sound callous. But then the villagers could mourn him, eulogize him, talk about how much they missed him around town, and eventually move on. That's probably what had happened, she told herself. Some unfortunate circumstance had tripped him up and cost him his life. After all, there was no real reason, no evidence, to assume it had been anything else.

But she also felt his sudden death was too coincidental to ignore, after what she'd just learned.

Could he have been involved in tapping the maple trees at the Milbrights' place? Had he been driving his red truck on the dirt road behind their property? *Was* there a connection?

"What the heck's going on?" Candy said out loud to herself, and stepped down a little harder on the gas pedal as she headed into town.

Even though there was a fairly important community event taking place this afternoon at the warehouse complex, the downtown streets weren't that crowded. Tourist season was still several months away, and on this mild, blustery day in March, the village had

56

a lazy weekday mid-morning feel to it. People were out running errands and taking care of business, meeting up and chatting, talking on cell phones and getting into and out of cars — all typical stuff, none of it done in a rushed or anxious manner. It was a small-town pace.

At least for the moment.

As she drove up Main Street toward the warehouses and marina, she noticed increased activity, and just as she was stopping at the northern intersection with the Coastal Loop, which paralleled the river, she saw a police car flash by directly in front of her. It was headed to her right, toward the river's mouth, where the English Point Lighthouse and Museum stood on the coastline.

She followed it quizzically with her eyes.

That was too obvious to ignore.

Even though the main entrance to the warehouse and marina area was to her left and half a block up the road, she hesitated only a few moments before turning the steering wheel to her right and falling into line behind the police car, just to see where it was headed.

It didn't go far. After a hundred feet or so, it swerved across the oncoming lane and pulled over to the side of the road, where it joined several other police cars. A jumble of them were on her left, parked in the open area along the river, doors open and light bars flashing. They were just across the street from the Unitarian church, the cemetery, and Town Park, where a small crowd had gathered to observe the sudden activity.

Traffic naturally slowed as gawkers craned their necks to see what was going on. Candy did her best not to stare too much as she drove past, more for safety's sake than anything else. She didn't want to rear-end the vehicle in front of her. But she allowed herself a series of quick glances, during which she spotted a group of officers with stern expressions gathered along the river's edge. The waterfront was relatively barren in this stretch of land, wedged between the warehouses and docks behind her, and the lighthouse and museum up ahead at the river's mouth. The officers were talking and pointing, and one of them, Officer Molly Prospect, whom Candy knew fairly well, appeared to be writing down something in a notebook. She also spotted a motorboat pulled up on the shore and a couple of men in wet suits standing at water's edge.

At first glance, it seemed to confirm all that Maggie had told her, and her heart sank.

She was still studying the scene when she heard the sharp burst of a siren behind her. Shifting her gaze, she caught the glimmer of flashing lights in the rearview mirror. The ambulance had arrived. Like the other drivers, she dutifully pulled the Jeep over to the side, but the ambulance was already headed off-road, in the same direction the police car had gone, angling away from her across the oncoming left lane, down off the asphalt, and onto the open space toward the cluster of police cars and officers.

Several horns beeped around her then, traffic got moving again, and she sped up a little. She followed the line of traffic along the curve of the Loop as it passed by the river's mouth and skirted the ocean's edge, until she came to the turnoff for the lighthouse's parking lot. Here, she flicked on her signal and made a left-hand turn, toward the museum buildings and tower on the point of rocky land where river and ocean met.

As she drove into the parking lot she could see the lighthouse up ahead, and the ocean beyond that. It looked glorious today, bright and windswept, the peaking waves trailing sprays of crystal blue water that fanned out in sparkling arches. The seagulls were out and active; the rocks shone blackly. The crowds were light but as energetic as always.

There were plenty of places to park, but she chose one as close to the river as possible. After shutting off the engine, she jumped out, pulling her trusty tote bag with her. She locked up the Jeep, slung the bag's strap over her shoulder, and headed off to see what she could find out.

FIVE

She took an indistinct path between the road and the river. It led her through mostly barren ground and low shrubs, strewn with alluvial sand and boulders. There had been some efforts over the years to renovate this riverside area of town, which many felt was going to waste. It was no doubt a prime piece of waterfront land, one of the few remaining undeveloped areas in town. A few old ramshackle buildings had once stood on the site, associated with maritime activities, but they'd been torn down years ago, and nothing had ever replaced them.

Few villagers wanted to see this area turned into a major development of any sort, such as a high-rise or an office complex. The ladies of the Cape Willington Heritage Protection League had been particularly adamant in their opposition to that idea, and skeptical of any improvements at all. Their preference, they'd said repeatedly at community events, public gatherings, town hall meetings, and anywhere else they had an audience, was to preserve as much of the riverside's natural state as possible. But they'd been open to hearing ideas about ways to make better use of the land, and after much discussion, accompanied by the promise of at least partial funding from a private foundation, a compromise plan was adopted to extend Ocean Walk in the other direction, northward from the lighthouse and museum, around the mouth of the river, then up along the riverside to the warehouses and marina — and right through this undeveloped area.

Construction on the new River Walk pathway was scheduled to begin as soon as the weather allowed, probably within the next few weeks, with a goal of finishing it before the tourists arrived en masse on Memorial Day weekend. A committee consisting of several members of the Heritage Protection League, as well as town council members and a few local residents, including Candy's father, was overseeing the project to ensure optimal access to this area with minimal disruption to its natural landscape.

Not that there was much to disrupt, Candy thought, looking around at the area as she passed through it. Mostly just dirt, as far as she could tell. She understood the historical and environmental value of it, but it could certainly use an upgrade.

So could the group of old buildings toward which she was headed.

As discussions for the River Walk were under way, many had suggested improvements to the warehouse and marina complex as well. Some floated the idea of reimagining it, turning it into an arts and crafts courtyard, with shops, studios, and restaurants. A new name was even suggested for the complex — River Walk Plaza.

Word had gone out about the idea, and it had circulated around town as rapidly as an infestation of black flies. Right after the beginning of the year, in a surprising development, one of the town's oldest families, the somewhat infamous and disreputable Sykes clan, had donated one of the abandoned riverfront warehouses to the town, and a plan was quickly hatched to turn the old warehouse into a much-needed community center.

Although nearly a hundred years old, the building was structurally sound, a local architect had determined, and both a historian and a preservationist were bought in to advise on the renovation. The project proceeded rapidly, as tradesmen offered their services, volunteers lined up to help, and donations of supplies and materials flooded in from local shops and businesses. Everyone wanted to pitch in on the project, and on a wave of enthusiasm and support, the renovation began just a few weeks later, in mid-January.

Candy's father became a fixture around the place, along with two members of his circle of close friends, whom Candy often referred to as his "posse" — classic car collector William "Bumpy" Brigham and eBay entrepreneur Artie Groves. All retired and in their late sixties or early seventies, they devoted as much time as possible to the project, bringing enthusiasm and experience with them. The group's fourth member, local theatrical producer and ex-cop Finn Woodbury, had even returned early from his annual winter pilgrimage to Florida to lend his skills to the renovation. Finn's wife, Marti, pitched right in to help, organizing group lunches and sometimes dinners in the community center to feed the workers and volunteers.

Candy had been inside the building a number of times during the renovation, and was impressed with what she saw. Gutted and almost completely rebuilt, it was designed to be a multifunctional space. A large open room on the main floor served as its focal point. The room had a stage at one end, so the town could hold large meetings and concerts in the space. There were a few smaller meeting rooms to one side of the main floor, as well as a commercial-sized kitchen at the back. Some additional offices and meeting rooms, as well as storage spaces, were located on a partial second-level floor.

Work had proceeded quicker than anyone expected, but despite the pace of the project — or perhaps because of it — all had not gone as smoothly as everyone hoped. Issues of time and money had to be hashed out, as well as the project's environmental impact and historical issues. The ladies of the Heritage Protection League, especially the group's cofounders and most vocal members, Cotton Colby and Elvira Tremble, had been particularly involved in the project, calling for a slower pace and a more cautious approach. Snags occurred amid attempts to fast-track permitting and inspections through the town's offices. Late-night calls were made about problem areas and potential roadblocks, in particular to the homes of Mason Flint, chairman of the town council, and other council members.

Owen Peabody, director of the Historical Society Museum, housed in the former Keeper's Quarters at the English Point Lighthouse, was called in to review and approve portions of the renovation project. He worked with architects and engineers, all on a voluntary basis, to make sure the work proceeded correctly, and sometimes held up operations to make sure everything was in order.

But, in the end, it had worked. And here they were, in late March, just two months later, with the facility ready to go, and getting its first big test this weekend.

A lot of credit for the successful completion of the project went to Mason Flint, the council's chairman, who had managed to navigate tricky waters to keep things moving and keep everyone happy. Candy thought she caught sight of him now, as she followed a rough, narrow path across the still-undeveloped stretch of land. He stood with a group of police officers off to her right, on the riverbank, a few dozen feet ahead of her. His straight posture and thick head of white hair were easily recognizable. On the ground near his feet, a black tarp was stretched over what must have been the body fished out of the water, probably via that boat she'd noticed anchored nearby,

66

and the men in wet suits.

Even from this distance, Mason looked windblown and haggard — not his usually confident self. As she angled in the group's direction and approached them, he glanced around and seemed to notice her. But one of the police officers had caught sight of her also. The officer broke away from the group, right thumb hanging on his belt near his holster. He held out the other hand as he started toward her.

"You can't come this way, miss," he called out to her, and pointed up toward the road. "You'll have to walk along the street. This area is closed to the public right now."

"What's the problem, Officer?" She pointed back up toward town. "I'm with the paper. I was just wondering if . . ."

But he wouldn't let her get any closer, and cut her off. "I'm sorry, ma'am, but this area is closed off. Please, you'll have to head up toward the road. You can't come any farther this way."

She stopped, craned her neck so she could see around him, but he took several steps sideways, blocking her view. He patiently swept a hand up the slope toward the street, two fingers extended, but the other hand continued to hover near his holster, she noticed. He pointed emphatically toward the street. "Please, ma'am. You'll have to head in that direction."

There were a thousand questions she wanted to ask. Who was the body under the tarp? Was it really Mick Rilke? How had he died? How long had he been floating in the river? Was there anything suspicious about his death? Or his body? Had he drowned? Had he died some other way. Had he? . . .

But the police officer's expression had turned grim, his mouth was a lipless straight line, and she knew she'd pushed her luck as far as she dared — at least, right now.

So she nodded and pointed up the slope. "I guess I'll head that way then."

"Yes, ma'am. Thank you, ma'am."

As she started off, she glanced over at Mason Flint to see if she could catch his eye again, but he was staring down at the tarp, shaking his head, as if he couldn't believe there had been another mysterious death in their quiet little village.

Candy knew exactly how he felt.

SIX

She found Maggie standing at the edge of a medium-sized crowd of about seventy-five people or so, arrayed loosely around the outside of the renovated warehouse along the English River. Almost instantly she noticed the subdued mood of the crowd. Conversations were hushed. Eyes darted furtively back and forth. Shoulders were hunched or sagging. No one seemed to quite know what to do.

They must have heard about the body lying on the riverbank nearby, Candy thought. That explained the hushed atmosphere, but why were they all just standing around? She checked her watch. It was shortly after eleven. The grand-opening ceremony should have started by now. Instead, she saw a mic on a stand near the front entrance to the community center, but no one was behind or near it. No officials or community leaders were in sight.

There must be a delay of some sort. She could guess why.

She came up behind Maggie and tapped her friend on the shoulder. "Hey there, Mags, have I missed anything?"

Maggie Wolfsburger spun around, chestnut hair flying. Her eyes widened at the new arrival. "Finally! You made it!" She leaned forward and gave Candy a quick hug. "I'm so glad you're here! And to answer your question, no, you haven't missed a thing — yet."

"Why, what's happening?"

A look of exasperation crossed Maggie's face. "Well, that's just it. Nothing! No one seems to know what's going on. There are a bunch of decision-makers huddled together inside the building but so far we haven't heard a word from anyone about anything. It's just been total silence. Thank goodness you're here. Maybe *you* can find out what's holding things up."

"I have a pretty good idea," Candy said as her gaze flicked back down along the riverbank.

Maggie leaned in close and lowered her voice. "It's shocking, isn't it? Just shocking! The whole ceremony has ground to a halt since they discovered that body. Have you verified that it's Mick Rilke? We still don't

70

know for sure."

"The police aren't talking," Candy said. "Trust me, I tried, but they wouldn't let me close. Mason Flint sure looks shaken up, though. Whoever it is, it's not good."

"No, it's definitely not." Maggie got an odd look in her eyes. "In fact, it couldn't have happened at a worse time. Of course," she added quickly, "there's no good time to get murdered, is there? And, as you can guess, the rumors are flying. You stand around with a bunch of people and a dead body turns up nearby, folks are bound to talk, right?"

"And what are people saying?" Candy asked, her gaze drifting around the crowd as they spoke.

"Well, that's just it. Crazy things! Weird things!"

"Like what?"

Maggie hesitated to add to the rumors and gossip, but in the end she couldn't help herself. "Well, you didn't hear this from me, of course. It's just the word going around. But there have been some general whisperings about . . . well, to put it bluntly, some folks are wondering if the missus did him in . . . if the dead person really is Mick Rilke, of course."

It took Candy a moment to process what

her friend was saying. "What, you mean Jean? Mick's wife? They think *she* had something to do with his death? But why?"

"Well, it would make sense, wouldn't it?" Maggie said, lowering her voice. "We all know he was a bit of a flirt, right?"

"We do?"

"And that he could be . . . well, pretty loud."

"He had a big personality, that's true," Candy conceded, "and he seemed to have a good time wherever he went. But why would someone murder him because of that?"

Maggie shrugged. "Don't know. I'm just a little fly on the wall here. It's what *they're* saying." She subtly waggled a finger at the crowd around them.

"And what else are they saying?" Candy asked, wondering if she should pull out her notebook and start taking notes.

"Well, that Mick had a tendency to rub some people the wrong way. They're thinking, if it wasn't Jean, then maybe he got on the wrong side of someone else."

"Like who?"

"No idea. It's just the general scuttlebutt."

"Sounds like the scuttlebutt is pretty chatty today," Candy observed. "Still, it makes sense, I suppose. Rumors start up pretty fast."

"People hear things and people say things," Maggie agreed.

"Apparently so." Candy was well aware of how fast a tasty piece of gossip could spread around their village.

"And, well," Maggie continued, "maybe there's some truth to those rumors, right? Who knows?" She forced a strained chuckle.

"Right, who knows?" Candy was silent for a few moments as she watched the crowd, thinking. Could there be any truth to what Maggie had heard? She was tempted to dismiss it all right out of hand as just the idle chatter of worried people. Still, Maggie's words echoed in her mind:

Maybe he got on the wrong side of someone.

Maybe he had.

What had happened to him? she wondered.

Candy turned her attention to the new community center in front of them. She nodded toward it. "So who are we waiting for? Who's inside there?"

"Well, your father, for one," Maggie said.

"Dad? He's here?"

"Sure is, along with the rest of them. Apparently, they're talking it over, trying to figure out what to do next, I guess."

Candy crossed her arms as she studied

73

the building. "Hmm, I guess."

"Of course, Mason Flint's not in there," Maggie said. "He's tied up with the police, as you've noticed, and probably will be for a while. Hence, the delay, and hence, that powwow taking place in there, without him. Sort of like a chicken with its head cut off."

"Trying to decide whether to go ahead with the ceremony or cancel it?"

"That's my guess." Maggie sighed deeply. "It would be a shame to cancel it, of course, after all the work and preparation that's been done. On the other hand, I suppose it's important to respect the dead."

"Yes," Candy mused, "I suppose it is."

She could understand their dilemma. They'd done a lot of work on the new community center, and it showed. Considering the condition of the building when they'd started the project two months ago, it looked surprisingly festive today. Brightly colored streamers flew from the eaves. A new sign had been hung on the front wall. The door and window frames were freshly painted. The place was all dressed up, but the intended celebration had been halted in its tracks.

At the moment, all the doors into the building were closed, including a large garage door around the left side. The windows were dark and lifeless. It was hard to tell if anything at all was going on inside.

"How long have they been in there?" Candy asked after a few moments.

Maggie checked her watch. "Maybe twenty or twenty-five minutes, something like that?"

"They should have reached a decision by now, I'd think."

"You'd think. But there are a lot of big personalities in there."

"Bigger than Mick Rilke's?"

"They'd certainly give him a run for his money."

"Let me guess." Candy turned back to the crowd, eyes darting from face to face, trying to figure out who was here and who was missing. "Well, we know my father's in there."

"Correct."

"And I assume the boys. I don't see them around." She was referring to Bumpy, Artie, and Finn, her father's friends.

"We can definitely assume that," Maggie agreed.

"And there's no Wanda Boyle in sight. I'm sure she's at this event somewhere, covering it for the paper. So if she's not out here, she must be inside."

"Again, correctomundo."

"And the ladies of the Cape Willington Heritage Protection League, most likely Cotton Colby and Elvira Tremble."

"They're there too."

"And who else?" Candy wondered. "No, wait, don't tell me." She thought a moment, peering back and forth. "If Mason Flint's over by the body with the police, then one of his surrogates must be representing him inside — most likely Carol McKaskie or Tillie Shaw." Carol was the council's new vice chair, while Tillie was the chair of the events committee and headed up the weekend's festivities.

"Both of them!" Maggie exclaimed. "It's like the clash of the titans! *Gott im Himmel!*"

"You're right about that — and you're starting to sound like your husband," Candy pointed out.

Maggie shrugged. "All that German stuff tends to rub off on you after a while. I've been working on my pronunciations."

"Keep at it. You're doing better. So, getting back to the subject — have I missed anyone?"

"As far as I know, you got them all. Of course, there could be a ringer inside. But, overall, I'd say your sleuthing skills have not deteriorated. Which is a good thing, possibly, unfortunately, depending on what happened to our local landscaper over there."

"You're right about that." Candy shifted her gaze back to her friend. "So what do *you* think happened to him . . . assuming it *is* him?" she asked curiously, interested to hear her friend's opinion.

Maggie let out a huge breath. "Honestly, I just don't know." Her tone softened and turned contemplative. "Maybe he just fell into the river somehow. Maybe it was just a terrible accident. Maybe he'd been drinking, not paying attention to what he was doing. It happens. But if not, if it was more deliberate, well, then you know what that means."

"What?"

"Well, you might be called on to solve another murder case."

Candy gave her friend a wary look. "You really think that could happen again? After what took place over at the Whitby estate last year? I thought we were all finished with this sudden-death business."

"Maybe it's a whole new business, something completely different," Maggie said thoughtfully. "Maybe Mick was involved in something we don't know about. Maybe he's got gambling debts or something like that. Maybe he was blackmailing someone and they retaliated. Or maybe someone was blackmailing *him.* Who knows? It could be anything."

She paused, a look of uncertainty crossing her face. "Or maybe I'm just overreacting. But you can't blame me for being skittish these days, can you? After the murder of our best man last year almost caused us to postpone our wedding?"

"No," Candy said honestly, "of course I can't. You're entitled to your concern. We all are. And it's not entirely misplaced. There's something strange going on here."

"Amen to that. So, just to be clear, you're thinking the same thing I'm thinking, right? That it wasn't accidental?"

Candy shook her head. "I'm not sure I know what to think at this point."

"Then maybe you should do what you do best," Maggie said. "Dig around. Ask a few questions. See what you can find out."

Candy arched an eyebrow. "I've been warned against doing anything like that, remember?"

"I remember. But that's never stopped you before, has it?"

"No, it hasn't," Candy reluctantly admitted.

Maggie turned and eyed her friend as a knowing smile crept across her face. "I'm surprised curiosity hasn't got the best of you."

Candy eyed her right back. "Who says it hasn't? I *am* curious to know what happened to him."

"You're not alone."

"The problem is," Candy continued, "it could be nothing, or it could be something. If it's nothing — if it really was just an accident — then that would be tragic enough. But if it's *something* — if it was premeditated, for instance — then I have to figure out what happened to him. And a good place to start is with the people inside that building."

Both their gazes were now focused on the new community center in front of them. "That's a pretty formidable crowd in there," Maggie warned her. "I'd be hesitant to disturb them while they're in the middle of their deliberations. But that's just me. You have family in there, so you have a reason for going in."

For a moment, at Maggie's cautionary note, Candy was torn. But she knew what she had to do. She sighed. "You're right about that crowd. They're formidable, all right. But I have to find out what's going on in there, no matter what the consequence. See which way the winds are blowing, if they've heard anything important. So . . . wish me luck."

"Good luck. Just take care of yourself."

Candy looked over at her. "You're not coming along?"

Maggie held up both hands in a defensive gesture. "No way. I'm not getting into the middle of that crowd. But I'll be right here, backing you up every step of the way, and holding down this spot right here, in case you need to make a fast retreat."

"Thanks — I feel so much better knowing you have my back."

"Hey, that's my job — being your side-kick."

"And you do it very well. So, I guess it's up to me then."

"I guess so."

Candy took a deep breath and focused on her destination. "No point putting this off any longer, is there?"

"No point at all," Maggie agreed.

Candy nodded, and without another word, she started toward the building.

SEVEN

She was a little surprised to find the main doors unlocked. For some reason, she thought all the villagers gathered around had been kept out of the building on purpose — locked out, to be honest, though she wasn't sure where she'd picked up that impression. But any one of them could have entered the building at any time. Just walked right in.

Apparently, they'd made a conscious decision to stay away and uninvolved, possibly out of a sense of self-preservation, until an official announcement of some sort was made.

Smart people, Candy thought.

Her, not so much.

She still wasn't sure she wanted to enter the building herself. It felt as if she were walking into a lion's den — an idea she didn't relish. She had no idea what to expect from those inside, how riled up they might be. They might not welcome an intruder like her. They might even become antagonistic toward her.

But, she told herself again, it had to be done. With what she'd learned earlier about the sap thief and the red vehicle seen from the woods, and now with the body of a red truck owner lying not too far away, supposedly fished out of the river, she felt she didn't have a choice. The links were too suspicious. The timing was suspicious. The whole thing was suspicious. Her instincts were humming.

The right-side door creaked a little as she opened it. She winced at the sound but didn't let it stop her. Inside, the building was dark and cool, with the lingering smells of old wood, varnish, and sawdust still hanging about. Tomorrow, when the pancakes and syrup were flowing, it would be a completely different aroma, she thought.

She stood for a few moments just inside the door, and almost immediately heard the voices. There were a lot of them, from the sound of it. Talking excitedly, some faster or louder than others, sometimes over one another. Some sounded exasperated. Some sounded like they were having trouble remaining civil. Most of the voices she could already identify. It sounded like battle lines were being drawn. And she could pretty much identify who would be on either side.

Great, she thought, and gave herself a final chance to back out while she could. But she knew she couldn't do that, so she steeled herself as she started forward.

Maggie had been correct. There were nine of them in all, gathered in one of the more shadowed areas of the main floor, in a narrow space on the left side of the stage. They'd formed themselves into a rough circle, though a few stood on the outskirts of the main group. Some of them she could clearly make out in the half-light as she approached. Others, she couldn't quite identify yet. But she could hear them, as she wound her way around and between the tables and chairs set up on the main floor.

"It's a mistake to go on with this fiasco," said one of them, a stiff, stern-voiced woman, in a disapproving tone that silenced the others. Candy immediately recognized the speaker as Elvira Tremble, of the Heritage Protection League. Elvira had roots in town that went back generations, and had some influence in local affairs, so the others around the circle gave her a few moments to speak her mind unchallenged.

"It would send the wrong message, and could ruin the town's reputation," Elvira continued, taking advantage of the end of the cross talk. She stood straight-backed, with her hands clasped firmly in front of her, as if she were a school principal addressing a classroom of rowdy students. "We should postpone any grand-opening celebration of any kind for as long as necessary — certainly at least a week or two, though a month or more would be best, until this unfortunate matter sorts itself out."

Her league companion, Cotton Colby, jumped in to voice her support. "Elvira's right," said the nicely dressed dark-haired woman with a firm nod of her head. "I'd find it highly inappropriate to proceed with today's opening event, after what's happened outside. Besides, I've been skeptical about this whole thing from the beginning. This building has historical significance, you know. It just doesn't seem right."

"Everyone's well aware of the building's historical significance, Cotton," said an older male in a placating tone — *obviously my father,* Candy thought, doing his best to sound the voice of reason, though she detected a hint of frustration in his tone. "Every move we've made with this place has been properly vetted. You know that. You were involved with it. We've considered everyone's reservations, and done our best

84

to accommodate everybody's wishes. It was a community effort, in every way possible. This is a place *for* the community. A lot of people contributed valuable time and effort toward getting it fixed up, and there have been a few hiccups, but it's done and we're finally ready to show it off."

He paused as he pointed toward the front of the building. "Now, we've got a lot of good people standing around out there, wondering what the heck's going on. They're just as invested in this place as we are. There's no harm in letting them come in, take a look around, and see what we've been up to. It's the least we can do. And we can keep everything toned down out of respect for the recently deceased."

"No point in postponing it now, after all the work that's been done," piped in Bumpy Brigham.

Finn Woodbury spoke up. "Plus, we have to remember that we have a pretty big weekend coming up, starting tomorrow morning, and we've got a lot of tourists flocking into town." He whirled a finger above his head. "This building and the pop-up pancake house operation we're about to open here are supposed to play a big part in the weekend's festivities. The tables and chairs are set up, dishware and utensils are ready to go, we've stockpiled all the flour, sugar, and syrup we need, and the fridges in the back are loaded up with butter, eggs, and milk. The griddles and skillets are standing by, ready to be greased up. We've got cooks and servers lined up to help out all weekend. If we call off this thing at the last minute, there's going to be a lot of wasted food and a lot of disappointed folks around town."

Elvira snorted. "You're talking about food at a time like this? Pancakes and eggs and syrup? For goodness sake, Finn," she hissed, "a man's dead!"

"And I'm sorry about that," Finn responded, standing his ground against Elvira's scorn. "I really am. But maple syrup is the lifeblood of this community at this time of year. You know that. It's part of the region's heritage."

Elvira frowned at this obvious attempt to verbally step on her toes, as she'd cofounded the Heritage Protection League. But before she could come up with a snappy rebuttal, Artie Groves spoke up, hoping to change the topic in an effort to head off a confrontation.

"Speaking of heritage stuff," he said, "we have that educational thing going on all weekend. We're going to set up a boiling demonstration out on the side lot, fire it up, show folks how we turn sap into maple sugar, talk to the kids about the history of sap collection. Only now . . ." His voice trailed off.

"Mick Rilke was going to help us set that up," Doc finished for him, addressing the group. "Of course, now that he's gone, that part of our weekend festivities is up in the air."

"This whole thing is up in the air," declared Elvira.

"You'll just have to cancel it," said Cotton Colby firmly, using the opportunity to press home her point. "This whole event should just be canceled."

"But what about the pancakes?" Bumpy asked, no doubt thinking of his own stomach.

"What about the tourists?" asked Finn.

"What about the community?" wondered Doc.

"And what about Mick Rilke?" said Elvira snidely. "Remember him? Doesn't he deserve some consideration?"

"Indeed he does," responded Cotton, "which is why we should call everything off and not let the masses make our decision for us."

"The . . . the masses?" sputtered Finn.

"You mean those *villagers* out there?"

Cotton's face hardened. "Don't try to put words in my mouth, Finn Woodbury. You know what I'm saying."

"Which is?"

Cotton looked put out to have to explain herself, but she did it anyway. "We can't let ourselves be swayed by those who would put money over people."

Finn drew back his head and squinted at that remark, and was about to respond, when a new voice spoke up. It belonged to Tillie Shaw, the events committee chair. She was a plump, red-faced woman with a generally sunny disposition that belied her no-nonsense attitude. "Whatever we decide to do," she said in a cheerful, singsong tone, "we must remember to be civil to each other. I know emotions are running high right now, but we must treat each other with respect, and keep positive thoughts. We can make it through this, people!"

"Oh, posh on your positive thoughts," groused Elvira.

"No, Tillie's right," said Carol McKaskie, the vice chair. "This is not a time to let differences divide us. We must work together to solve this . . . *thing.*" She shifted her eyes, searching for a better word. "This . . . problem. This situation." She paused as she

88

licked her lips and gathered her thoughts before she went on. "Now, let's face it. In many ways this is a no-win situation. No matter what we decide to do, we're going to be criticized for it. If we go ahead with the event, we'll look bad. If we don't, it'll cause a financial setback for the town — and no matter what you say, Cotton, that's something we have to consider. We'll lose revenue and might have to postpone the River Walk project, which will affect other plans and budgets in turn. Again, the town will look bad, especially those of us on the council. It's damned if we do, damned if we don't."

"So what do you suggest we do?" asked Doc.

"I suggest," Carol said hesitantly, "that we get this thing over with as swiftly as possible. Just do it and suffer the consequences, whatever they might be." She folded her hands across her abdomen. "Open the doors and let those folks in here. That's what I say."

Another voice broke in — spoken by someone Candy hadn't noticed. A man stepped out of the shadows. She realized he had been there for a while, listening.

It was Owen Peabody, director of the English Point Lighthouse and Museum, who had helped out with the renovation.

"That's one option, I suppose, Carol," he said, taking a few steps forward out of the shadows, "and a very interesting approach. But don't you think it might be better to dismiss the crowd today, sleep on it overnight, and decide what to do in the morning, when we all have clearer heads?"

"I think that's a fabulous idea," Elvira Tremble said.

"I concur," said Cotton. "Who knows what happened to that man out there? We have to find that out before we do anything else."

"Can you imagine," added Elvira ominously, "what would happen if his death was premeditated — not an accident? We'd have a dark cloud hanging over the village for weeks, if not months. It could ruin everything!"

"Now, Elvira, let's not jump to conclusions," warned Doc. "No point in spreading rumors."

"They're not rumors," said a new voice, this one belonging to Wanda Boyle, the paper's managing editor. She looked up from her smartphone at the faces around the circle. "It appears there's something suspicious about the body — at least, according to my sources," she said. "I just got a report."

"From who?"

Wanda turned. Candy had come up behind her, unnoticed.

Surprised to see the blueberry farmer, Wanda took a few moments to recover, but she quickly gathered her wits and responded. "As I said, a source of mine, down by the river, who overheard a couple of the police officers talking about Mick Rilke."

"So they've confirmed it's him?" Candy said.

"They have. Apparently, he'd gotten all tangled up in a fisherman's net — something that had fallen off or been left behind by one of the fishing boats around here. At first they thought it could have been accidental. Maybe a heart attack, and he'd fallen into the river and drowned. But there's a problem."

"And what's that?" Doc asked.

Wanda turned toward him. "They said his hands and feet were tied up."

There were a few gasps of shock around the circle. "Tied up?" Bumpy repeated. "What does that mean?"

Wanda gave a noncommittal shrug. "It means his death was premediated, I guess."

The group was silent for a few moments, until Candy spoke up, summarizing what they all were probably thinking.

"In other words, you're saying he was murdered."

EIGHT

Ten minutes later, Candy was back outside, in a bit of a daze.

She didn't want to appear unsettled or, worse, shamble around in a zombielike state, especially when some of the villagers were eyeing her curiously, probably because she'd just come from inside the community center, where decisions of importance were apparently being made. But she wasn't ready to talk to any of them right now. She wasn't sure what to say. Instead, she wanted to carefully think through what she'd just learned.

She returned to the spot where she'd left Maggie, but her friend was gone. Candy quickly scanned the crowd but there was no sign of her. She probably had headed back to the bakery, Candy assumed, so she looked around for a place to sit, catch her breath, and organize her thoughts.

Trying to appear as casual as possible, and

gently declining to answer any questions from those gathered around the building ("Someone will be out soon to answer your questions," she told the more persistent ones), she wound her way through the crowd, which seemed to part for her as she headed toward the river, to the outskirts of the gathering. There she spotted a weathered bench along the side of an adjacent building with an open spot at one end, next to an older couple talking softly to each other. Gratefully, she settled into it, her mind whirling.

There was a lot to absorb.

Naturally, everyone inside had been unsettled by Wanda's revelation — and Candy's somewhat blunt assessment of the situation. There had been whispered words around the circle, expressions of regret and disbelief, looks of concern and uneasiness. They all knew what it meant — another cloud hanging over their village, another murderer on the loose at the worst possible time.

Most of the contentiousness had gone out of them then, and in a more agreeable manner, they'd collectively decided to take Owen Peabody's suggestion, with a slight modification: They'd dismiss this morning's crowd and postpone the opening ceremony until the following morning, when they'd hold a greatly toned-down version.

The plan was to open the pancake house operation at seven A.M., as originally scheduled, with a small grand-opening ceremony on the stage inside the main room at nine. The pancake house would remain open until four P.M., when events would shift to Town Park. And they'd decided to continue with the weekend's other Maple Madness festivities, though in a somewhat subdued manner.

Most had agreed it was the best solution, and even Elvira and Cotton had finally given their grudging approval. Cotton had tried one final time to have the entire event canceled, but soon realized she was outnumbered, and reluctantly gave up on her efforts.

Carol McKaskie volunteered herself as the proper spokesperson to inform the waiting crowd of the group's decision. It seemed a fitting choice, given her position on the town council. So until Carol made her appearance, Candy sat and waited. She'd become a little overheated inside. The damp air here along the river felt good in her lungs and soothed her skin. She took a deep breath and leaned back in the bench seat.

It had been a busy day so far — not at all what she expected when she'd slid out of bed that morning. She'd planned to do a few chores around the farm, then drive into town and enjoy the show at the community center. After that, she was going to head over to Town Park with Maggie to help with preparations for the Maple Marshmallow Roast, scheduled for tomorrow evening. They were going to set up a booth Maggie and Herr Georg had rented, where they planned to sell a limited range of their wares, including Chocolate Maple Brownies, created especially for the weekend. Herr George was probably baking away right now, Candy thought, and the smells emanating from his shop must be glorious.

All his efforts, though, and Maggie's, and everyone else's, could be in vain. Everything associated with the weekend threatened to fall apart. *One* more revelation, she thought, *one* more unfortunate event, and it could all go up in a whirling funnel of maple-laced smoke, to be swept away by the strengthening wind.

All because they'd pulled Mick Rilke's body from the English River, apparently drowned, wrapped in a fisherman's net, his hands and feet bound together.

That last part gave her the most concern. The conclusion seemed obvious. Mick's death had been no accident. No drinking too much and falling off the back of a boat, or tumbling off the edge of a dock. No heart attack or dozing off while out in a canoe or kayak. Those might have been possibilities at one time, when they'd first discovered the body, but after Wanda's recent disclosure, they no longer were.

His death had been caused, at least in some part, by an intentional act.

It meant, as she'd said inside, that someone had murdered Mick Rilke.

Someone in this town, no doubt. Someone who knew him, who could get close to him, perhaps take him by surprise. There was no other way to incapacitate him. He was a landscaper, a working man who did physical labor for a living. He was big and husky, with a solid build. Not easy to take down. It meant some sort of subterfuge must have been involved. Maybe it was someone he trusted. Someone he had antagonized in some way.

But if it was someone around town, who could it be?

She'd been looking down, at the cracked asphalt between her shoes, but now she raised her head and swept her gaze across the faces in the crowd around her. Some of the villagers were starting to peel away, moving up the slope toward the main road, headed back to their cars and their daily lives. But many still remained.

Who, she thought again, could have murdered Mick? Who knew him well enough to get close enough to deliver some sort of fatal blow?

Everyone, she thought, and the realization made her shoulders sag.

It could be just about anyone, because he knew just about everybody in town, at least by sight. He probably knew most of the villagers by their first names. Due to his various seasonal jobs, he got around a lot, met a lot of people. He was generally a nice guy — as a businessman, he had to be — but as Maggie had said, he was known to rub some people the wrong way, due to his somewhat boisterous personality. Maybe he'd turned his back on the wrong person at the wrong time. Maybe someone had jumped him, caught him off guard, surprised him, lured him into a trap.

However it had happened, she thought as her gaze swiveled to her left, out past the warehouses, docks, and boats to the water beyond, *someone* had tied him up and cast him afloat on the river. Obviously from somewhere upstream.

But why had he been tied up that way? Why wrap him in a fisherman's net? And where was his red truck? Had he abandoned it somewhere, near where he'd been dumped into the river? Was it still at his house? If so, how had he wound up where he did? Had he walked? Had someone picked him up and driven him to some remote location, where he'd been ambushed and taken down?

How long had he been dead? she wondered. Since yesterday? Since last night?

Did his wife, Jean, know of his death yet? When was the last time he'd been seen alive?

Her thoughts turned to the other mysteries she'd heard today. Did his death have anything to do with the red vehicle spotted behind the Milbrights' farm yesterday? Or the alleged stolen sap, tapped from the Milbrights' highly productive maple trees?

Or was it something completely different? Something unrelated? Something random?

Was it linked in any way to the town's questionable history and the deadly feud that occasionally erupted between two of its wealthier families, the Sykes and Pruitt clans?

That last thought made her shudder.

The town had dealt with a number of recent tragedies, including the death last year of the village's beloved historian, Julius Seabury. She'd felt, after his death, and the unveiling of the murderer, as well as those behind the plot, that at least some of the conflicts that had plagued the community over the past eight years or so had finally been resolved, at least in some part. She'd hoped they'd put all those mysterious deaths behind them, and anticipated a brighter future.

But here they were again. Another day. Another dead body.

Her gaze shifted back around the crowd before focusing in on the community center's main doors. With those around her, she waited for the vice chairwoman to emerge like a groundhog from its burrow, to make a major announcement.

"I wish they'd hurry up in there," said a voice from the bench beside her. "It's sure taking them a long time to make up their minds."

Candy looked over at the older couple seated next to her. She'd become so absorbed in her thoughts that she'd forgotten they were there.

"I'm getting a chill from sitting here so long," said the woman, frowning as she pulled her sweater a little more tightly around her. "And my legs are getting stiff. I can't sit here much longer."

"This is very troubling, don't you think?"

said the husband. He had leaned forward to look around his wife as he spoke.

Candy could only nod and agree with them. "It is," was all she said.

"I can understand the delay, after what's happened," the man continued, "but it's been going on too long." He pointed toward the building. "Do *you* know what's going on in there?"

Candy hesitated before giving them her standard response. "Someone's going to make an announcement in a few minutes," she replied, somewhat robotically, and checked her watch. It was after noon, closing in on twelve fifteen. She'd been here for an hour.

"Well, I certainly hope so," the woman said with a shake of her head. "I just don't know what's happening here in the village anymore. This used to be such a safe, peaceful place. Now look what's happening. Bodies in the river. Crazy drivers on the roads. People stealing sap from maple trees. It's insane!"

"Madness!" the husband agreed.

Candy turned back to the couple with renewed interest. "What did you say?"

"People are going insane!" the husband said. "We just don't know what's going on in town anymore."

Candy pressed him. "You said something about crazy drivers? And stolen sap?"

"Well, everyone knows about the stolen sap," said the woman confidently.

Candy was surprised. "They do?"

"We heard about it at the general store, just a little while ago," the husband said.

At this revelation, Candy was even more surprised. "You did?"

"Sure, word gets around. Can't keep secrets in this town for very long."

"And, of course, Stuart is still upset about what happened yesterday," said the woman.

Candy surmised Stuart was the husband. She looked over at him. "Why, what happened?"

"Well, we were almost run off the road, that's what happened!" said Stuart, his voice rising and his expression turning blustery at the memory. "Darnedest thing I've ever seen. This old red truck came out of nowhere, swerving back and forth across the road, like he owned both lanes. Obviously not paying attention to where he was going. Nearly scared the wits out of us. There should be a law against things like that! I'm thinking of reporting it to the police!"

NINE

"You saw a red truck?" Candy sat straight up, and her gaze zeroed in on the couple as all other thoughts fell out of her brain. They had her full attention now. "When was this? And where? Tell me everything, exactly as it happened."

"Everything?" Stuart hesitated and licked his lips. "Exactly?" He looked suddenly unsettled, and he seemed to be thinking back over his words, as if he might have said something wrong. "Well, I don't know, exactly," he finally hedged.

"In your own words," Candy said in a softer, more persuasive tone, realizing she might have spooked him by her urgency. She calmed herself a notch, hoping it would translate to Stuart. She gave him an encouraging smile. "Just tell me what you remember."

"Well . . ." Stuart's pale blue eyes darted about. He seemed to be carefully considering his words now. "Like I said, it was yesterday."

"What time yesterday . . . if I may ask?"

When Stuart continued to hesitate, his wife spoke up, filling in the information. "It was late afternoon or early evening. A little before sunset," she said, glancing at her husband before looking back at Candy. "Right around six fifteen or so. I remember checking the time, just in case we wanted to report it. Like Stuart said, the truck was swerving back and forth across the lanes. Almost ran us off the road. We had to pull over to avoid getting hit."

"That must have been very unsettling," Candy said.

"You bet it was!" Stuart piped in emphatically, getting his voice back.

"Where did this happen?"

"A few miles north of town, up on the Coastal Loop. Not too far from Route 1."

"So near Judicious Bosworth's cabin?"

Stuart scrunched up his face. "I don't know who that is."

Candy waved a hand. "It doesn't matter. What about the truck itself? What do you remember about it?"

"It was a little beat up," the woman said.

"An older truck then," Candy clarified.

The woman nodded. "And red. That's

104

about all I remember."

"Did it have a snowplow in front?"

"Sure did," Stuart said. "That's what made it look so scary. That huge chunk of metal coming at us, barreling down the road like it was out of control. Like Audra said, we just tried to get out of the way."

"What about the driver? Could you identify him?"

Stuart paused only a moment before he shook his head. "The truck was going too fast. It was all over the place. We couldn't see into the cab."

"Did it look familiar?" Candy pressed. "Have you seen that truck before?"

The two took a moment to think about this, and shook their heads almost in unison. "We're not regular villagers, you know," Stuart explained. "We live north of the cape, up past Gouldsboro. We got a little cabin up there, and a few acres. We don't get into town much anymore. We just ran down here yesterday to pick up a few supplies at the garden center and visit some friends. Today is the second time we've been here in two days, you know, which is a lot for us. We came down today to see the grand opening of the community center, of course. We're pretty excited about it. We've heard they're starting a number of clubs, which we've thought of joining. Audra loves playing bridge, you know. But, well . . ." Stuart's voice trailed off.

The woman had been watching Candy with growing curiosity during this exchange. As Candy considered her next question, Audra asked, "Do you think this could be important? With us and that truck, I mean?" She pursed her lips and subtly tilted her head toward the river. "With what's happened?"

"I don't know." Candy said, and it was an honest answer. "Maybe."

"Do you think we should report it to the police?" Audra wondered.

"We've thought about doing that," Stuart added, "but, well, we really don't want any trouble."

Candy was still considering her response when she heard murmurs from the crowd and looked over to see Carol McKaskie emerge from the community center's main doors. The vice chairwoman was closely followed by the others who had been inside, including Tillie and Wanda, Owen Peabody, and Cotton and Elvira, with Doc and his buddies bringing up the rear. Bumpy was the last out the door. Somewhere he had found a chocolate doughnut, which he'd already half eaten.

Outside, Carol squinted in the brighter light as she stepped to her right, toward a microphone on a stand that had been set up for a more celebratory address. She held a sheaf of papers in her hand. Pink-framed reading glasses perched on her nose, with a long silver neck chain draping along the sides of her face. She tucked a few strands of her shoulder-length hair, which was being tossed about by the riverside wind, behind her ears.

At the microphone she looked around for a switch, flicked it on, blew into the mic, backed her head away as it squeaked a little, tentatively blew into it again, and finally tapped on it with a couple of fingers. "Can everyone hear me okay?" she asked, louder than necessary, for her voice nicely came through the speakers hanging under the building's eaves in a number of places, a last-minute addition to the design, for events just such as this. "Can you hear me okay in the back?"

A bearded gentleman in jeans toward the rear of the crowd waved an arm. "Yup, we hear ya just fine! So let's get on with it!"

There were a few twitters of laughter around him, and a few groans. Carol studied the bearded man for a moment, as if fixing his face in her mind. "Okay then," she said finally, and looked down briefly at the papers she held in her hand. She cleared her throat, looked up, and began. "Attention, fellow Capers. May I have your attention, please? I have an important announcement to make."

"We know that," the same gentleman shouted back. "That's why we've been waiting around here for an hour and a half!"

Carol kept her expression carefully under control as she backed away from the microphone briefly. She waited patiently for a resurgence of whispered comments and conversations to die away before she stepped back up to the mic and started again.

"For those of you who don't know me, my name is Carol McKaskie. I'm vice chair of the town council. Chairman Flint can't be with us at the moment, due to unexpected circumstances, so I'll be making the announcement in his place." She paused, checked the papers in her hand again, and continued. "Now, as all of you know," she said, looking around the crowd, "we've gathered here this afternoon to celebrate the grand opening of our town's newest facility, this building right here behind me, which is now called the English River Community Center."

She paused again as a smattering of applause rippled through the crowd like the sound of waves breaking, then plunged on. "The opening of this center is a major achievement for our community. Many people have pitched in to renovate the building and make this event happen today, and we're grateful for all their contributions. Everything is set up inside and ready to go tomorrow morning for Operation Pancake, as we like to call it. However, due to the unfortunate tragedy that struck our village today, we've decided to make an adjustment to our schedule."

A wave of moans and groans swept through the crowd, and a general restlessness seemed to seize those gathered about, as if they were all getting ready to sprint to their cars to beat an expected mini-rush of traffic.

Carol noticed what was happening and picked up the pace before she lost her audience. "We've decided to cancel today's event and reschedule the grand-opening ceremony for tomorrow morning at nine A.M., on the stage inside the main function room here behind me. The restaurant itself will open at seven in the morning to serve our early birds. We're expecting a big crowd all day tomorrow, so if you've volunteered to help out at the community center, you can check the schedule with myself or one of the other folks up here. It's also posted on the town's website, so you can check that. We appreciate everyone's help in pitching in to make sure this event goes off without a hitch."

A general buzzing sound arose from the crowd, causing Carol to speak louder as she continued. "As many of you know, the maple sugar shack tours will kick off at ten A.M. tomorrow morning from Town Park. We're asking volunteers to gather in the park at nine for final instructions. We'll have two buses running, on the hour. That will allow ninety minutes or so for each tour. Tickets, of course, are ten dollars, and can be purchased at the booth we're setting up in the park, as well as at the opera house, the general store, and various businesses around town."

She glanced down again at the sheets in her hand, and her voice rose another notch as she continued to talk above the growing restlessness. "Tomorrow we'll be lighting the bonfire in Town Park at four P.M. for the Maple Marshmallow Roast, with live music starting shortly after. A bunch of food and craft booths will be open all afternoon and evening, plus we'll have activities for the kids. So we hope you'll join us here again first thing tomorrow morning as we kick off our first annual Maple Madness Weekend. We're looking forward to seeing all of you there! Oh, and remember, we still need a few volunteers to help with . . ."

That was as far as she got. Folks had started moving, and the chatter continued to rise as the crowd broke apart and everyone started heading for the exits, around the buildings and up the slope to the parking lots and their cars. Carol had a few more words she wanted to say, but finally gave up and clicked off the microphone, turning back to the others standing behind her.

From her place on the bench, Candy watched the crowd disperse, vaguely keeping an eye out for Maggie. But her thoughts quickly returned to the conversation she'd been having with the older couple before Carol appeared and gave her speech.

"So," Candy said, trying to pick up where they'd left off, "now that that's all over with, where were we? I think we were talking about . . ."

But when she turned her head, she was addressing an empty bench.

The couple had slipped away without her noticing — and she didn't even get their last names. Stuart and Audra something, from north of the cape up near Gouldsboro.

That's all she knew.

Whoever they'd been, they'd provided her with a new and possibly important addition to the puzzle that had been growing larger all day.

A red truck with a snowplow in front had been spotted late yesterday afternoon, just after six P.M., on the northern section of the Coastal Loop, apparently headed out of town, destination unknown. Could it have been Mick's truck? It certainly seemed possible, even probable. There weren't that many trucks like that around town, especially with a plow. And he'd been swerving across the lanes. Why? What had he been doing?

She could think of a number of possibilities, none of them good.

It could, however, help establish a timeline of his death. If Stuart and Audra were to be believed, the driver of that truck had apparently been in a hurry to get somewhere — or could he have been racing away *from* something? Or *someone*?

Of course, someone other than Mick could have been driving the truck. That was a very real possibility. He had not been positively identified as the person behind the wheel.

Could she trust the reporting of an elderly

couple from somewhere up near Goulds-boro? Had there really been a snowplow on front? She could have put that thought in their mind. She'd mentioned it first, if she recalled.

Had the truck even been red?

Honestly, she thought, her shoulders slumping, it could have been anyone. An out-of-towner, maybe. A visiting farmer. A sightseer.

But something told her there was a link here, some tie to Mick Rilke's death. It was more than coincidental, she thought. There was more going on. She just had to find out what it was.

She took a few moments to ponder her next move, and made a quick mental list of potential avenues of investigation. She'd have to be cautious, she thought as she worked out the best approach to take — work under the radar, stay on the down-low. She'd been warned repeatedly by Cape Willington police chief Darryl Durr to stay out of these matters. She didn't want to break any laws or get herself back in hot water with the chief. But somehow she found herself in the middle of another murder case — or, at least, involved in some way. She thought of going to the chief with what she'd learned, but decided to hold off for now, until she had something more concrete to go on.

So with a nod of her head and a vague plan in mind, she pushed herself off the bench and began to navigate her way across the open space in front of the community center. It was still swarming with people, some hovering in small groups as the crowd cleared out. The mood was not the convivial one she'd anticipated that morning. *But maybe I can change that,* she thought determinedly as she headed toward her father and his buddies.

She was still approaching them when she caught the eye of Finn Woodbury, the ex-city cop. He had his head close to Doc's, and the two of them seemed to be whispering about something. They stood apart from the others, off to one side. When he saw her, Finn made a slight gesture with his eyes, beckoning her over. Then he gave her another signal with his eyes, flicking them toward Carol, Tillie, and Wanda.

Candy got the message: *I have something to tell you, and it's not for public knowledge.*

She knew right away something was up. Perhaps Finn had heard back from his secret source inside the police department.

As nonchalantly as possible, so as not to draw attention to herself, she slowed her pace, drifting through the crowd, and in a leisurely manner circled around the main group in front of the community center, coming toward her father and Finn at an angle.

The two of them waited patiently until she'd sidled up beside them. "What's up?" she asked softly, her head bent low.

"Got some information for you," Finn said solemnly. "Inside stuff. You have to keep this under your hat."

Candy nodded firmly with her chin. "What have you heard?"

Finn's eyes hardened. "Well, we just got confirmation. Mick was murdered, for sure. There's no question about it."

Candy felt a chill go up her spine. She steeled herself as she asked, "What happened to him?"

"Well, it appears our friendly local landscaper was literally stabbed in the back."

TEN

Candy knew she should be shocked by the news, but she wasn't. In fact, she'd almost been expecting to hear something like this. In an odd way, it made complete sense to her.

Mick Rilke had been a big guy, over six feet tall and well over two hundred pounds. He had a bit of a gut and a fleshy, weathered face — probably from eating too many hamburgers and drinking too many beers. He also had big shoulders, muscular arms, and thick legs. No one could have tied him up and wrapped him in a fishing net without taking him down first.

A blow to the head would have worked — or a stab in the back, especially if it pierced any of his vital organs. But how had it happened? Stabbing was a close-in action. How had it been done? Had he been ambushed? Taken by surprise? Or had someone he'd known, perhaps trusted, waited for the opportune moment to catch him unaware?

"Do they know anything specific about the murder weapon?" she asked after a few moments, breaking the silence that had followed Finn's revelation.

The ex-cop shook his head. "Just that it was a blade of some sort. It was a deep wound, lower back, left side, from what I've heard. Might not have been fatal in itself, but it was enough to incapacitate him."

"Long enough for someone to tie up his hands and feet, wrap him in a net, and roll him into a river," Candy said, and Finn nodded.

Doc shook his head in disbelief. "Can't imagine who would do such a thing, in a fashion like that," he said. "He must have crossed the wrong person somehow."

"Who could it be, though?" Candy asked.

"Mick was controversial, we all know that," Finn said. "He sometimes rubbed people the wrong way. And he probably had a few enemies around. They're checking on all that right now."

"But what could he have done that would make someone want to kill him like that?" Candy continued. "It sounds like a premeditated act. Something that must have been planned."

"Maybe," Finn said. "They'll know more

117

when they figure out where the murder took place and can investigate the scene."

"Somewhere along the river," Doc surmised. "Possibly on a fishing boat."

"Or in a fishing *camp*," Candy said, "with nets and a few boning and skinning knives lying around."

That image pushed all three of them back into silence. Finn tilted his head thoughtfully, while Doc grimaced and rubbed his lower back, as if he could almost feel what it must have been like for Mick. As Candy considered her next questions, her gaze shifted, taking in the area around them. A few of the villagers lingered, milling around the community center, peeking in through the windows, while Carol, Tillie, and the other decision-makers were beginning to head off in different directions.

Inexorably, Candy's gaze was then drawn to the riverside, to the spot where Mick Rilke's body had been pulled out of the water. Though it was a little far away to see any details, and the scene was obscured in part by shrubbery and some of the buildings and warehouses in the marina complex, she could see the silhouettes of the officers and officials still milling around, although the EMTs and ambulance were gone, hauling Mick's body to a morgue somewhere, where it would be poked and prodded for additional clues to his death.

"Do they know anything about his whereabouts this morning?" she asked. "Or last night? Any idea of where he might have been last seen?"

Pulled out of his reverie, Finn said with a bit of a croaking voice, "Not that I've heard of. Again, I'm sure they're checking into that."

"I'm sure they are," Candy said, her mind working. "And what about that red truck of his? The one he drives in the winter, with the snowplow in front?"

Again, Finn shrugged and shook his head. He frowned, and his silence answered her questions.

The police, as he'd told them, were following up on all the obvious leads. They'd be talking to those who knew Mick closely, interviewing his wife, his family, work associates, and customers, looking for a suspect, a motivation, someone who might have had a grievance with him.

Candy knew she could do the same. She could talk to a few people who knew Mick. She could knock on a few doors and stop by a few workshops. She could ask questions at the hardware store or garden center, which she knew Mick frequented. She could flag down Wanda Boyle, who was probably headed back to her office by now. As the newspaper's managing editor, Wanda had her ear close to the ground and heard all the latest gossip from her shadowy network of spies and informants around town, which she'd carefully developed and nurtured over the past few years as she continued to solidify her position as one of the town's more powerful voices.

And that's why Candy decided to avoid those avenues of investigation — at least for now. She doubted she'd learn anything new at the local stores or shops, and she wasn't sure she was quite ready to tangle with Wanda in a case like this again. In the past, Wanda had helped solve a few similar murder cases in Cape Willington, and had even been closely involved in one or two of them herself. But even though the two of them had worked together in the past, they were hardly BFFs. Though the animosity between them had leveled off, Candy knew Wanda still had a temper with a hair trigger and could turn unpredictable at times.

Besides, she had a better idea: to follow the trail of clues back to where this whole thing had started, just a few hours ago.

"So what are you thinking?" her father asked.

When she turned to him, she saw that he was eyeing her curiously. So was Finn.

She took a moment to glance back down along the river, and out toward the backs of the departing crowds, and to the traffic on the Coastal Loop, before she turned her gaze inland, in the general direction of Sugar Hill Farm.

"I think," she said, with a tilt of her head, "I need to go maple sugaring."

Eleven

For the second time that day, Candy navigated her way along the lane that led to the house, barn, and sugar shack at the Milbrights' place.

She kept a relatively light grip on the steering wheel, letting it slide easily in either direction through her fingers as the road jerked and twisted the front wheels, but she was ready to clamp down instantly should the Jeep swerve too far off track. As a farmer herself, she was used to roads like this. She drove them all the time. This one wasn't as muddy as some she'd been on over the past couple of weeks, but she noticed still-melting ice crusts rimming the sides of the road, and puddles all along the way, and knew it could turn sloppy real fast if it received too much traffic, as it probably would this weekend. Hutch had anticipated that, she saw, dropping down a mixture of gravel, straw, and topsoil in some of the muckier places to help firm them up. He'd also finished placing signs along the dirt lane and out on the main road, pointing tour buses and anticipated visitors toward his maple sugaring operation, which would be running at full steam all weekend.

The road twisted and dipped, and she drove through a cluster of sugar maple trees with the sap buckets still attached to them and a chaotic network of clear tubing running from the buckets to a collection tank somewhere nearby.

As she came out from under the trees and approached the house, she spotted a large, hand-painted sign up ahead that read PARKING. A red arrow directed visiting vehicles to a roped-off lot to the right of the barn. A little farther along, a banner hanging across the front of the barn announced, WELCOME TO SUGAR HILL FARM AND OUR WORLD-FAMOUS SUGAR SHACK.

She was doubtful of the second half of that particular statement, but supposed some visitor from across the pond, maybe Scotland or Ireland, had stopped by the sugar shack at some point in the past, and that gave Hutch and Ginny reason enough to profess their international recognition. After all, in maple sugaring, as in most things in life, marketing was important.

There were more signs around the house and barn, pointing visitors to the maple sugar shack back toward the tree line on the right, and inside the barn, where the Milbrights planned to sell bottles of their maple syrup on tables they'd set up.

They've been busy, Candy thought as the pulled the Jeep to a stop in front of the barn. The place looked like it was nearly ready for the maple sugaring tours. As she'd just heard from Carol, a number of volunteers had been lined up to help out with the tours, so the Milbrights could focus on boiling the sap and monitoring the sales table in the barn. Candy would be helping Neil do the same thing tomorrow over at Crawford's Berry Farm.

From the driver's seat, she quickly surveyed the place, looking for Hutch and Ginny, but unlike earlier when she'd been out here, there was no one around. A white Ford Explorer, probably ten or fifteen years old, was parked in the driveway. That was primarily Ginny's vehicle, Candy knew. Hutch sometimes drove an old green farm truck; she could see its tail end sticking out behind the barn. The tractor was gone, though, and the sap collection wagon — just like over at Neil's place. Obviously, the Milbrights were out in the woods making last-minute sap collections.

Candy pulled up beside the barn, stopped the Jeep, and shut off the engine. Again, in the absence of anyone here to talk to, she pondered her next move.

She could head back to Blueberry Acres and let the whole thing go for now — let the authorities handle it. They were the experts at this sort of thing. That, she thought, would be her best move, and probably her smartest one. She had plenty to do over the weekend to keep her occupied without getting herself involved in an amateur murder investigation.

Or she could drive into the village, to the newspaper's office on Ocean Avenue, and find out if Wanda Boyle had heard anything new about Mick's death. That was still an option, though still not a good one. She could hunt down Maggie and head over to Town Park, as they'd originally planned. She could make another trip over to Crawford's Berry Farm and try to track down Neil and Random. She could, of course, head over to the police station and report what she'd found. Or she could just give the chief a call — and get herself in hot water with him, all over again, for the nth time in a row.

She could do any of those things.

She was still thinking it over when the mobile phone buzzed in her back pocket. She leaned forward in the driver's seat, reached behind her, pulled out the phone, and looked at the screen.

She'd received a text — from the chairman of the town council, no less.

Can you solve this ASAP? read the message from Mason Flint, the town council chairman.

That was it. Nothing more. Candy blinked several times. She really didn't need to read more. She knew what was behind his request.

Mason had relied on her before to help solve some of the past murders that had taken place in Cape Willington — unofficially, of course, off the record. But his entreaties in those instances had been urgent. In addition to ensuring the safety of the villagers as much as possible, his goal, as always, was to protect the town's reputation — and its business community — as best as he could.

The sooner this is solved, he'd probably tell her if he was sitting in the seat beside her, or leaning in the side window, *the better for us all.*

As she sat in her Jeep in the driveway at the Milbrights' place, she considered her response. After a few moments she texted him back.

I'll do what I can.

Then she keyed off the phone and slipped it back into her pocket, gazing out at the woods around her as she did so.

She knew what she had to do. She'd avoided it, hoped the situation wouldn't call for this, but ultimately she knew it would. There was no getting around it. If she wanted to solve the mystery of the sap thefts, and determine if there were any links to Mick Rilke's death, she had to see the place where the whole thing had started that morning. She had to find those illegally tapped trees out in the Milbrights' woods and search the area herself, to see if she could locate any clues that might lead her to some answers.

So she hopped out of the Jeep and walked around toward the back, where she opened the rear hatch. She slipped out of her tennis shoes and pulled on calf-high rubber mud boots, which she always kept with her at this time of year. She also grabbed wool ear warmers and gloves, just in case she got chilly, and made sure she had her compass with her. She didn't want to get lost out there.

When she was all set, she closed the hatch,

locked up the Jeep, and set off into the woods behind the sugar shack.

TWELVE

The wind died and the sun receded as dark trunks closed in around her. They nudged in from the sides, while overhead a canopy of entangled limbs began to block out the sky. It was far from gloomy in the woods, however. There was a certain brightness to it today, a glistening, and a surprisingly fresh scent. The birds were out and active, singing high in the trees and flittering about, and she heard the typical cracking and sighing sounds as the snow and ice still left on the ground disintegrated, creating soggy spots she was careful to avoid.

Other than the muddy patches, her path, as it turned out, was a relatively easy one. Once behind the sugar shack, at the edge of the trees, she'd spotted a well-trodden track leading back into the woods, a trail created by the frequent passages of Hutch's tractor and cart as he went back and forth on his sap-collecting trips. In the early sections the trail was relatively dry, just loose gravel and dead leaves and flattened vegetation where the tractor's wheels had passed. She encountered the soggy spots a little farther in, where the tractor and cart had left deep ruts that dug into the crusty ground cover. In those places she stayed to either side, seeking high ground when possible, or sometimes walking in the center of the track between the two ruts, always looking for the least soggy footing. Still, her boots soon became encased in mud and muck and clumps of moist earth and dead dry leaves and twigs. She was glad she'd worn them.

Despite the mud and muck, she made good time. It wasn't quite as chilly here in the woods as she'd thought it might be. The land was warming. There was a low, misty fog in some of the swampier places, but in others the sun shone through the trees.

A few hundred yards in, she came across the first offshoot from the main trail, headed to the north and apparently looping around toward the east, to her right. But it looked like it hadn't been disturbed in several days, perhaps a week, so she stayed on the main trail, which took a more westerly route, through the trees and occasional clearings, and along a rocky ridge.

As she moved farther into the woods, she

thought she might hear the hum and sputter of Hutch's tractor, or maybe the echoes of its passage through the trees. But for the most part the woodsy silence remained unbroken, except for an occasional animal call or the brisk clatter of branches overhead as a burst of wind shot through them. She hurried on, not exactly sure where she was going, but keeping an eye on the ground for clues as to Hutch's whereabouts.

She soon came upon a small clutch of tapped trees to either side of the trail. There were perhaps ten or fifteen sugar maple trees in a fairly tight area, all with white plastic collection buckets hanging from them. No real need for a network of plastic tubing here, leading to a collection tank on the ground — as a larger operation might have — since the trees were close enough together to make collecting the individual buckets a fairly quick process.

On an impulse, Candy darted to one side and checked several of the buckets. They were mostly empty, though she saw the sap was still flowing freely today, with a steady drip coming from many of the trees. Empty buckets meant Hutch had collected the sap recently, she thought, especially if the sap was still flowing at that pace.

Looking down, she focused her gaze on

the disturbed earth around the trees, and soon spotted what looked like traces of fresh footprints pressed into the ground in a few places — a heel here, a boot toe there. Probably made by Hutch's boots. So he'd been through here, but how long ago? An hour, or two? She'd seen him just a few hours ago. So he must have come through here recently. He must be close by.

She looked around again, turning a complete circle, her ears sharpened to every sound.

Was he still out here, somewhere just ahead of her? Or had he looped around back toward the sugar shack?

At the moment, she thought, it didn't really matter where Hutch had gone. The goal was to find the illegally tapped trees. So she pressed on.

She walked for another ten minutes, past two more turn-offs. Nothing. She knew she was somewhere near the back of the Milbrights' property. She hesitated. Was she close to the illegally tapped trees? Was she even in the general vicinity? Should she go on, or turn back?

She checked her watch. It was nearing one thirty. She felt time slipping away, and she had other things to do. She wanted to find out what had happened to Maggie and head

132

over to Town Park to help her set up the booth. She wanted to stop back by Neil's house to let him know about the Milbrights' accusations, so he wasn't blindsided by them. She had to catch up with her father.

"Five more minutes," she told herself, "and then I'll turn back."

It didn't take five minutes. She found the trees in question just over the next rise in the trail, only a few hundred paces farther on.

THIRTEEN

She knew it right away. There was no mistaking it.

Hutch had cordoned off the area in a general fashion using yellow police crime scene tape he'd picked up somewhere. He'd marked the boundaries with stretches of tape ten or fifteen feet in length, creating a partially enclosed octagon of sorts. And she noticed a few outliers here and there — trees outside the ring with yellow tape tied around their trunks. None of the trees she could see, in or outside the ring, had sap collection buckets attached to them. Some-one had removed those. But she could see darker spots on some of the tree trunks, disturbed areas that could indicate some tampering.

From where she stood on a high spot along the track, the slope stretched away from her, downward for twenty or thirty feet before leveling out. This part of the woods was relatively clear of underbrush, with a soft carpet of dead leaves, pine needles, dry bracken and grasses, and a few heavy patches of moss, which looked silver today and matted down, like tightly packed steel wool. Small rocks were strewn everywhere, and farther along she could see larger boulders bordering the trail, which eventually veered to the left, back toward the farm.

A quick scan of the area revealed no sign of Hutch or his tractor. But she saw tractor tire marks in the damp ground just a little ahead of where she stood. He'd been here and moved on.

But she was hesitant to move on. She wanted to survey the scene first.

Instinctively she edged a little closer to a nearby tree as she studied the landscape. Leaves rattled at her feet and the forest shuffled and sighed around her. Something about this place made her feel uneasy. It was as if she'd wandered into a crime scene of sorts, though no one had died here — at least, no one she knew of, except perhaps a tree or two. A whispering wind rattled the tops of the branches above her, and while the rest of the woods had seemed sunny and bright, there was a shadow here. She looked up. Just a cloud passing by, blocking out the light, filtering it strangely. A temporary thing. It would pass. And hopefully her uneasiness would pass also. Still, she thought it best to be cautious.

For a final time she looked in all directions. Then, moving carefully and quietly, she started to her right, stepping gingerly as she began to circle around the outside of the ring. Aware of any footprints she might be leaving behind, she tried to stay to the leafier or rockier spots, to the clumps of pine needles or the crusty patches of leftover snow, which were melting and would soon take with them any signs of her passing. She knew she was probably being overly cautious, but she didn't want to make any mistakes, given the unknowns about the current situation.

She wished, in that moment, that she'd brought someone along with her. Maggie, perhaps, or her father. Someone for backup — or to run for help, just in case. It had never crossed her mind, until just now, as she was creeping through the woods alone. She wasn't sure it was the brightest thing she'd done, and briefly considered turning back, but she quickly shook that thought away. She'd come this far. Might as well finish what she'd started.

After she'd made her way halfway around the ring, she swung to her right to inspect one of the outlier trees, which stood apart from the other maples in a nest of low pine trees and shrubs. She could see right away that it had multiple taps in it, one larger than the others. A deep wound digging into the ragged bark, it looked nearly an inch across. A mass of congealed sap had gathered around the intrusion, as if trying to heal it. The overflow had left cloudy, clumpy streaks running down the bark, but it appeared the tree had dried up. There was no fresh, glistening sap.

She moved on, seeing the same thing on other trunks. While the sap was still flowing on the trees she'd passed earlier, here the sugar maples had nothing left to give. They looked as if they'd been tapped out — and seemed to confirm what Hutch had told her earlier in the day.

She also noticed, on closer inspection, that the ground was disturbed in some places around the trees. Dead leaves had been shoved aside, and she saw heavy bootprints in the churned-up earth. *Someone* had been tromping around a lot out here.

She moved from one tapped tree to another, crouching down at times to inspect a print closer, until she found what she was looking for, around a small cluster of sugar maples. All had been heavily tapped, and the ground was low and soggy. Here, she found two different pairs of footprints in the mud. They were almost side by side, though headed in opposite directions. One was larger than the other, possibly a ten or eleven shoe in a men's size, but both were wide, with deep heel marks. Different treads were on the bottoms. The smaller one had a wavy pattern, and the larger a blockier design made up of geometric shapes, like trapezoids and parallelograms.

Two different bootprints, two different shoe sizes.

She tried to recall the bootprints she'd seen earlier along the track. They'd been the ones with the wavy pattern, on the smaller boots. Were those Hutch's prints? Or someone else's?

On an impulse, she pulled her phone from her back pocket, leaned in close, and snapped a few pictures of each print.

So two people had indeed been out here at some point over the past day or two. But were the two people adversaries? Or had they been working together? Hutch and Ginny, for instance? That could explain it. Simple enough. Ginny had been helping her husband collect the sap; hence, two different sets of footprints in two different sizes. But if Hutch's boots were the smaller ones with the wavy pattern on the bottom, did that mean the larger ones were Ginny's? Or had the prints been made by someone else?

Both sets of prints looked fairly fresh, though it was hard to be sure about these things. Also, there was no way to tell if they'd been made at the same or different times.

As Candy pondered the possibilities, her gaze wandered, shifting around the woods, and a sudden thought came to her:

Where had this alleged sap thief taken the buckets of maple sap once he or she had stolen them?

How would the thief have transported the sap away from this site? Where had it gone?

It was an intriguing thought.

The sap couldn't have been airlifted away, so it must have been taken out on the ground. Possibly by a tractor and cart, like Hutch used, although that meant there would be signs of a second tractor out here. If, for instance, Neil Crawford had driven his tractor over here from his farm, there would be imprints of it somewhere around here. Even though she'd seen no evidence of that, it was one possibility.

Another option was just as simple and more likely: a pickup truck parked nearby, with collection tanks in the truck bed.

Hutch had said there was a service road behind his property. That would make it easy to access this part of his woods and transport the stolen sap out of here.

So she began to search again, on the far side of the ring of yellow tape, toward the back of the Milbrights' property. She knew what she was looking for — a singular footpath, or perhaps a series of paths, leading away from the tapped trees toward the service road.

She followed several, which turned in various directions, until she spotted one that led off into the woods at a right angle, away from the Milbrights' farm. It seemed to take almost a direct line from the tapped trees to the back of the property.

She knew right away this was the path she was seeking.

It appeared as if someone had traveled back and forth along the path a number of times, and here she recognized a third set of bootprints, with ringed circles about the heels and balls of the feet.

A third set of prints. So there *had* been someone else back there — Hutch, Ginny . . . and the sap thief.

FOURTEEN

Hutch had been right. This appeared to be the evidence needed to support his claim, that someone *was* stealing his sap.

But who? And why?

The path, she thought, might hold an answer. Those new bootprints might as well, if she could identify the owner.

She tried to remember what type of boots Neil wore, and what type of patterns they had on the bottoms. But she'd never taken the time to look that closely at them. She'd never had a reason.

She put that thought aside for now as she studied the path and the footprints in front of her.

The boots with the circles on the bottoms had made several trips through here, going back and forth. She looked behind her, back the way she'd come, and then in the other direction, following the path with her eyes until it disappeared into the woods.

Time to find out where it led.

As confident as she'd ever be out here, she started off through the woods again. She moved as silently as possible, placing her feet carefully as she went. Rather than walk directly on the path, she moved in a line that took her parallel to it. She wanted to avoid disturbing any potential evidence — and possibly incriminate herself by mixing her footprints with the sap thief's.

Back into a denser part of the woods she went. The foliage rose up again and closed in around her, a mixture of taller bushes, thicker stands of trees, and knee-high vegetation. A few times she thought she'd lost her way, and she was beginning to become worried that she'd get turned around in these woods. But then they thinned again, the open sky returned, and the path ended. Quite suddenly, she stepped out of the woods into a cleared space — an unpaved road.

The service road. The one at the back of the Milbrights' property. The place where Hutch had allegedly spotted the red vehicle.

The road was more mud than dirt at this time of year, she noticed right away as she looked in both directions. It was slightly wider than a single lane, edged in tightly on the sides by the encroaching woods. At both ends, a hundred feet or so on either side of her, the road curved around, to the right in both directions, with the two legs headed away from each other.

At the moment, it was empty. Nothing of interest in sight. Just trees and mud, with the sky above.

She looked down to see if she could spot any tire tracks through here, or tractor tracks, or anything that might give her some clue about the vehicles that might have passed this way recently. She saw some tire markings, but nothing stood out. Any number of vehicles could have passed through here. There were mud ruts all along the way. But at the same time, it was obvious that the road was not heavily traveled. Just a back access road, as Hutch had said.

She wanted to get a better look at the tire tracks and mud ruts on the far side, so she hopped over a muddy spot to more solid ground in the middle of the road. There she paused, looking down at the ground around her, searching for anything interesting. Her gaze was focused on the muddy road, and she wasn't really paying attention to anything else around her. The wind picked up, and she heard it humming low in her ears. And, strangely enough, it sounded like it was getting louder — like it was coming closer, toward her.

She looked up. The wind appeared to be rushing. A tornado, perhaps? But on a clear day?

She heard other sounds then — what sounded like the revving of an engine, the spinning of wheels. A sort of whipping sound, a rush of oncoming air.

The hum grew louder, and she realized it wasn't the wind.

She turned her head quickly back and forth, her gaze shifting first one direction, then the other. She spotted it then, and was somewhat shocked by its sudden appearance in these quiet woods. It came around the curve to her left, emerging from behind a screen of trees like a lion on the prowl. And it sounded like a lion too, its hum building into a roar, blocking out the natural sounds around her.

Going too fast for this type of road, it swerved around the curve. Its back end slid out a little in the mud, and the rear wheels spun with a high whine, until the tires finally caught on something solid and the vehicle lurched forward. It straightened and came right at her, down the center of the road, its black tires deep in the mud ruts. As it approached, it seemed to accelerate, the engine revving higher, the tires kicking up sprays of wet, dark mud in their wake.

As she stood there in the middle of the road, unbidden words echoed through her mind, words Mick Rilke had spoken to her a couple of weeks earlier, said with a laugh.

In snow, drive slow; in mud, drive as fast as you can.

She'd put that in her column in this week's issue of the paper. The driver of the approaching vehicle must have read it, because he or she was following Mick's advice. The vehicle was going as fast as it could on this back road, coming straight toward her.

Momentarily she froze, and her heart seemed to stop as her brain struggled with what she was seeing. Her thoughts were scattered, indecisive. She expected the vehicle to slow down or veer off, to try to avoid hitting her. But it didn't. It just kept coming, though it was swerving back and forth in the mud ruts as it approached, almost rocking on its springs. It looked — and sounded — like it was out of control. She couldn't get a good read on it, and was suddenly afraid that, no matter which direction she went, the vehicle would follow her.

It barreled forward with alarming speed, its engine roar filling her ears. At this point she couldn't quite register what kind of vehicle it was, just a blunt nose and a mass of dark steel, gray glass, and faded chrome bearing down on her, looming larger and larger as it came on. There was no blast of a horn, and the face behind the windshield was obscured by glare. She thought she might have seen someone wearing sunglasses, maybe a hat or a flannel shirt. But everything was happening too fast. It was a blur.

She didn't take any longer to look. She had to move. More on a survival instinct than anything else, she jumped forward, taking big leaps as she hopped across the muddy road toward the far edge and the shelter of the woods.

Much to her shock, however, the vehicle followed her. It accelerated and zeroed in on her as she ran, and for an instant she registered the disturbing image of the driver twisting the steering wheel in her direction. The wheels spun on the mud and popped out of the ruts, making the vehicle rock so violently on its springs she could hear them creaking in protest.

She lost her footing as she reached the edge of the woods and fell, holding out her hands to cushion her landing on the mushy ground. Then she continued to move, scrambling away even farther, back into the shelter of the trees, hoping the big trunks on either side would protect her from the berserker vehicle that had appeared out of nowhere.

As she moved, she jerked her head back over she shoulder. The big vehicle was still coming toward her, but it was being jostled by the uneven road. It started to whirl around, as if the driver was losing control, and she thought it might even tip over. But at the last moment it found its footing and finally veered off.

As it sped past her, only a few feet away, she yelled something incomprehensible at it, though whether in fright or anger, she didn't know. She felt a rush of wind as it passed by, enough to tousle her hair. It skidded a little on the edge of the road as the driver turned the wheel the other direction, back toward the center of the narrow lane. Its back tires spun in the muck, again flinging up sprays of mud and dirt and gravel, and the engine sputtered as a cloud of black smoke erupted from the tailpipe. The vehicle swerved first one direction, then the other, until the tires settled back down into the mud ruts, and the vehicle accelerated again.

With a final belch of noise, it lunged down the road, swooped around the far curve, and was gone.

In its wake, it left only an echoing hum and the soft smacking sounds of disturbed mud ruts coming back together and airborne fragments splattering to the ground.

Candy was in shock as she watched the vehicle go. She realized her heart was racing, and she was breathing deeply. Her skin felt moist, and her legs felt numb. Her mind was a whirl of thoughts and emotions, but she finally registered what she'd just seen.

It was a van. An old van, probably twenty years old or more. And not red, but faded purple. It had looked like a giant withered grape.

Other images flashed through her mind of what she'd just seen. Mud-caked wheel wells, a number of nicks and dents. Rust around the grille and down along the sideboards.

And, as it drove away from her, she'd spotted an old Maine license plate attached to its rear, with six letters spelling out two words. It created a disturbing message that was instantly imprinted on her mind:

RIP DIG.

back. She didn't want to face another attack today.

She still wasn't quite sure if that's what
had happened. Maybe it had been a mistake,

FIFTEEN

"What the heck was *that*?" Candy practically shouted at the settling sprays of mud,
feeling the rush of the moment. Her chest
was heaving, her mouth was dry, and her
palms and knees were damp. She took a few
moments to calm herself, then rose un-
steadily. She brushed hair out of her face
and dashed her hands across her clothes,
trying to clean herself off. She had some
mud stains around the knees and elbows,
and some dead leaves and twigs snagged in
her fleece jacket. Her hands were trembling
and her stomach felt a little queasy. But
otherwise she was fine. Just shaken up.

Her first instinct was to get off this road
and out of these woods as quickly as possible. And that's what she did.

She didn't run. She didn't rush. But she
moved deliberately. As she crossed back over
the service road and reentered the woods
on the other side, she kept a sharp eye on

the road, in the direction the van had gone. She wanted to make sure it wasn't coming back. She didn't want to face another attack today.

She still wasn't quite sure if that's what had happened. Maybe it had been a mistake — an accident. Maybe the driver had looked away for a few moments and hadn't realized someone else was on the road. Maybe the driver had fallen asleep at the wheel. Maybe it had been a completely innocent act.

And maybe not. Maybe it had been deliberate.

But, she thought, it couldn't have been premeditated. Who knew she was going to emerge from the woods at this particular time, on this particular spot? No one, not even her. It didn't make any sense. It must have been a purely coincidental incident.

Whatever had just happened, she'd sort it out later, once she was in a safer place. Right now, it was time to retreat.

Rather than try to find a new way out of the woods, she decided to go back the way she'd come. She followed her own footprints, moving as quickly and silently as possible. As she went, she kept a constant lookout both ahead of and behind her. She wasn't ready for any more encounters. She'd had enough excitement for one day.

Time to get back to something more normal, around people she could trust.

She had no trouble finding her way out. Retracing her steps was simple enough. And the trip back seemed shorter than the one going in. She made good time, and was soon back at the Milbrights' farm.

Here, at the edge of the woods, she paused, giving herself time to scan the area first, but she saw nothing out of the norm. The place still looked deserted. Hutch and Ginny weren't around — nor anyone else, for that matter. At this point she wasn't quite sure what she'd say to them, since she still felt too flustered to explain what had just happened, and she decided she wanted to think through everything first before she talked to them again. It would probably be best to just slip away for now, unnoticed.

She didn't hurry as she made her way out of the shelter of the trees and into the open, but she didn't dawdle either. The sugar shack, as she passed it, was closed up, with no tractor and cart in sight. The barn was empty. The house looked dark. Everything appeared the same as it had been when she'd gone into the woods.

A few minutes later she was back in the Jeep. She took a final look around as she started the engine, but seeing nothing to cause her to stay, she backed up, hit the gas, and headed out to the main road.

SIXTEEN

As she drove into town, she tried to make sense of it all.

Now that she was away from the isolated woods behind the Milbrights' place and back among the living, she found she could focus her thoughts better. Naturally, the events of the past few hours had her feeling a little rattled, but she pushed aside her emotions and steadied her hands as she tried to unravel the myriad questions that had become entangled in her mind.

On some level, her encounter with the purple van on that isolated back road seemed surreal, almost dreamlike. She had a hard time believing it had actually taken place, since it had been so sudden, so unexpected. There was an otherworldly quality to it. *Had it really happened?* she wondered.

But of course it had happened. There was no doubt about it. Her imagination had not been running wild. *Someone* had almost run her over — that part she knew for certain. Whether it had happened on purpose or not — *that's* what she had to figure out.

The randomness of the encounter was a key point, she thought. Why that time of day? Why that exact moment? And what had the van been doing on that muddy back road in the first place? Where had it come from, and where had it been going?

It had passed by her from left to right — generally, she figured, on an angle from the southwest to the northeast — before it disappeared around the curve. She didn't know where that particular road came out, on either end. Most likely it connected to the Coastal Loop on its northeast end, if she had her bearings right, but in the other direction it could conceivably run all the way to the peninsula's other side, to the western coastline, or it could just terminate somewhere, at someone else's farm or property, or dwindle into a turnaround or a dead end, or even a cow path.

She decided that, at some point very soon, she'd have to go back and investigate that road, drive its length to become more familiar with it, find out where it began and where it ended. But not right now. She wasn't ready to make that commitment at the moment. She needed time to recover, to collect herself, to try to figure out what it meant. And she wanted to make sure she proceeded cautiously from here on. She didn't want to put herself back in a dangerous situation like that again — at least, not if she could help it.

In her mind, she could still see the image of the van as it bore down on her. It had approached with alarming speed, like an animal charging, headed straight for her from the moment it appeared. That part, at least, made a certain amount of sense, since initially she'd been standing right in the middle of the road. She'd been in the way of traffic. There wasn't a lot of maneuvering room on that road. It seemed plausible that the old van would appear to come at her like that.

But why hadn't the driver simply braked when he or she spotted someone standing in the middle of the road? Why appear to increase speed, or at the very least, make no attempt to stop? And why deliberately angle the steering wheel toward her when she tried to move out of the way? Why not stop to make sure she was okay?

Because, Candy concluded, it had been a deliberate attempt to run her down.

Who had been behind the steering wheel? Why come at her like that? Did it have anything to do with her investigation of the alleged sap thief?

She didn't have the answers right now, but she believed she'd been purposely targeted by the driver of that vehicle — which meant, she realized with a chill, that it *could* have been the actual murderer behind the wheel of the van.

Was she onto something? Was she getting too close to finding a few answers? Had Mick's murderer just tried to kill her also, to keep her from discovering the truth?

Who was it? Who killed Mick Rilke?

She'd caught a glimpse of the driver through the windshield, but not enough to make a positive identification. She remembered sunglasses and a hat. Possibly a round face. Possibly bearded, possibly not. Possibly hair sticking out the sides of the cap. Wearing? A dark top, a shirt or jacket of some sort, maybe a flannel shirt, maybe a fleece or cloth coat, brown or dark blue or black, with a hood.

Who might fit that description? Honestly, it could be any one of two dozen people she knew. Or someone she didn't know at all. Farmers, fishermen, landscapers, teachers, tradesmen, even business people and professionals, as well as other townsfolk around the cape, and across Maine, essentially all dressed the same, casually and comfortably, usually in jeans or khakis, sneakers or boots or low-heeled shoes, fleece jackets or sweaters, often with a ball cap, knit cap, or other hat of some sort, just as it appeared the driver had been wearing. In other words, an average Mainer.

So, she asked herself, what *did* stick out? She racked her brain, trying to recall any distinguishing features, but nothing came to mind. She hadn't been able to get a good enough look at the driver. She remembered things only in flashes. It had all happened too fast.

So what did she have? Not much. Too many generalities. Nothing concrete. Nothing at all.

Except for the color of the van. And its age. And its license plate.

RIP DIG.

That, at least, was something she could follow-up on, though what it might mean, she didn't know. She assumed the *RIP* part might mean *rest in peace,* but what about the *DIG?*

The plate had been on an old purple van, one she hadn't seen around town before, as far as she could remember. But then again, she saw so many old cars and work trucks everyday on the cape, she didn't know if she'd remember if she *had* seen it. It probably would have just blended in anywhere it went. Other than the color, which was washed out, there wasn't anything unique about it.

But if it did belong to someone in town, she could find out easily enough.

Still, as she turned onto Main Street and headed past Gumm's Hardware Store on her right and the House of Style on her left, she knew one thing for certain — whatever she did, she'd have to proceed more carefully from here on. Try not to put herself into a precarious situation. But she wasn't about to give up on her investigation, no matter what threatening moves were made against her. She'd figure out this mystery one way or another. She just needed to keep digging, keep talking to people, keep asking questions, and keep searching for that red truck.

Right now, however, she just needed to find a parking spot.

Not surprisingly, given the upcoming weekend's activities, the improving weather, and the fact that it was a Friday afternoon, the town was busier than usual. But she managed to snag a spot in front of the

158

general store not too far from the bakery and bookstore. She pulled the Jeep to a stop, shut off the engine, grabbed her tote bag, and locked up the vehicle before heading up the street.

Usually at this time of year, in late March, the windows of the bakery would be dark and the ovens cold, since Herr Georg, when he'd been a single man, had wintered in Florida, returning to Cape Willington in mid-May to prepare his shop for the busy summer season. But today, Candy knew, she'd find light in the windows and warmed-up ovens inside. Newly married just a year ago, the Wolfsburgers had again spent some time in Florida this winter, but they'd returned early to open the shop for the upcoming weekend's festivities. After that, they planned to keep it open on a limited basis through April and May — four mornings during the week with extended afternoon hours on Tuesdays and Thursdays — before going full-time around Memorial Day and staying open right through the fall season.

As Candy passed the shop's large front window, emblazoned with the words BLACK FOREST BAKERY, EST. 1988 in an Old World–style typeface, she peered inside, but she saw no one in the front of the shop, behind the counter, or around the display cases. So she walked to the front door and tried the handle. To her surprise, she found it unlocked.

With a tilt of her head, she pushed open the door, which set off a tinkling bell above her, and stepped inside.

SEVENTEEN

The aromas coming from the bakery's kitchen in the back almost made her swoon. Just inside the door, she paused and rocked slightly on her heels, her head going back as the scents overwhelmed her. She always loved coming into this place, and every time she entered, she knew why. For the moment, thoughts of sugar shacks and tapped trees and wayward vans drifted to the back of her mind.

"Hello?" she called out, still seeing no one in the front of the shop. "Anyone home?"

She'd worked in the bakery herself several years ago, before Maggie took over for her behind the counter, so she knew her way around the place. The scents enveloping her were coming from the kitchen, so obviously that's where all the action was taking place. She headed in that direction, but before she could push through the swinging door into the back, Maggie came through from the other side, emerging in a flurry of flour.

"Oh, there you are!" Maggie said, brushing her hands together and then wiping them on her apron. "Thought I heard someone come in. Sorry to desert you earlier while you were inside the community center, but duty called — or, rather, Georg texted me and said he needed some help." She aimed a thumb behind her. "He's in full-press mode. I've been kneading dough and running the mixers for an hour. We've got all the ovens fired up. He's been baking all day."

"So I noticed," Candy said, sniffing deeply again. Scents of chocolate, maple syrup, and cinnamon were particularly strong. She pointed behind her. "The front door was unlocked. Are you open for business?"

"Not officially, but if someone walks in, we'll serve them. Helps me get my fingers warmed up on the cash register. Good practice for the busy season."

"What time are you opening in the morning?"

"Eight," Maggie said, "until three, when we move over to the park." Her eyes flicked to the cuckoo clock on the wall near the door. "Speaking of which, we're still heading over there in a little while to set up the booth, right?"

"Right. That's why I'm here."

"Good." Maggie nodded. "It shouldn't take too long. Ray's helping out, of course." She was referring to Ray Hutchins, a local handyman, who had assisted them with his carpentry and fix-it skills numerous times in the past at the bakery and out at Blueberry Acres. "He called just a little while ago. He's already at the park, unloading some stuff and getting everything set up for us. I just need to finish a few things here real quick and we can be on our way. You, um" — she pointed toward the kitchen behind her — "you want to try a sample of what he's making back there?"

"Do you have to ask? Let me guess what's on the menu. Chocolate Maple Brownies?"

"The moistest, most scrumptious, most maple-y brownies you've ever had in your life, I promise you that!" Maggie said, her eyes widening. "So, can I tempt you with one — or two?"

"When it comes to anything Herr Georg makes, I'm easily persuaded, as you well know," Candy said, and she held up her finger and thumb, a short distant apart. "Just a smidgeon, though. I'm trying to watch my weight. The older I get, the harder it is to keep the pounds off."

Maggie padded her burgeoning waistline.

"You can say that again. You know what it's like working here. If I don't watch out, I'm going to have to buy myself a bigger apron. Keeping my girlish figure is the hardest part of the job. That, and the early-morning hours."

"I thought you were getting used to that," Candy said as she started moving around the counter toward the kitchen door.

"Daylight saving time," Maggie replied, and she pulled a face. "That was hard to get used to this year. Sets my time clock out of whack. I'm still not really sure what time of the day it is anymore when I look outside. Why do we do that anyway?"

"Because, apparently," Candy said as her phone rang in her back pocket, and she reached around to fish it out, "it saves daylight."

"Hmm, well, there ain't much daylight when I get up in the morning, so I'm not sure we're saving anything," Maggie mused as she reached the kitchen door and began to push her way through. She continued talking over her shoulder as she went. "But Georg says he still loves me, despite the few extra pounds and all the yawning during the day. He's started calling me his little cupcake. Isn't that funny? And appropriate, I suppose, since I do love cupcakes. The icing especially. It's one of my Achilles' heels. Of course, I've lost count of how many of those I have, especially working here!"

She glanced behind her with a smile, to gauge her friend's reaction to her latest comments, but Candy had stopped in the doorway. She was studying her phone's screen with a questioning look on her face.

"Who's that?" Maggie asked, stopping also.

Candy shook her head. "I'm not sure. I don't recognize the number, but it's a local area code." Curious, she swiped at the screen and held the phone to her ear. "Hello?"

"Is this Candy Holliday?" a quasi-familiar female voice asked.

"Yes. Who's this?"

"It's Jean Rilke. Mick's wife." She said it almost as if nothing had happened and this was a completely normal day, though Candy detected a slight hitch in the other woman's voice.

"Oh, of course! I should have recognized your voice. Hi, Jean." Candy's eyes flicked to Maggie as she instantly switched her tone to a more empathetic one. "I'm so sorry to hear about your loss. Mick will be greatly missed around the village. He was a wonderful person. If there's anything I can do. . . ."

165

"Yes, well, that's why I called," Jean interrupted in a flat tone. "I wonder if you and I could speak. In person. As soon as possible."

Candy tried not to sound surprised. "Um, well, of course. I, ah, I'm sure we can figure out how to do that." She paused. "What would you like to talk to me about — if I may ask?"

Jean's voice turned a little hoarse. "It's a . . . private matter." She cleared her throat before she proceeded. "We can discuss it when we meet. When can you get here?"

It was such a forthright request that Candy was caught off guard. Absently, she rubbed her brow and turned toward the front door, her gaze unfocused, as she considered how to respond. "Well, I'm not sure, honestly. I have a current engagement and I . . ."

Jean interrupted, and her tone was more firm now. "Candy, I wouldn't ask if this wasn't important. I need your help with something and, frankly, I don't know where else to turn." She paused, and in a voice that sounded suddenly desperate, she added, "You see, it appears I'm being investigated by the police for the murder of my husband."

EIGHTEEN

A few minutes later, Candy keyed off the call with a look of uncertainty on her face.

Despite Jean's request and her revelation about the police investigation, Candy had given the other woman a noncommittal answer. Then she ended the call as graciously as possible, asking for some time to think it over.

But Maggie set her straight. "You're going, of course," she said after Candy filled her in on the details.

"I don't know." Candy was torn. "She wants to see me as soon as possible, but I was going to help you with the booth this afternoon."

Maggie waved a hand. "Oh, don't worry about that. Ray's on the scene. You know how he is. He probably has the whole thing assembled by now anyway. Honey, this is the *widow* of a dead man they just fished out of the river! She wants to see you. You *have* to go. We can meet at the park afterward and you can tell me *everything* that happened."

Maggie was right, of course, so Candy called Jean back, told her she'd be right over, and with a quick good-bye to her friend, headed outside to her Jeep.

The Rilkes lived on the crest of a low hill, a few miles outside of town, at the end of a long stony lane that wound its way inland from the main road. Candy had driven past the lane to their house numerous times, but had stopped in here only a few times before. There was never much of a need to come out here. Mick was usually somewhere around town, in one of his two trucks. He could be flagged down if his services were required. He was often spotted at the Lightkeeper's Inn, where he helped out with the landscaping and snowplowing, and could be seen hanging around the garden center or the hardware store or the Main Street Diner, where he favored an end stool at the counter, usually with a half-eaten doughnut or a slice of pie in front of him.

Jean, on the other hand, was a homebody who kept the place running in her husband's absences — which at certain times of the year tended to be a lot, as Mick was often away from dawn to dusk. In the winter, from what Candy had heard through the local grapevine, Jean holed up inside the house, weaving and sewing, reading or cooking. But during the other seasons she was outside most of the time, maintaining the property's extensive gardens and its small apple orchard. Their dog, a black Lab named Velvet, kept her company and went everywhere with her around the property. Jean showed up sometimes at community events and public meetings, where she stayed on the periphery of crowds and rarely spoke up, maintaining a watchful gaze instead. She was most sociable during harvest and canning season, since she was a card-carrying member of the village's Putting Food By Society. But at other times of the year, and especially during the winter months, she could almost disappear, never leaving the homestead for days or even weeks at a time.

Which was why Candy had been surprised by her call. Now, as she drove up the well-kept lane, she was uncertain of what to expect.

The Rilkes' home was a typical New Englander, a two-story white clapboard affair in relatively good condition, with a peaked tin roof, tall narrow windows, and a small front porch. Behind the house stood a windbreak of tall pine and a few thin-trunked deciduous trees, and just beyond that, a low stone wall trailed off down the slope and into the woods. Huddled next to the house, on its right, windward side, was a collection of outbuildings, including a white barn and a low-roofed garage and workshop, connected by a covered breeze-way. There were a couple of smaller buildings as well, which were used for storage, Candy recalled. Today, their tiny windows were dark.

On Candy's previous visits, Mick had done most of the talking, in part because she'd been there to interview him for various articles she'd been working on at the time. Jean had rarely spoken during those visits, and had generally drifted away after the interviews had started. They'd seen each other around town on occasion, and had acknowledged each other with eye contact, perhaps a nod, but nothing more than that. They'd never had a real conversation together. They'd never been friends, barely even acquaintances. It was obvious Mick had been the extrovert of the couple, while Jean was his polar opposite.

An odd couple of sorts, with very different personalities, but nothing really out of the norm.

Velvet, keeping a watchful eye from the side lawn, spotted the Jeep coming and was instantly on her feet, sounding the alarm. Moments later, Jean's pale face appeared in the side door's window. Her dark, hollow eyes followed the vehicle as it pulled to a stop, and watched as Candy hopped out of the Jeep and crossed the driveway toward the house. Jean's face disappeared then. Candy stopped to greet Velvet, giving her a few scratches behind the ears, before climbing the stairs and knocking on the door.

"It's open," said a muted voice from within.

As Candy turned the handle and pushed open the door, she heard the voice add, "Let Velvet in, would you? And lock the door behind you. I don't want anyone to walk in on us unexpected. We can talk in the living room."

Through the half-open door, Candy saw a shadowy figure rise from a chair at the kitchen table and shuffle across the linoleum floor. On the other side of the room, the figure headed around a corner and out of view.

Candy hesitated in the doorway. *Who would walk in on them?* she wondered. *And why such a mysterious greeting?* But she didn't think about it too much, given the circumstances, and did as the grieving widow asked. She opened the door a little wider and looked behind her. She was about to call out but didn't have to. As if on cue, the black Lab bounded up the steps, scooted around her legs, and dashed inside, ruffling against her jeans. Almost faster than she could follow it with her eyes, the dog zipped across the kitchen floor and dashed around the corner after Jean, also disappearing from view.

"Well!" Candy said to no one in particular. Overly cautious because of Jean's cryptic warning, she took a final look behind her, at the driveway and yard, just to make sure no one was hanging around out there. Then, with a shrug, she followed the dog into the house.

She took a step or two inside before she stopped and turned to lock the door. It was an old lock and required some finagling to get it right. She had a feeling they didn't lock the door much, or the mechanisms inside would have moved more smoothly. Apparently, when Mick was around, they didn't worry much about someone unexpected walking in on them. Once it was locked, she tugged on the door, just to make sure it remained shut tight, and turned back to survey the kitchen.

She needed a few moments to let her eyes adjust to the darker interior. All the blinds had been pulled down, giving the place a sad, gloomy feel. Jean probably just wanted to block out the whole world at this point. Certainly understandable, Candy thought.

It was a large kitchen, typical of a house of its era, perhaps sixty or seventy years old. Cabinets and appliances were located along the two exterior walls, interspersed by a trio of tall windows. A small breakfast table, piled with newspapers, magazines, and unopened mail, stood to one side. Boots and sneakers were neatly lined up on mats beside the door. The linoleum floor was worn but clean. Dishes were washed and drying in a rack. A kettle had been put on the gas stove to boil.

Candy didn't allow herself the time to look around too long. Trying to organize her thoughts, she crossed the kitchen to the dining room, where the linoleum gave way to heavily varnished old wood floorboards. All the blinds had been pulled down in here as well.

She turned the corner, where she found a short dark hallway that led toward the front of the house. Candy followed it and came to an archway on her right. Here, in the living room, she found the widow of Mick Rilke.

"Jean," she said as she stepped into the room, "I came as quickly as I could. I was so sorry to hear about your loss. You have my deepest condolences."

"You're very kind," said Jean Rilke in a low, thick voice, as if her throat needed to be cleared. "Now, please, sit down. As I said on the phone, we need to talk."

NINETEEN

"Um . . . of course, Jean."

It was admittedly a lame response but it was the best Candy could come up with at the moment. She spoke the words softly, in a whispery tone, as if she were in a library, for in some ways that was how it felt in here. Hushed, still, closed in. This whole thing was odd and a little unsettling. She wasn't quite sure what she was doing here. But, she thought, she'd see it through, find out what Jean wanted, and do what she could to comfort the other woman.

She paused in the archway as she searched for an appropriate place to sit. As in the rest of the house, the shades were pulled down here, too, plunging the room into shadows. But her eyes had started to adjust to the gloominess. She could see well enough, though the colors were muted and some of the shapes indistinct.

Jean had ensconced herself in a dark easy

chair tucked into the opposite corner. A series of shelves, bookcases, and cabinets lined the wall on the right. In the center of the room was a coffee table of dark wood, also covered with magazines and books. Along the left wall, under a shaded window, sat a brown corduroy sofa with large throw pillows at either end. That's where Candy headed.

She took a few steps into the room, trying to tread as quietly as possible, so as not to disrupt the somber atmosphere, but still a few floorboards creaked under her heels. She had to hold herself back from verbally apologizing.

Velvet, seated at her mistress's feet, watched their visitor the entire time with curious brown eyes. Then, as Candy reached the couch and turned to sit, the dog vigorously scratched herself behind the ears with her hind leg. Her collar chain and tags rattled noisily, breaking the silence. At the same time, the kettle whistled impatiently in the kitchen.

With a few soft-spoken words, Jean rose from her chair, passed in front of Candy, and disappeared around the archway. Velvet hopped up and followed closely on Jean's heels. Candy found herself alone in the dimly lit room.

"Well," she said to herself again as she settled uneasily onto the edge of the sofa. For a moment she was tempted to follow Jean into the kitchen, but she decided to stay put. Better to let the other woman proceed at her own pace. She'd talk when she was ready.

As Candy waited, her gaze wandered around the room, centering on the wall of shelves, bookcases, and cabinets on the other side of the room. At first glance she couldn't make out much on those shelves. She desperately wanted to open a window and let in some light. *That might help Jean's mood,* she thought, *and would make it easier to see in here.*

On an impulse she rose, stepped around the coffee table, and crossed to the shelves. She stopped in front of them, her eyes sweeping over the book spines, interspersed with vases and candles and keepsakes, before settling on several framed photographs arranged on one of the cabinet tops to her right.

Not surprisingly, Mick Rilke was well represented in the photos. There was one of him with all his fishing gear at some secluded spot along the river, in front of what looked like a boathouse. Another showed him in front of his gray landscaping truck.

Mick sported a huge, toothy grin in the photo, which looked a decade or so old. He'd had more hair back then, and his paunch wasn't quite so pronounced.

Her gaze shifted. Two other photos drew her attention. One was recent, while the other looked much older. The first showed Mick in front of the new community center. There was still quite a bit of snow on the ground, so it must have been taken in late January or early February, when a trio of storms had blown through the area, one right after the other. It looked like it had been cold that day. Hands were tucked in pockets and cloud breaths emerged from mouths. Mick was standing with a group of bundled-up people, including Mason Flint, Carol McKaskie, Elvira Tremble, Cotton Colby, and Tillie Shaw. Candy's father was absent, but Finn Woodbury represented the posse. She saw a few other familiar faces, including Ginny Milbright's, but no Hutch. Ray Hutchins, the local handyman, also stood in the background.

Good company, she thought. Mick certainly ran in the right circles.

The other photo, the older one, took her a few moments to decipher. It showed a group of perhaps forty to fifty students, all in caps and gowns, standing on a set of risers set against a brick wall, maybe in a cafeteria or gymnasium. A sign in front of the group identified it as the CLASS OF 1981, CAPE WILLINGTON HIGH SCHOOL. This was the entire class, she knew. The high school claimed fewer than three hundred students total, in four grades. She scanned the faces, figuring the photo must be here for a reason. Some of the students looked vaguely familiar, but most didn't. And then she spotted him. He was young, and his face was still changing, but she noticed the distinctive features. It was a teenage Mick Rilke, standing toward the end of the top riser. He'd been husky even then, though his face was more boyish, his hair an uncontrolled mop. Just in front of him, on a lower riser, was a pleasant-looking young woman. She had a round face and kept her dark hair short even then. It was Jean, Candy realized. She stood next to another young man, this one with a beard. She knew right away who it was. He'd been a big lad even then, though his features had matured over the years, but the same basic structure was there. It wasn't hard to identify him as Hutch Milbright.

So they'd all been in the same graduating class, Candy thought. Something she hadn't known. Interesting.

She moved on, continuing to scan the shelves, and spotted a photo of Jean and Velvet toward the far end. Other than the high school graduation photo, this was the only one with Jean in it. For some reason, the lady of the house wasn't well represented in this photo gallery. Looking back across the bookshelf, Candy confirmed that Jean wasn't in any of the photos. No wedding photo even. No images of her and Mick dating, or hanging out as a younger couple. Most of them were of Mick.

That's odd, Candy thought. *Jean must be camera shy.*

She heard footsteps then, approaching along the hall, and returned to her seat on the sofa just as Jean and Velvet came around the corner of the archway.

Without a word, Jean set a tray on the coffee table and poured tea for both of them, before returning to the easy chair with a teacup in her hand.

"Now," she said in a flat tone, as Velvet settled at her feet, "on to business."

TWENTY

"First of all," Jean said as her eyes took on a defensive glint and her whole demeanor hardened to New Hampshire granite, "and before you ask, no, I didn't kill my husband. Just let me make that clear right from the start, okay?"

She said these last few words emphatically, in sharp contrast to her earlier somber tone. "It's what I told the police, and it's what I'll tell you. I don't know what happened to him. I don't know how he wound up in that river, wrapped in a net like that. I don't know where he was when . . . . well, you know, where he spent his last minutes on earth."

She paused as her carefully maintained manner threatened to crumble, and averted her eyes as she fought to keep her emotions in check. Her mouth quivered a little, but a few calming breaths seemed to settle her. Candy caught a glimpse into the woman's anguish and hesitated to speak, afraid she'd make it worse. Instead, she waited patiently as Jean gathered herself, which she soon did.

"We were happy early on, the two of us," she finally continued, her gaze distant, her voice turning wistful. "We were high school sweethearts, you know. And there was some competition for him, back in those days, I don't mind saying. But I was the lucky one who managed to snag him. We got married a few years after graduation, and we've had some good years together, but like many couples who've been together as long as we have, we'd grown apart. He had his interests; I had mine. I like keeping to myself, and he liked to get out and talk to other people. He was quite a talker, as you're probably aware. And he knew lots of folks. Most of the time, when he wasn't here at the house, I had no idea where he was at. Of course, on weekdays he stopped in at the diner for lunch, and he usually swung by Rusty's tavern after work, to hang out with the guys. The rest of the time he was on the road somewhere, at other people's houses or tending to commercial properties. He moved around a lot. It was hard to keep track of him. It was his job, you know. It took him all over the cape. He could have been anywhere, really, when it happened.

That's what I told the police."

She paused, and gulped, and focused her gaze back on Candy. Her voice lowered and turned hoarse again as she continued.

"At first, when the police came out here to talk about Mick, I thought it was just going to be routine stuff. I thought they'd just ask me if I knew what had happened to him. Maybe comfort a grieving widow a little. But that wasn't why they were here. Instead, they asked me where *I'd* been this whole time. Well, I don't mind telling you, that question surprised me. I knew right away what they were implying. And I told them point-blank they were on the wrong track. I did indeed."

She emphasized the statement with a firm nod of her head. There was silence in the room then, and Jean seemed to have run out of things to say for the moment, so she looked expectantly at Candy, who cleared her throat before she spoke.

"Thank you for telling me all that, Jean," Candy began. "I know this must be very hard for you. It's especially troubling that the police think you were somehow involved. But if I may ask, what was their response when you told them you didn't do it?"

Jean made a distasteful face. She could be

183

quite expressive, communicating a lot without saying a word. "They didn't believe me, of course. That seemed fairly evident. I could see it in their eyes. I'm pretty good at reading these things. Besides, I know what they say. The spouse is always the primary suspect in cases like this."

"I'm sure they're not thinking that in this case," Candy said.

"I beg to differ," Jean said sternly.

"But why would they think you had anything to do with Mick's death?"

"That's the question of the hour, isn't it?"

"Maybe it's just procedure."

"Maybe. But they seemed pretty interested in my whereabouts lately."

"Did they give you any idea of why they might suspect you? What did they say, specifically?"

Jean shifted in her seat, and Velvet moved restlessly as well. "They asked me where I've been lately. I told them I was right here the whole time."

"If I may clarify, what time frame are they looking at? When do they think . . . well? . . ."

"Since about six P.M. last night," Jean answered, giving no indication that the question bothered her. "They said they've established the time of death around early

184

evening, last night. Seven or eight, something like that. I told them I was here at the house all day yesterday, all last night, and all day today. But they weren't interested in taking me at my word. They wanted corroboration."

Candy nodded. "Whether anyone saw you here during that time. Whether someone stopped by the house, or you talked to one of the neighbors."

"Or if I sent any e-mails, made any calls on the landline or cell phone — to prove I was here, I suppose. Again, I'll tell you the same thing I told them. I spoke to my brother in Concord late yesterday afternoon around five. That's the Concord in New Hampshire, by the way, not the one in Massachusetts. People tend to get the two mixed up. We talked for maybe twenty minutes. Other than that, I haven't made any calls. I was online this morning but didn't send or receive anything. I'm not on any of that social media stuff. Just not my cup of tea. I haven't had much contact with other people, I'll admit. But I was here, the whole time, by myself. Well, except for Velvet, of course. She can back me up, can't you, girl?" Jean reached down to scratch the dog's neck, and Velvet leaned into her hand gratefully.

Candy considered all that, and decided it was time to get to the heart of the matter. "Again, I appreciate your telling me all this, but I'm not quite sure what you'd like me to do. Why, if I may ask, did you invite me over here today?"

The other woman's gaze turned flinty again, drilling into her guest. "It's simple. I want you to find the real murderer, of course. I want you to help me clear my name, so the police — and all the other people in this town — don't think I did something terrible to my husband. I know how the gossip mill in this town gets all ginned up. Some of those ladies, like the ones in the Heritage Protection League, can get pretty judgmental real fast. I know I'm already a topic of conversation around town. They're always spreading rumors about villagers — including Mick."

"Mick? About what, if I may ask?" Candy had some idea of what Jean was referring to, but she didn't run much in the local gossip circles these days, and since she'd left her job at the paper a couple of years ago, she was out of the loop on a lot of the hottest information floating around town.

"Oh, you know, typical stuff," Jean said, almost casually, as if it were old news. "He's running a shady deal. He's working under the table. He's fooling around with this person or that. He steals other people's tools. He can't be trusted. It's all complete rubbish, of course."

"Of course," Candy said. She'd heard a little of that herself over the years, but not all of it. Still, she wasn't completely surprised by Jean's revelations. She knew how small towns were, and Mick certainly had been a controversial figure. "When was the last time you saw him?"

Jean shook her head. "That's just it. I haven't really seen him much over the past few days. He's here in the mornings, of course, but even then he dashes out sometimes before I'm up. I saw him yesterday morning, briefly. I think he was back here in the afternoon for a while but he was out in his workshop the entire time. He didn't come into the house. I never noticed what time he left, but his truck was gone by four or so. Anyway, as best I can remember, it's been about a day and a half since I've actually talked to him. Thirty hours or more, is my best estimate. That's what I told the police."

"When he left yesterday morning, did he say where he was going, or what he was doing? Did he mention any names?"

"The police asked me the same thing. The

answer is no. I didn't keep tabs on his schedule, and he didn't mention it much, unless he was seeing someone we both knew."

"What truck was he driving when he left here yesterday?" Candy asked. "Was it the red one, with the snowplow in front?"

"His truck?" Jean seemed a little surprised by the question but answered nonetheless. "Sure, that's the one he's driving right now. The plow truck."

"Do you know if he's been over to Sugar Hill Farm?"

"The Milbrights' place?" Jean fell silent, uncertain of this line of questioning. So Candy tried a different approach.

"Let me ask you this: Did Mick have any enemies who might have wanted to do him harm?"

Jean's facial expression showed her tiredness. Candy knew she'd have to wrap this up soon. The widow had been through a lot today.

"He ran a business," Jean answered matter-of-factly. "There were always some hard feelings here and there with a customer or two. But nobody stands out — no one who could do something like this."

"What about the project over at the community center? He was going to run their sugaring demonstration, I've heard."

"He's dabbled in that from time to time, though we don't have a sugar shack of our own," Jean admitted. "Some years he'd just set up a temporary boiling operation out by the garage, with a big iron pot over a fire pit. But we didn't bottle enough syrup to make any money off it. It was just for personal use, and for friends. He was always doing something or other like that."

Candy pressed on with a few more questions. "Do you know where he was getting the sap for the demonstrations this weekend?"

"The sap?" A look of irritation flashed through Jean's eyes. "What has that got to do with anything?"

"I don't know yet," Candy admitted, "but it could be important. What about Mick's work schedule? Did he keep any sort of calendar of his daily activities? Anything that might show his whereabouts over the past few days?"

"The police asked me that too," Jean said. "He keeps most of that information on his phone, though some of it is on his work computer too, out in the workshop. I think the police took that and they're looking at it."

"Do you know if they've found his phone?

Forgive me for asking this, but was it on his body?"

Jean shook her head. "I don't know. I don't remember what they said about it. I was too upset by their line of questioning and, honestly, a lot of what they said just didn't register."

"I don't suppose he left it around here somewhere? It could provide some clues as to who did this to him."

Jean's response was subdued. "I haven't seen it. Far as I know, he had it with him when he left."

Candy paused to think. There were more questions swirling around her mind, but she didn't want to bombard Jean too much at the moment. Her gaze turned toward the window, which faced the side yard and the barn and outbuildings. Finally, she spoke again. "You said Mick had a workshop. I assume it's one of those buildings out there."

Jean nodded as her gaze turned toward the window as well. "The low building, next to the barn. He's got an office in there too, and a woodstove, and a fridge and TV. He can hole up in there for a while. He slept out there sometimes, in his workshop, when he was out late — so he didn't disturb me, he used to say. Like I said, we lived our own lives."

Candy studied the buildings. Mick's workshop. Where he'd spent a lot of time.

She'd never been in there.

"Do you mind if I have a look around inside?" she asked.

Jean made a face. "The police have already checked it out. They hauled off a few things, like his computer, as I said, and probably some of his business books and papers. I'm not sure what's left. Do you think they might have missed something?"

"I don't know," Candy said. "Let's go have a look."

TWENTY-ONE

They went out to Mick's workshop together, into the rustling mid-afternoon, with Velvet leading the way.

Even though it was just a short trip across the driveway and yard, it took Jean a while to get herself ready. It was starting to cool off outside, the temperature dropping back into the upper thirties, so she scrounged around in her bedroom for a sweater, but she couldn't decide which one to wear. Candy could hear her muttering to herself, comparing colors and styles, and caught the impression that the woman was stalling. Perhaps she wasn't ready to look around her deceased husband's workshop — which made perfect sense. Candy was about to volunteer to proceed alone, but Jean finally appeared, wearing a brave face and a ragged old light green wool sweater with a large collar she could fold up around the back of her neck. "It's comforting," she said looking down at the sweater. "Reminds me of the old days."

The breeze had indeed picked up, just as the forecast had predicted. The windbreak of trees dispersed some of it, along with the slanting sunlight, but it still buffeted them at times in quick bursts, tugging at their clothes, tossing about their hair. Jean ducked down into her sweater and made little sounds of annoyance in the back of her throat as she hurried along in quick steps.

As they passed the barn, Candy peered inside. It was used primarily for parking and storage, rather than anything typically farm related. She noticed Mick's other truck — his gray summer landscaping vehicle — parked to one side, along with a small lawn tractor and a detached red metal cart, bags of dirt and loam stacked high, pallets of stone and brick and fencing, lawn mowers and edgers, hoses and garden tools. Rows of empty black plastic pots and buckets of various sizes waited to be filled. Mick had been in the midst of preparing for the upcoming busy season when his life had been snuffed out.

As they moved on, Candy saw a small greenhouse and garden space behind the barn, on the other side of the connecting breezeway, which led to the low-roofed, single-story workshop and office, painted white like the barn. The door to the workshop was closed tight, the windows dark. Jean stopped before it and fetched a small brass key from the top of the wood frame above the door. "Never locked it much," she said. "Mick always kept it open, day and night, so he could dash in and out whenever he wanted. But the police insisted that I lock it up now, considering what's happened."

She turned the key in the knob, pushed open the door, and returned the key to its hiding place before standing aside. "You first," she said, doing her best to disguise her trepidation, "if that's okay."

"Sure." Candy patted her supportively on the shoulder, peered into the gloom, and stepped across the threshold.

She stopped a few feet inside, again letting her eyes adjust to the dimmer light, as she'd done in the main house. Jean shuffled inside behind her, and an instant later Velvet dashed into the place, nose to the floor, zigzagging back and forth. She quickly disappeared from view, into the far area of the shop.

"We get critters in here sometimes," Jean explained as she flicked on the overhead lights. "Voles and field mice, mostly. Red squirrels in the winter." They heard a clatter

194

toward the back of the shop. "She's on the hunt. Sounds like she might have cornered something. I'd better go have a look."

As Jean wandered off toward the right in search of her dog, Candy moved to the center of the shop, where she stopped and surveyed the place.

It must have been fairly organized in here at one time, but it was obvious the police had been through the place. Items were scattered about, pieces of furniture were askew, and stacks of old boxes looked like they'd been moved, examined, and hastily restacked. Drawers in a trio of ancient filing cabinets, wedged together in one corner, were half-opened, the dusty files inside fingered and in disarray. A nearby metal desk also had open drawers, with some of the contents piled on the desktop. The desk chair was pushed to one side. Piles of newspapers and magazines had tumbled over and spilled across the floor. Mementos and keepsakes on cheap metal shelves had been rearranged or toppled over. In the opposite corner, a small lounge area, with an overstuffed chair, black futon, and wooden coffee table made from old crates, looked largely untouched, though some recent reading material, along with abandoned coffee cups, plates, saucers, and even a few

195

beer cans, were scattered across the table-top.

She saw no actual workshop or benches in this part of the building. Those must be in the back section, where Velvet and Jean had headed. This was more of an office and lounge area for Mick.

Other than the typical disarray of a police search, Candy noticed nothing unusual or particularly interesting at first glance. If there was some clue here, some evidence that pointed toward what had happened to Mick, it would take closer inspection to find it. And, of course, she had no idea what the police might have found and already carted away. The computers were gone, as Jean had said, and other electronic items, so for the time being, those were out of reach.

She started moving around the shop, her gaze running over the items she saw, searching for anything that stood out. She stepped forward or crouched when something of interest caught her eye, digging through papers and bills, and paying particular attention to Mick's scattered notes, many written on small slips of paper or sticky pads. Most were dates and appointments, phone numbers and first names, streets and addresses. She saw some names she recognized, others she did not, but most looked old and crinkled, the noted dates and times apparently long past. Again, she imagined the police had looked through these and considered them of little interest.

She moved on, her gaze focusing tightly on the photos, pictures, and posters Mick had hung on the walls around his shop. He'd apparently been a collector of sorts, something she hadn't known about him. Rather than collect movie posters or some such thing, though, he seemed to favor Cape Willington memorabilia. She saw old street signs, Maine license plates, political materials, and black-and-white photos of the town's historic buildings. She also noticed awards and recognition plaques, snapshots of him and his buddies, and the usual humorous tavern signs with various slogans and sayings.

Definitely a man cave.

She looked around for a wall calendar. That might give her a clue as to his recent activities. But she saw none, only a rectangular space that was paler than the rest of the wall, where it had no doubt hung. The police had taken that as well.

She spotted the phone on the desk, a landline by the looks of it. She stepped over toward it, eyeing the desktop for a notebook, address book, Rolodex, or to-do list. Again, nada.

Hmm, she thought, the police had been thorough. They hadn't left much behind.

She spent several more minutes surveying the place, as she heard Velvet and Jean banging around, but in the end she came up empty.

Maybe there just wasn't anything else to be found.

She was about to give up when a splotch of color caught her eye. It was just on the periphery of her vision, an anomaly in a mostly dull, dusty place. She turned her head, her eyes searching.

There it was, a mark of sorts on one of the posters on the wall.

Not a poster, she realized a moment later. A map. An old one, stylized with a sort of fifties or sixties design. Its colors were faded now, and it was a bit frayed around the edges. But there was a mark on it, in red, brighter in color than the surrounding text and images.

She approached the map slowly, her gaze wandering around it, from side to side and corner to corner. It was obviously some sort of tourism marketing map from half a century ago. It showed a few of the highlights around the cape, including the opera house, the Lightkeeper's Inn, Town Park, the library, and the marine and warehouse district along the river.

The red mark was high on the map, up along the northern leg of the river, near the intersection of the Coastal Loop with Route 1, far out of town.

Candy squinted at the mark. It was a hand-drawn *X* in red ink, circled several times, with a line of writing next to it, at a crooked angle. It looked as if it had been written hastily. Just a few words scribbled down, but they gave her a jolt.

VIP 5 DIG.

TWENTY-TWO

For what seemed like the longest time, but was surely only a few seconds, Candy stared at the message on the map. Her heart fluttered as she wondered what it meant. Or if it meant anything at all.

But of course it does, she realized as she thought it through. It was too obvious to be coincidental. Her eyes flicked over the handwritten message again.

VIP 5 DIG.

DIG. The same initials she'd seen on the license plate of the purple van that had tried to run her down an hour and a half earlier. Mick had written those initials on the map in his workshop. That seemed to tie him to the van in some way. But how? He couldn't have been driving today on that back road. So who had been behind the wheel?

Maybe, she thought, the answer was right there in front of her, in the rest of the message, the *VIP* and the *5.* It appeared Mick

200

had written the message as a reminder to himself. Had he planned to meet someone, a VIP — a very important person, apparently — at that spot along the river, marked on the map with an *X*? But who specifically? And *when* was the meeting supposed to take place?

That was the question, she knew. Had the meeting already happened, or was it yet to occur?

How old was the message itself? When had it been written? The ink appeared to be fairly fresh. Could it have been written in the past few days? Certainly. In the last few weeks? Of course. Sometime in the last few months, or even years? Not out of the question.

Problem was, the message was hard to date. It could be a few days, or a few months, old. Something about it, though, made her feel it was recent. Maybe the way the overhead light reflected off the letters. It made them look new.

VIP 5 DIG.

She wondered what that number meant, tucked there in the middle. Had Mick been planning to meet five VIPs? Was it some sort of community thing?

She thought of the group photo she'd seen inside the Rilkes' house, the one that showed Mick standing with a group of people in front of the community center. Mason Flint. Carol McKaskie. Tillie Shaw, Elvira Tremble, Cotton Colby, and a few others. Certainly those people were among the village's VIPs.

So what did it mean, assuming the message was recent?

She leaned in closer for a better look, focusing on the *VIP,* bringing up her finger to trace the lettering — and was startled when a voice spoke behind her.

"Find something?"

Candy jumped and backed away from the map quickly, turning deftly on her feet as she did so. "Oh, Jean, hi! There you are. I was wondering where you'd gotten to. I was just . . . well, I was just" — she pointed over her shoulder toward the map — "admiring your husband's choice of décor."

"Oh, that old thing." Jean waved a dismissive hand and looked behind her before she fell into a chair. "He found that at a yard sale somewhere, I think. Same with all this old stuff. Junk, most of it. But this was his place. He was happy out here. He could do whatever he wanted with it."

"Yes, I see that," Candy said, glancing around the office before returning her attention to the map. "Does it have any significance?"

Jean scrunched up her face. "Other than being an old map of Cape Willington? Not that I know of."

"What about some of these markings?" Candy pointed. "Like this writing up here near the top?"

"What writing?" Jean squinted at the map from her chair.

"This here." Candy indicated the red *X* and the three words written in capital letters. "See? It says *VIP 5 DIG.*" She turned toward Jean. "A strange message, don't you think? I wonder what it could mean."

Jean planted her elbows on the chair's side arms and leaned forward. Her mouth worked as she studied the map. "I don't know," she said finally. "He was always scribbling down things like that, little messages to himself. It all had to do with his clients and such."

"And this message in particular doesn't ring a bell?"

Jean leaned back and shrugged. "I don't know. I couldn't tell you much about it. I don't come in here that often, to be honest. It's Mick's place — or was his place."

"Did he say anything about a job he had along the river — or someone he might be meeting there? Maybe a local VIP?"

At these questions, Jean suddenly looked exhausted. "If Mick wrote that, he didn't tell me about it or what it meant. Like I said, we didn't talk much about those things. I didn't keep track of his schedule or who he might be meeting with. He knew a lot of people. He's been in this town a long time."

Candy had more questions, but sensed it was time to give the other woman a break. She was obviously drained, both emotionally and physically. She needed to rest. So, instead, Candy reached into her back pocket and withdrew her phone. She took a few quick snapshots of the map, zeroing in on the red X and the writing next to it. Then she turned and took a few additional photos of the workshop itself, of anything she thought might be of even remote interest. She studied the map a final time, to fix the location of the red mark in her mind, as she slipped the phone into her pocket and turned back to Jean. "Okay," she said, "I think I'm done in here."

"So you'll look into this for me?" Jean asked as she rose wearily from the chair. "See if you can figure out who killed my husband?"

Candy nodded. "I'll tell you the same thing I told Mason Flint a little while ago.

I'll do what I can."

Jean seemed satisfied with the answer. "That's all I ask."

TWENTY-THREE

Five minutes later, Candy was back out in her Jeep, headed north along the river in search of an *X* on a map.

She drove with her hands firmly on the steering wheel, eyes straight ahead, as recent events and discoveries whirled through her mind. A lot had happened since she'd received the phone call from Ginny Milbright that morning. It had been only seven hours ago, she thought, working back in her mind through the day, and so much had happened since then. She'd been going on an almost pure adrenaline rush ever since, bouncing around from place to place and, among other things, almost getting run over by a purple van.

Now here she was, at half past four in the afternoon, with only a couple of hours of daylight left, still running around, headed off in another direction, like a pinball hit by a series of flippers, chasing down another obscure clue. On her own. When she had other things she should be doing right now.

She found herself glancing repeatedly at the digital clock on the dash. Each time she did so, she coaxed the Jeep faster a notch or so. She sensed an urgency, the press of time. She was missing the setup activities in Town Park. She'd promised to help with the pancake operation at the community center. She had chores to do at home, chickens to check, paperwork to finish. She wanted to get out and walk the property around Blueberry Acres, start spring cleanup.

She wanted to find out where Neil and Random had gotten to. She wanted to figure out who had tried to run her over, and who had rolled Mick Rilke's body into the river, wrapped in a fishing net.

Her thoughts returned to that red mark on the map. According to the admittedly limited information she'd heard, Mick's body had been launched into the river from somewhere upstream.

Did X mark the spot? Could she have just stumbled onto the scene of Mick's murder? The idea made her pulse quicken, but at the same time she didn't want to speculate too much. It could be nothing more than a coincidence.

But it was *too* coincidental, and she

sensed she was onto something. She felt it in her bones.

Traffic was moderate, and perhaps even a little heavier than expected for this time of year, with long lines of cars backed up behind slower vehicles — a delivery truck at first and then, a little farther on, a tractor pulling some type of motorized farm equipment. But eventually the way opened up before her, and she couldn't help goosing the pedal another increment.

Fifteen miles an hour over the speed limit, she hurtled northward.

Not too far out of town, she zipped past the turnoff to the riverside cabin belonging to Judicious F. P. Bosworth, the town's local recluse, philosopher, and sometime mystic. She hadn't seen Judicious in a while, since he'd been in self-imposed hibernation for the winter. But she wondered if it might be worth paying him a visit. He lived along the river. Maybe he had heard or seen something that could be useful. Maybe he knew who owned a purple van with a license plate that read RIP DIG.

She put that on her to-do list, and drove on.

She continued for ten or twelve minutes without paying much attention to where she was going. The closer she came to Route 1, though, the more she focused her attention on her surroundings. Her eyes swept back and forth across the road in front of her in a methodical fashion, like the Terminator's in the search for John Connor. She wasn't quite sure what she was looking for. In fact, she had no idea. She was chasing an obscure mark on an old map, indicating a place unknown. Who knew if it was approachable from the main road, or even which side of the road it might be on? Or what signage might point out the spot to her? Or whether it was identifiable in any way? More than likely it was hidden away somewhere, nondescript and isolated. She was looking for a residence, perhaps, or a commercial building of some sort, or even a beat-up old garage. At the very least, a narrow side road, a bent-over mailbox, a rusted gate, or perhaps a stone wall. Anything that might catch her attention, spark an association.

As the traffic thickened again, her foot played on the brake pedal. Her attention was pulled back to the cars in front of her, so she wasn't able to keep an eye on the sides of the road as much as she would have liked. She saw a few markers and small signs sweep past her peripheral vision on either side, but couldn't take her eyes off the traffic long enough to read them. She also noticed a few narrow driveways and homes tucked in among the shrubbery, trees, and vines along the river, but they were quickly lost from view.

The road swerved inland then, before entering a low area and stretching out before her. The trees and vegetation on either side opened up, and suddenly she was joining a line of cars stopped at the intersection of Route 1, the main coastal artery in this area of the state. She watched the northern sky as she waited for the traffic light to turn green. The clouds were drifting eastward with a lack of urgency that made her envious.

Soon she was moving again. Most of the cars in front of her turned either left or right, headed west or east, downstate or up the coast. But Candy drove straight ahead, still going northward, onto a road less traveled.

Narrower and more pockmarked than its southern leg, it again angled toward the river, skirting it at some places. There were a few picnic and fishing spots along here, and low cabins with sloped tin roofs and stacks of firewood piled under dark windows. She could see narrow wooden piers jutting out into the river in some places. Sail- and motorboats were tied up to some of the docks, and a few canoes were pulled up on the shore. There would be fishing poles and equipment in all these places — and fishing nets too.

She knew she was close to the spot marked on the map. It certainly fit all the criteria of a possible crime scene location: river access, fishing equipment, a sense of isolation yet just off the main road, making a clean getaway possible. The beats of her heart intensified.

She finally slowed and pulled over to the side of the road. She wanted to check the spot on the map again, to see if she was in the right location. As she fumbled for her phone, she glanced in the rearview mirror, just to make sure there was no stray van out there. But she saw no cars or people, either in front of or behind her. She had a few moments alone, to orient herself.

She brought up the photo she'd taken of the map in Mick's workshop and zoomed in on it. The old map clearly showed Route 1 and the Coastal Loop. And the bridge over the river, though it looked older than the current version. In the map's illustration, there was a boat on the river below the bridge, and a trio of low log cabins on the river's bank. A stylized boy in a straw hat and yellow shirt, looking much like Tom

Sawyer, fished from one of the docks. An old woody station wagon, an icon of the fifties, was crossing over the bridge, and above that, a passenger airplane flew low in the sky.

The red *X* was right there, hovering over that spot. But she couldn't tell if the location it indicated was north of the bridge or south of it.

She puzzled over that for a few moments. It wasn't much to go on.

After checking the mirrors again, she switched off the engine, opened the door, and climbed out of the Jeep.

Her best bet at the moment, she thought, was to make a quick reconnaissance.

Hands tucked into the pockets of her fleece jacket, she tried to look as inconspicuous as possible as she crossed an area of low grasses and shrubbery, headed toward the river's bank. There were two low cabins to either side of her, but both were some distance away, a few dozen yards at least. And they both looked dark, abandoned for the season. She doubted anyone was around to notice her.

She'd expected a somewhat typical sandy riverbank, with a gradual slope down to the water, but instead it was rougher and rather rocky along this stretch of the river, with the bank a few feet above the water's edge. Good for keeping the cabins high in case of a flood, but not ideal for rolling a body wrapped in a net into the water.

She turned and looked downriver. That was a better prospect, she could see almost immediately. The bank lowered a little farther along, and she noticed a few locations that might be what she was looking for.

With a quick glance around, she dug her hands a little deeper into her pockets and started off along the riverbank.

TWENTY-FOUR

She walked slowly, headed downstream, choosing her steps carefully. She didn't want to lose her footing on the uneven, debris-strewn, and sometimes slick surfaces and injure herself, but she also wanted to make sure she didn't miss anything. As she moved, she kept her head low and her hands in her pockets. Her eyes flicked back and forth, across and around, on the lookout for anything unusual, anything that might help her unravel the meaning behind the *X* on the map. She was quiet and cautious. She didn't want to look like she was snooping. She just wanted to appear . . . casual.

Not that it mattered much. As before, it seemed no one was around. She appeared to be all alone in this tiny corner of the world, so close to civilization yet also off on its own, hidden away from view. All the small riverside cabins and shacks along here, spaced generously apart to give them plenty of maneuvering room and privacy, looked deserted and locked up — with actual padlocks, in some cases — as she passed them by. Some had small signs on their properties, down close to the river-bank, announcing to anyone who might be traveling along this stretch of the river the names of the owners of this cabin or that one — Bell and Donovan, Cook and Kimball, Robinson and Pooley, she read as she passed them by. But the owners were all absent today. No smoke swirled from the chimneys. No one peered out a window, no voices spoke in the distance. There were no cell phones ringing or TVs or radios playing faintly in the background. Only the sounds of the wind and the cold river kept her company as she progressed downstream.

The Route 1 bridge soon appeared in the distance, looming over the trees a quarter of a mile or so ahead. She could hear the faint whoosh and echoes of cars and tractor trailers speeding by. The river gurgled. Birds called in the trees.

Candy turned first one direction, then the other, still cautious. She listened as well as looked. But she saw, and heard, no one.

She had to admit, it felt a little . . . spooky.

After a few dozen more steps she finally came to a stop to catch her breath and have another look around. She checked behind her to see how far she'd come, then looked ahead again before continuing on at a more purposeful pace. She decided she'd go just to the other side of the bridge before turning back. Maybe she'd move the Jeep and search farther downstream. Maybe not. Maybe this was nothing but a waste of time. Maybe —

She stopped so fast her feet nearly slid out from beneath her. She'd spotted a subtle change in the ground a few feet in front of her. At first her mind didn't quite register what see was seeing — only that it was an aberration of some sort, a disturbance in the patterns of leaves and twigs and stones and matted vegetation. A shallow indentation, she realized as her brain began to make sense of it. That's what it was, stretching perpendicular to her in either direction, a very shallow trench of sorts, like a smear across the land.

It looked as if something had been dragged through here. Something heavy, like a huge sack of potatoes.

Or a body.

That thought caused a tingling sensation to crawl up the skin of her arms, but she mentally brushed it away, along with any feelings of trepidation. Instead, she took a step closer and leaned in for a better look. Her gaze narrowed as her breaths came almost to a standstill.

Yes, she thought, *something definitely has been dragged or rolled through here.* Long, thin scrapes stretched through the dirt, and she noticed that the still-dead grasses over which the object had been dragged were pushed down or flattened completely, all in the direction of the river.

Her gaze shifted to that direction.

The indentation, scrapes, and flattened ground cover all led right to the water's edge.

It seemed obvious that whatever heavy object had been dragged through here had wound up in the river.

Her brow furrowed in thought. Could she have found the scene of the crime? It had all the makings of it. So far everything seemed to fit.

How long would it have taken a body to float down the river from this point to the place where Mick Rilke had been found this morning? A few hours? Overnight? A day or two?

She straightened, took a step back, and turned to look inland, away from the river.

The vegetation was thick in this area, but she thought she could spot something back there among the trees. She started in that direction warily, following the drag marks as they stretched across the landscape. Again she moved slowly, and as she went, her eyes scanned the ground.

She stopped a short distance along. It looked as if a jar of strawberry jam had been spilled across this area. Some of it had soaked into the ground.

She thought she knew what it was, and quickly backed away. There she froze as she considered her next move. She wanted to leave this area completely undisturbed just in case it was . . . well, in case it was what she thought it might be. When she finally started off again, after giving herself a few moments to recover, she skirted the area by a wide berth.

Here, on the other side of the suspect spot, the drag marks disappeared — or, rather, they simply ended at the reddened ground she'd just encountered. That made sense. She hesitated a moment, trying to imagine the scene in her head, before she continued inland.

She'd gone only a few more paces when she saw it — a small, weathered wooden sign, attached to a low post pounded into the ground half a dozen feet in front of her. Faded red letters hand-painted on the sign identified the place.

GULLY'S BOATHOUSE, it read.

She shifted her gaze from the sign to the fringe of brown vegetation before her. There was an upspring of thin trees here, intermixed with dense berry bushes and ferns, backlit by the dying light of the day.

She squinted at the foliage. What was hiding in there? She spotted what appeared to be a side wall of some sort. A small building, perhaps a cabin or a shack, was hidden back behind the screen of still-hibernating nature. It was well camouflaged, painted a sort of faded grayish color with brushes of green and brown that helped it disappear into the landscape. You had to look carefully to see it.

The boathouse, apparently. Belonging to someone named Gully.

She pondered the name but it didn't ring a bell. She'd been in town awhile now, and knew most of the villagers, but there were still some she didn't know and hadn't run into yet. Gully — whoever he or she was — apparently fit into the latter category.

It didn't matter, though. She had enough evidence to contact the police. This appeared to be the scene of the crime. At the very least, *something* had happened here — a fisherman had cleaned a few fish, possibly, or someone had dressed wild game he'd killed, maybe a small animal like a rabbit or squirrel, or maybe even a duck or wild turkey, which were often seen around here this time of year.

But something told her it was more than that — possibly the result of an argument that had escalated too far, resulting in a physical confrontation and eventually leading to violence.

From the evidence she'd seen, and from what she'd learned over the course of the day, she could begin to assemble the pieces in her mind, to visualize what might have happened here. Sometime late yesterday afternoon or early evening, possibly around six P.M., Mick had driven up here to meet someone. For some reason he'd driven too fast and was swerving across the lanes, according to Stuart and Audra, the couple she'd talked to at the community center. Apparently Mick had been on his way to meet a VIP, or possibly five of them. Maybe he'd been late for the meeting, and that's why he'd been driving so fast headed northward on the Coastal Loop. But when he arrived here, something had gone wrong. There'd been an argument or misunderstanding. Tempers had flared. At some point, for whatever reason, the tide had turned against Mick. He'd been attacked from behind, ambushed, and overpowered. Stabbed in the back, the police had said. She'd possibly just seen further evidence of that. While he was down, his hands and feet were bound, he was wrapped in a net, and then he was dragged or rolled into the river. He'd floated downstream overnight to the marina area, where his body had been discovered this morning.

Had Mick known he'd been walking into danger? Had he known his attacker? It seemed likely, she thought, though the opposite could also be true. Mick could have been the instigator himself. Maybe he'd come here with vengeance on his mind, intending to harm someone else, only to have his plan backfire on him.

Backfire.

Stabbed.

A sharp weapon of some kind, she thought. There could be any number of items that fit that description around a camp like this. A hunting knife, a carving knife, a boning knife, a simple pocketknife, possibly even a machete. Maybe something from a tackle box, or the toolbox of a riverboat? The weapon that incapacitated Mick Rilke could be anything like that.

She looked around with renewed interest

221

as she reached into her back pocket for her phone. No sense delaying this any longer. If there was anything else to be found here, such as a possible murder weapon, it was up to the police investigators to locate it.

She'd swiped at the screen and was searching for the number of the Cape Willington Police Department when she heard a banging noise echoing through the vegetation in front of her. It was a low, ominous, metallic thump of some sort, followed by a frustrated yap of a bark and a series of sharp scraping sounds.

Candy froze, her eyes ricocheting back and forth across the landscape before settling on the half-hidden boathouse nestled into the thick fringe directly in front of her.

Gully's Boathouse.

The sounds came from in there, she thought. She was almost certain of it. The tingling sensation returned to the skin of her arms. *Someone could be trapped in there,* she thought. The bark had sounded desperate.

She glanced down at her phone, slipped it back in her pocket, and set off to investigate.

TWENTY-FIVE

Several paths led through the dense underbrush in front of her. She chose the one that
was slightly to her left and started toward it
at a cautious pace. It was the widest, most
traveled path, which she figured was also
the one where she'd least likely encounter
an ambush of some sort — say, from a river
snake, or something more treacherous.

The path wound among the still-dormant
trees, bushes, and ferns in a serpentine pattern for a short distance before depositing
her in a clearing occupied by several small
buildings. In addition to the boathouse,
which was the gray-painted building she'd
spotted, she saw a narrow lean-to hitched
up against a trio of trees, with a short
shingled overhang that protected a dwin-
dling pile of seasoned firewood; a small
outside workstation, also between a couple
of trees, with a well-used thick wood plank
for a counter, presumably used for cleaning

fish; an outdoor grill next to a weathered picnic table; and a small tin garden shed set off by itself on the far side of the boathouse, back toward the edge of the woods.

She also noticed the big, black maple sugaring pot set up between the boathouse and tin shed, right next to the picnic table. The pot looked ancient, as if it had been boiling sap since the turn of the previous century. It was nearly two feet across at the mouth, with a scorched, bell-shaped bottom. It hung from a tripod formed by thick tree branches, leaned together and lashed at the top with a length of twine. Beneath it was a circular fire pit rimmed with blackened rocks.

She didn't need to be told twice what had been happening: Someone had been boiling sap here, in this isolated spot — perhaps recently.

Could it be the same person who had collected sap from the illegally tapped trees over at the Milbrights' farm? And who was this Gully person? Could he, or she, be responsible for everything that had happened in the past day or two, including the murder of Mick Rilke?

She half expected to see an old purple van with a license plate that read RIP DIG parked nearby, partially hidden in the trees or ditched behind the back side of the boathouse. Or even Mick Rilke's missing red snowplow truck. But there was nothing. No vehicles, no sign of anyone around, just as she'd seen at every other place she'd passed along the river.

She turned her gaze back toward the boathouse — which, she thought, was oddly named, since it wasn't on the waterfront, as most similar structures were. Typically, she thought, the idea was to drive or haul the boat inside so it could be repaired. This place, she thought, was too far away from the river to haul a boat inside easily.

She supposed it might be more of a workshop and general guy's hangout than a boathouse, and a sign over the iron-hinged dual swinging front doors, now tightly closed and latched together, seemed to confirm that.

MARINE AND MECHANICAL FIX-IT, the sign read in faded block letters across the top in an arcing fashion, and underneath that, in smaller letters, EST. 1963, IRVING GULLIVER AND SONS, PROPRIETORS.

Hmm. She made a mental note to check that out as soon as she had a chance. But for now, she wanted to find out where those thumping and scraping sounds had come from.

She wondered if she should sidle close enough to the boathouse to have a look in through the small window in the building's side door. Maybe that's where the sounds had come from. She was still considering her next move when she heard the barks again. Several quick yaps and more low, thumping sounds.

At first she thought the sounds were coming from the boathouse. But no, she realized a moment later. Not the boathouse.

They were coming from the tin garden shed over near the woods. And, she thought, she recognized those particular barks. They had a certain tone to them, a deepness and timbre, along with an inherent sense of communication and connection.

Random.

Neil Crawford's dog.

And if Random was here . . .

She hesitated no longer, starting across the clearing at a quick pace. But a sudden thought occurred to her, so as she went, she scanned the ground around her. Seeing nothing useful, she veered back toward the edge of the trees. She didn't want to leave herself completely unarmed, depending on what type of encounter she might have coming up in a few seconds. She needed to protect herself, just in case. She needed a weapon of some sort — anything, really. After a quick search, she settled on a heavy tree branch lying on the ground nearby, about the length and thickness of a baseball bat.

It would have to do for now, she thought as she bent over to pick it up. She wielded it a few times like a sword, to test it, then hoisted it up above her shoulder, ready to defend herself if she had to.

Cautiously, she moved forward, eyes roaming restlessly across the scene in front of her. She approached the boathouse warily, keeping a good distance from it initially. She didn't want to walk into a trap. She circled the building twice, making sure there were no surprises on the unseen sides of it, before she changed direction and approached the tin shed.

On the way, she passed by the picnic table and the black maple sugaring pot hanging from the makeshift tripod. She took a quick look inside, but the pot was empty, though a little slick and gooey around the sides and the bottom. The fire pit looked cold. Just a pile of gray ashes and a few charred shards of wood, no more than small chunks and slivers, remained.

On an impulse, she bent over and put the flat of her hand on the ashes. She felt a small bit of warmth emanating from beneath the top layer. At some point over the past few days, she guessed, it had been fired up.

She brushed her hand off on her jeans as she rose, and once more hefted the thick branch.

It was time to check the tin shed, and find out who — or what — might be trapped inside.

TWENTY-SIX

"Random?"

She used a reassuring tone, to try to placate the animal as she approached the shed. She gripped the tree limb tightly in her right hand and held her left out in front of her, as if keeping the dog at bay, even though she couldn't see him through the shed's walls.

Now that she was closer, she saw that, rather than tin, it was made from sheets of corrugated steel, with a metal sliding door in front, now closed. The shed had once been painted some shade of green but, like the boathouse, had faded to an almost gray color over the years. It was perhaps six by eight feet in size. There were no windows.

She took a few steps forward. "Random?" she called again. "Are you in there? It's me, Candy. You know who I am, right?"

She heard a series of ruffs and whimpers in response, and more metallic scrapings.

Random was apparently pawing at the inside of the door. "Just hold on," Candy said, "and let's see if we can get you out of there."

There was no padlock on the door, but it was held shut by a length of wire looped through the latches in the door and frame.

A few more steps closer. "Now, just hang on, and stay calm," she told the dog through the door. "I'm going to see if I can open this."

To do that, she needed both hands. She hesitated only a moment before dropping the tree branch to the ground. She made quick work of unraveling the wire and slipping it out of the latches.

"Okay," she said, stooping to pick up the tree branch and again holding it in her right hand as she reached for the door handle with her left. "Now, don't get too crazy. Remember, it's only me."

The reaction was almost instantaneous. The door had slid open only a mere slit when a wet black dog's nose appeared in the narrow space, frantically trying to push the door open farther. Candy could hear his paws skipping on the floor inside, seeking purchase.

"Easy now, easy now," Candy said, pulling the door open a few more inches, before it was finally flung aside by the persistent dog, who scooted out in a flurry of wild eyes, flying fur, and a flapping tail.

He threatened to run her over. All Candy could do was get out of the way. She juggled the tree branch as she jumped aside, out of the path of the charging animal.

Random was a big shaggy dog, mostly white with splotches of black on his thick winter coat, which he hadn't yet shed. He was normally a friendly dog, who loped along in a casual manner or chased rabbits and squirrels through the fields and woods, but today he seemed obsessed, focused. He paused to sniff only an instant at her feet, and gave no sign he recognized her as he circled her twice before dashing off in a lather.

He ran straight to the boathouse and began to claw wildly at its foundation. He ruffed several times in the back of his throat as he did so, and paused at times to expel dirt and debris from his mouth. He shifted his spot after a few moments, digging again at a different location, as if trying to get inside.

"What are you doing?" Candy asked as she went after him, but she quickly realized what he was telling her. "Is someone inside?" she asked, inching forward in a sideways manner, almost crablike. She held up the tree limb with both hands this time, raised over her right shoulder. There was no time to get backup, to call the police. She was on her own. She had to see it through herself.

So as Random dug at the foundation, Candy moved closer and closer to the boathouse's side door. It was closed but didn't look like it was locked. As before, she took the tree limb solely in her right hand and held out her left to the door's black metal latch.

She grasped it, flipped it open, and pushed at the door.

Random was instantly at her feet, scrambling around her, desperate to get inside. He was gone in a blur. She heard him sniffing and then barking softly inside.

"Random, what is it?" she asked as she cautiously entered the boathouse. The light was dim inside, and shadows were gathering in the corners. But she could make out the counters, shelves, and braces, the steel scaffolding leaned against one wall, the piles of ropes and canvas, the small industrial machines, the white plastic buckets . . . and the large wooden canoe in the center of the building, mounted on sawhorses, as if in for repair.

She found Neil inside, under a pile of canvas.

And the murder weapon in the boat with him.

Twenty-Seven

In her dreams she saw the flashing red lights, heard the sirens, looked into all the stern, solemn faces, listened to all the voices and questions and beeps and buzzes and phone calls and shouts, a chaotic mishmash that threatened to overwhelm her senses. She saw the body of Neil in the canoe, heard the frantic barks of Random, felt her head spin and her stomach churn, and had that dark, empty feeling deep inside her as she thought, in those spare, incomprehensible moments, that the worst had happened to one of her closest friends.

Neil.

That thought, that single name, worked on her subconsciously, making her eyes flutter for a few moments in the darkened room, as her thoughts continued to swirl in her dreamlike state.

Her *boyfriend,* Hutch Milbright had called him, when she'd been talking to him and

Ginny out at Sugar Hill Farm yesterday.

Her boyfriend? Is that what everyone thought about the two of them? That they were a couple? Romantically involved?

Candy's subconscious sensed there was some truth to that, and if pressed, she'd confess that she had a true affection for Neil, but she'd never really considered him her boyfriend. Sure, she loved him, and Random, in a certain way, as close friends love each other. And although they'd spent a lot of time together, and shared meals together, and hugged, and touched in a friendly, mostly nonromantic way, they'd never officially dated, or even kissed. For some reason, their relationship had always remained platonic and had never progressed beyond that. Of course, at times she'd given some thought to what it might be like if they really did start dating seriously. It would, she'd thought periodically in the past, be fun.

But a *boyfriend*? She wouldn't describe her current relationship with Neil that way.

Could she be wrong? Were Hutch and Ginny right? Were she and Neil really that close?

If so, she felt as if she was the last to know.

Or maybe she was simply denying her own true feelings. Maybe she was burying those emotions, unwilling to face them, and what they might mean. Maybe she *knew,* deep down inside, how she really felt about Neil, but never admitted it to herself, due in part to the emotional scars of a previous relationship that lingered, and in part because she was perfectly content to live with her father at Blueberry Acres.

She'd had a few suitors over the past six or eight years or so, since she'd moved to Cape Willington following the breakup of her marriage, years ago, and her descent into a downward spiral of depression upon the death of her close friend, when she was still living in Boston, working for a high-tech marketing firm.

There had been Ben Clayton, the previous editor of the *Cape Crier,* who had given her the job as community correspondent at the paper, replacing the late Sapphire Vine, who had turned the column into a gossip fest. Candy and Ben had become close, until his abrupt departure from the paper and his decision to head west, to San Francisco. They'd tried to stay in touch, but over the years, life had gotten in the way. They rarely communicated now.

Then there was the wealthy, handsome, and somewhat elusive Tristan Pruitt, whom she'd met a few years back while running a

Halloween hayride with Maggie. There had been moments when she'd thought that she and Tristan might actually have a future together. He had hinted at it himself, and they'd both enjoyed the time they spent in each other's company. But nothing serious had ever come of it, and she eventually had to let those feelings go. He was too busy, too occupied with family business in Boston, and gone from Cape Willington too much for them to build any sort of relationship, let alone a life together.

So she'd accepted her life as a single woman, a farmer working beside her father, and had come to depend on the friendship and support of the villagers for any sort of social life, such as it was.

And, now, this had happened to Neil.

What to make of it? What did it mean for him, and for her?

In her dreams, her feelings were as chaotic as everything else, the images and sounds coming and going in random patterns, thrashing against one another in a building cacophony. She shifted uneasily in her chair, felt part of it digging into her muscles and bones. She brushed the back of her hand across her forehead, felt a small drop of drool in the corner of her month.

The overhead fluorescent lights flicked on.

Footsteps approached on the beige tile floor. Candy's eyes blinked open and shut several times.

"Oh, hello," said a female voice. "What are you doing here? I thought you were in the waiting room."

Twenty-Eight

It took a few moments for Candy's eyes to adjust to the sudden brightness. She held out the flat of her hand to shield her eyes from the white glare of the overhead fluorescents — much as she'd held out a hand to try to calm Random. That had been hours ago — and eons ago. Now, she squinted up at the lights before eyeing the dark-haired nurse who had just entered the room.

"I'm sorry?"

Candy said the words dully. She was still coming out of her restless, dream-filled sleep, and her mouth couldn't form the words quite right.

"Miss Holliday, as I explained earlier, Mr. Crawford needs his rest. It's best not to disturb him right now," the nurse said as she busied herself around the bed. Her tone was generally positive, though persuasive. "Besides, you'd be more comfortable in the waiting room, wouldn't you?"

Candy shifted uneasily in the lightly padded hospital chair, and looked up at the clock on the wall, but the hands and numbers were too blurry. She rubbed at her eyes to try to get them to focus. "What time is it?"

"Four A.M.," the nurse said in a pleasant, bedside tone. "We have to draw a little blood from Mr. Crawford's arm. For lab work."

"Of course. Lab work."

It all came back to her then. She was in a hospital room. Neil's room, where he'd been brought after they'd examined him and run some tests on him. The room was on the third floor of a community hospital near Ellsworth, she now recalled. Forty-five minutes from Cape Willington and the boathouse. Her trip here was a blur, as were the hours that followed. She thought she'd arrived here sometime around eight the previous evening, following the taillights of the ambulance that carried Neil. That meant — her mind struggled to work out the numbers — she'd been here eight hours.

Eight hours.

She looked over at Neil. His head was heavily bandaged, and there was a thick patch over one eye. He had a concussion, they'd told her. A moderate to severe head injury, resulting in prolonged unconsciousness, which could result in confusion, dizziness, and temporary amnesia once he woke. But he was alive, and he would eventually recover.

That thought made her heart swell, though for a few minutes there, she hadn't been so certain of his survival. And it had caused a panic to flood through her like she'd never felt before.

Her first thought, upon discovering his body, was that he was dead. His face was still and ashen, his eyes were closed, and he didn't move. But when she'd thought to check at his neck and wrist, she'd found a fairly healthy, though slightly erratic, pulse in each spot. That had given her some small comfort as she'd finally called the police.

The next twenty minutes or so, as she waited in the boathouse, had been nerve-racking ones, though she knew she had Random there to protect her if worse came to worst. Her efforts to rouse Neil had been unsuccessful, though his eyes had fluttered a time or two, but never fully opened. Random had been frantic. Trying to keep him under control had taken all her efforts. She'd closed the boathouse door, just in case whoever had attacked Neil was still around, but there was no way to lock it from the inside. So she'd tied it off with a length of rope, which took her some time to remove once the police finally arrived. They took over the scene immediately, ushering her out of the boathouse, though Random refused to leave the side of his master. Two of the police officers, with Candy's help, eventually had to carry the dog out physically. There was no place else to put him other than in the backseat of a patrol car, and he wouldn't stay there alone, so Candy sat with him. Chief Durr scooted in beside them from the other side, with Random wedged in between the two humans. It took a while, but they finally got the dog to settle. Candy could sense the anxiety in him and tried her best to calm him down, stroking the fur on the back of his neck reassuringly as she told the chief what had happened. He'd listened grim faced, not saying a word as she went through the entire day, from her meeting with Hutch and Ginny Milbright to her discovery of Neil's unconscious body.

"Fine," the chief said when she was finished. "Stay right here."

Then he'd left the car without another word.

Her father arrived shortly after that, with

242

the boys in tow, and she told them the same basic story, though a simplified version. Doc had taken Random off her hands — "I'll keep an eye on him until Neil's back on his feet" — while she jumped in the Jeep and followed Neil's ambulance to the hospital. Then she'd waited for what seemed like hours outside the emergency room, waiting to hear about his condition. "He doesn't have anyone else," she'd told the nurses and doctors. "I'm his . . . closest friend."

She'd almost said *girlfriend,* but held that word back, for now.

He hadn't needed surgery but he'd been sedated overnight. He hadn't woken since she'd found him. Once he'd been taken to his hospital room, she'd hovered in the waiting room until the hallway was clear, then scooted quietly into his room and settled herself in a chair, where she'd promptly fallen asleep.

"Maybe you should just head home and get some sleep," the nurse suggested. She was leaning over Neil's bare arm, drawing blood from him. "From what I've heard, you've been through a lot yourself. We'll take good care of Mr. Crawford until you get back. You can visit him again, during regular hours. As I said, he needs his rest now, and we don't want to disturb him any more than we have to."

Candy carefully moved her mouth. Her jaws practically creaked. Her lips were cracked and her throat was dry. She felt groggy, and drained. She wanted to say, *Well, you're disturbing him right now,* but she held back. She didn't want to make any enemies here, or give them any reason to prohibit her from visiting Neil later on. After all, she wasn't family. For all they knew, she was barely a friend. Best to keep the peace.

"When will he wake up?" she asked finally.

"The doctor will see him in the morning, and then they'll make a determination on how to proceed next." Her work completed, the nurse slipped around the bed and patted Candy gently on the knee. "There's not much we can do at the moment. As I said, he . . ."

". . . needs his rest," Candy finished for her, and realized maybe the nurse was right. She'd been sitting in this uncomfortable chair for so long her bones ached. Her own bed sounded pretty good right about now. Besides, she thought, she should check up on Random, to make sure he was getting through this okay.

She stopped in a bathroom and splashed water in her face in an effort to wake herself up. Out in the parking lot, the air was damp and chill, shadowing her mood. She wondered if she should even drive, and thought about calling her father, but he was too far away, and probably asleep himself right now.

She started the Jeep's engine and put the heater on high. She was about to pull out of the parking spot when she remembered she wanted to do something first — something important.

She leaned over and slipped her mobile phone out of her back pocket. In the hysteria that had enveloped her at the boathouse and on the way to the hospital, she'd silenced the phone, which had been pinging and ringing, to keep it from distracting her and her focus on Neil. She hadn't had time to check her messages and calls since then.

As she suspected, there were quite a few, but she bypassed them for the moment. Instead, she pulled up her photo app, scrolled through some of the images she'd taken recently, and found the last photo she'd snapped.

In the boathouse. Of the murder weapon.

It had been lying next to Neil's body, and it was why she'd initially thought he might be dead.

It had been a knife. A sharp, ferocious-looking one, with a long blade of perhaps ten or twelve inches, made from old steel, now stained and pockmarked and tinged red. The knife's edge didn't look that sharp anymore, but the point could pierce just about anything. The handle was made of wood, now stained dark and cracked, and had a metal handguard perhaps an inch wide along the length of the handle, obviously to protect the fingers of the wielder. It certainly wasn't a new knife. It looked like the type of thing she'd see in a museum. An antique. Certainly not something you'd expect to find in an old boathouse — or then again, maybe it was.

At first she'd thought Neil had been stabbed with it, but upon inspection, she'd found no knife wounds in his body, fortunately. Still, she suspected the knife might have been the one used to kill Mick Rilke. What it was doing there, lying beside Neil's body, she didn't know.

She'd left the knife undisturbed when she'd found it, except to make sure it posed no threat to Neil. She knew the police would want to examine it. But she'd taken a photo of it with her phone's camera before the police arrived. Because something about it had caught her eye — something that had given her a chill.

Toward the back of the knife's handle, near the spot where the metal guard attached to the hilt, the letters *S.S.* had been neatly carved into the old wood.

It had been a shock, seeing those initials, because she'd seen them before, carved into an old wooden treasure chest she, her father, and Neil had dug up on the Crawford property a few years ago. A treasure chest that had held a variety of valuable items, including gold, jewels, and some important land deeds to properties in Cape Willington.

The box, they'd determined at the time, had belonged to a long-dead scoundrel named Silas Sykes, who had frequented this part of Maine more than a hundred and fifty years ago.

Now, here was a knife — potentially a murder weapon — with the same initials carved into its handle.

Where had the knife come from? How had it gotten into the canoe beside Neil? What was the significance of those initials? And, most important, who had it belonged to?

She thought she might know a way to find out.

While she'd been watching the EMTs load Neil's stretcher onto the ambulance at the boathouse, she'd heard two of the police officers talking. "It looks like a collectible of some sort," she'd heard one of them say.

A collectible. She hadn't thought much about it at the time, but the words had swirled through her consciousness as she'd been in her dream state in the hospital room. It was only when she'd stepped out of the building into the cool night air that the connection had suddenly popped into her mind.

Artie Groves. One of her father's buddies. Artie had experience buying and selling items on eBay and other online auction and shopping sites. He dealt with all kinds of memorabilia and collectibles like this. He might know where the knife came from.

Her thumbs moving swiftly, she texted the photo of the knife to Artie with a quick note attached, asking him if it looked familiar and if he'd seen anything like it before.

Then, knowing she'd done all she could do tonight — or, rather, this morning — she dropped the phone onto the passenger seat, popped the transmission into gear, backed out of her parking spot, and drove home on an empty road through the dark, misty night.

TWENTY-NINE

A commotion woke her — and the feeling that she was slowly being suffocated. She tried to move her legs but couldn't. It felt as if a bear had her pinned down, lying heavily across her lower body and part of her chest.

She struggled to turn over but couldn't. She tried to pull the blankets up closer around her neck and shoulders but they wouldn't budge. Something was on top of them, holding them down.

Groaning, sleepy eyed, she struggled to lift her head and tried to pry open her eyes to see what was going on.

A heavy, furry something scooched up on her, thick paws pressing gently on her upper arm and shoulder. A big wet tongue appeared out of nowhere and licked her chin and neck.

She pulled her head back instinctively, under the covers, as she realized who it was.

"Random," she breathed, and settled her head back down on the pillow. The dog had fallen asleep last night at the foot of her bed, but sometime during the night he had climbed up onto the bed with her. She'd been so far gone she'd never noticed his presence.

She tried to pull the blankets up around her again. "You have to give me a little breathing room, buddy," she muttered as she closed her eyes again. "I just need . . . to sleep . . . a little longer."

She closed her eyes and tried to settle back down, but the dog snuggled up closer to her, nudging at her through the blankets and sheets with his nose.

"What?" she asked, her mouth working dryly. "Don't tell me you have to go out."

She wondered what time it was, and was just about to poke her head over the covers to check the bedside clock, when she heard footsteps outside her bedroom door and a quick rapping sound. "Candy? You up?"

It was her father. He knocked again, more urgently. "It's me. Are you decent?"

She could feel Random's head jerk up, suddenly alert, and his body tense, but he didn't move — for the moment.

The knob turned and the door pushed open a crack. "Hello?"

Candy wrenched her head up and turned it vaguely toward the door. "Dad?"

Her mind was still groggy. After her restless, uncomfortable doze at the hospital and the nearly hour-long drive back to the cape, she'd fallen into a deep, dreamless sleep once back home and in her own bed. She'd lost all track of time. It felt as if she'd been out for days. "What time is it?"

Her father opened the door a little farther and poked his head around the corner. "Just after eight thirty. Saturday morning, to be specific. I came up to see if Random wants to go out. And you have a visitor."

At the sound of his name, Random ruffed softly in the back of his throat. A moment later he was on his feet, taking a shaky stance on the soft, unstable mattress before making a lumbering and not altogether graceful leap off the bed. He landed heavily, his big paws thumping into the wood floorboards. In a fairly relaxed manner, he ambled across the room and out the door around Doc's legs.

"There you go, boy," Doc said as the dog passed by him and rumbled downstairs. "I'll be right down."

Candy finally was able to rearrange herself in the covers, but as she resettled herself, tucking the blankets in behind her knees,

251

she had a feeling she wouldn't be staying here for long. "Thanks for taking him out," she mumbled. "Who's the visitor?"

"Artie. He says he has some news for you."

"What about?"

"Not quite sure. Something to do with a photo you sent him last night. He said he wouldn't talk about it until we were both downstairs together."

"A photo?"

She remembered now. The photo of the possible murder weapon — the old knife with the long blade and handguard — which she'd sent to Artie the night before.

It all came back to her in a rush. She sat up suddenly in bed, the covers still wrapped around her, her mind instantly alert.

Neil.

She looked over toward the door. "How is Neil doing? Any word?"

Her father shook his head. "Finn called over there a little while ago, but he wasn't able to get through to the room. The nurse just said he was resting. Apparently he's been out most of the night. Now he's headed over to the berry farm."

"Who? Neil?"

"No, Finn."

"Finn's doing what?" Candy looked confused.

Her father clarified. "Sorry, pumpkin, it's been a busy morning so far. Lots going on, you know. It's Maple Madness Weekend, remember? We've got a bunch of tourists coming into town to watch sap boiling and taste fresh maple syrup on pancakes. We can't have one of our only two sugar shacks down at the most important time of the year. So, with Neil out of it for the moment, Finn went over to the Crawford place to see if he could get the sugar shack going. That's why he called over to the hospital — to talk to Neil and get his approval. And some last-minute pointers. But he couldn't get through, so he's winging it over there. He thought, well, he wondered if you'd be willing to help him out, once you're up and running, since you've worked with Neil in the sugar shack before."

"Of course. But what about the community center? The pancake breakfast? I was planning to help out there this morning."

"Bumpy's got it under control for the moment, along with a bunch of other volunteers. I talked to him just a little while ago. He said there's a pretty good crowd already. I'm headed over there myself shortly. Artie's going too, as soon as he's had a chance to talk to you, though he says he might split his time between the sugar shack and the community center — wherever he's needed most."

"So who's with Neil?"

"At the moment, no one, other than the police."

"The police?" She'd barely woken up, but already her head was spinning.

"That's something Finn *did* find out," her father clarified. "The police are at the hospital right now. Apparently they want to talk to Neil as soon as he wakes up. See if they can find out how he wound up in that boathouse, and if it might have something to do with Mick Rilke's death."

"Mick Rilke?" Candy could feel her heart thumping as her mind jumped ahead.

Did the police think Neil had something to do with Mick's death?

I need to get over there, right away, she thought, *to see how he's doing — and to run interference for him. He could probably use a friendly face in his corner right about now.*

And he's probably missing Random.

Unaware of his daughter's thoughts, Doc continued. "I know, it's getting crazy out there, isn't it?" He shook his head as he chuckled softly. "Looks like we came up with the right name for this Maple Madness Weekend thing. We've got tourists flooding into town with all these plans and expectations. We've got a sugar shack whose owner is in the hospital. We've got another man in the morgue. We've got this pancake breakfast going on at the new community center, and the marshmallow roast in Town Park later today. And we haven't even started talking about tomorrow and the scavenger hunt." He shook his head, which was still craned around the end of the door as he leaned forward, one hand on the doorknob. "Sorry to get you out of bed so early, pumpkin, after all you went through yesterday with the boathouse and all, which probably has you shaken up, but there's a lot going on. Why, it's been so busy, I haven't had my coffee yet!"

Despite all she'd just learned, Candy couldn't help but smile. If her father hadn't had his first cup of coffee by this time, she knew it was a busy morning indeed.

Time for her to get up and get moving.

She couldn't help groaning a little as she threw the covers back and swung her legs over the side of the bed. "I'll be right down. Give me ten minutes."

Downstairs, she smelled freshly brewed coffee, and Doc was making eggs and toast. Artie Groves was already munching away. He was chewing on a piece of toast thickly layered with homemade blueberry jam as she walked into the kitchen. He waved and she waved back, wiping the sleep out of her eyes as she stopped at the coffeepot to pour herself a cup. Doc had his cup close at hand. Half was gone already. It seemed her father was quickly catching up on his morning routine.

She grabbed a three-day-old banana nut muffin from an old metal tin on the countertop before sitting down opposite Artie at the kitchen table. She launched right into it.

"So, you're here to talk about the photo, right? What have you found out?"

"Yeah," Doc said, for a moment turning away from the stove to look toward their guest. "We're both here now. So what gives? What's this big mystery of yours?"

Artie nodded, swallowed another bite of toast, licked a dollop of blueberry jam from a fingertip, and took a quick sip of coffee before he reached for his phone. "Right, the photo of the knife you sent me last night," he said, pulling it up on the phone's screen. "I didn't get a chance to look at it until this morning. I usually have the phone on silent mode overnight, you know. And you sent this to me at, what, four A.M. or something like that?"

"Something like that," Candy said, trying to stifle a yawn.

He nodded. "At first, when I looked at it, I didn't really register what you were asking," Artie said with a somewhat apologetic tone. "I thought you were forwarding something from one of my eBay people, so I didn't pay much attention to it. Sometimes I help them buy and sell items like this, so I thought that was the case here — you wanted me to help someone do that, or to get my opinion about something."

"That's why I sent it to you," Candy confirmed. "The second part, actually — to get your opinion about it."

"Right. As I said, it took me a few moments, but then I realized what it was. And yes, I know a few people who collect knives like this." Artie's brow furrowed, and he reached up with an index finger to push his wire-rimmed glasses higher on his nose. His eyes became a little bigger as he looked across the table at her. "I assume you came across it last night in that boathouse where Doc said you found Neil?"

Candy nodded. "You assume correctly."

"So I suppose it could be tied somehow to Mick Rilke's murder?"

"It could be."

"The murder weapon?"

257

Candy avoided the question for the moment. Instead, she said, "I found it in the canoe right next to Neil's body."

"And the police have it now?"

"They do. I didn't touch it. I just took that photo of it, left the knife right where it was, and called the police."

"Well," Artie said, "then they may already know where it came from, and who it probably belongs to."

"And who *does* it probably belong to?" Doc asked with a strained expression, sounding as if he wasn't quite sure he wanted to know the answer.

"Actually, it's pretty easy to trace," Artie said, and he held up his phone, showing Doc the photo Candy had sent to him. "It's a Civil War–era bowie knife. Decent shape. Oak handle with this very nice handguard. I believe it came with its own leather scabbard, when it was first delivered."

"And how do you know all that, about this particular knife?" Doc asked, tilting his head toward the image of the weapon.

"Because of these initials here on the handle." Artie pointed with his pinky. *"S.S."*

"S.S.?" Doc's voice cracked a little as he spoke. "That can't be right."

Candy turned to her father. "It's true, Dad. I saw it myself. In fact, it's the first thing I noticed." She looked back at Artie. "I don't suppose those initials refer to the person I think they do."

"None other than Silas Sykes," Artie confirmed. "That old scoundrel and pirate who lived around here a hundred and fifty years or so ago. I know, because I researched the provenance of this item myself."

The revelation surprised Candy. "You did? When was this?"

Artie shifted in his chair. "Two or three years ago, after you found that treasure box buried out at Crawford's Berry Farm. After everything that happened with that box — the gold and the deeds and everything else — there was a surge of interest in collectible items once belonging to Silas Sykes. Their value went up quite a bit. Verifiable personal items belonging to him or items with some historical significance were the most sought after, of course." He paused, swallowed. "The bulk of the interest came from a certain local individual. A collector of these sorts of things — mostly knives."

"So you're saying you helped purchase this item for him or her?" Candy asked.

Artie's eyes were dark beads as he looked across the table at her. "That's exactly what I'm saying. That's why we have to contact the police."

"And who might this certain local collector of antique knives be?" Doc asked warily.

Sighing, Artie said, "It's Hutch Milbright."

THIRTY

"We already had it ID'd, so we know all about Hutch Milbright and that knife you found," Chief Darryl Durr told Candy in a guarded tone an hour and a half later as they stood in a hospital corridor outside Neil's room. Neil wasn't currently inside, though, as he was being wheeled away on a gurney for a CT scan. "We appreciate Mr. Groves's call, of course, and the details he provided, but it just confirmed what we already knew."

A man in his late fifties, Chief Durr had been with the Cape Willington Police Department for more than twenty years. Most of that time had passed with few major incidents, but this recent spate of murders in the village had taken their toll on him. His close-cropped steel gray hair had lost some of its steel, going mostly white, and the crags around the corners of his eyes and mouth had deepened. Never an ebullient

261

person, he looked decidedly weary today, as if he'd been up most of the night — which he probably had — but she could see the determination in his firmly set mouth and razor-sharp gaze.

Candy had spent a few minutes with Neil in his room before they'd taken him away for his tests, and as she listened to the gurney clatter down the long, bustling hallway, she thought about how his eyes had fluttered open and closed as she stood beside him just moments before. He'd obviously recognized her, but he'd still been groggy, only half-awake. Looking into his gray-green eyes, holding her hand gently against the side of his bearded face, she leaned in close as she told him Random was safe, and that Finn was covering for him at the berry farm, cranking up the sap-boiling operation, and that she was headed there next, but she wanted to check up on him first. He hadn't said much in return, but she could tell he understood her from the trace of a smile on his bluish lips. With his eyes closed, he'd reached up tentatively with a callused hand and placed it over hers, so she could feel its warmth against her skin.

She'd felt it then, something new, something deep within her heart, or maybe somewhere just behind her heart, an awakening of emotions she hadn't quite felt about Neil before. She realized, with some surprise, how much she really cared for him, and how close they'd become over the past few years. She realized how much he and Random meant in her life right now. And she realized how much she'd miss him, and how devastated she'd be, if he were suddenly gone from her life.

"It wasn't hard to track down the ownership of that knife you found, since it was well documented," the chief continued, breaking into her reverie, "but I guess you know that already." He checked his watch. "We've dispatched a couple of officers to pick up Hutch for questioning. Should be happening right about now."

Candy wasn't surprised to hear this information. In fact, she wouldn't have been shocked if the police had arrested Hutch outright and hauled him off to jail in cuffs. They had the presumed murder weapon in their possession. They knew who owned it. Hutch's fingerprints were probably all over it. They had the evidence they needed. Case closed, right?

But, for some reason she couldn't explain, she didn't believe it was that simple. Something about the whole thing bugged her. That's why she'd asked Chief Durr if he had a few minutes to talk. So now, in a low voice, her brow furrowed in concern, she said, "But do you really think Hutch could have done something like this?"

For a moment, the chief's carefully constructed granite expression broke, and Candy thought she saw the real person behind his facade. "Honestly, Ms. Holliday, I've learned to reserve my judgment in situations like this, when it involves someone I've known for years, and who's been an upstanding member of our community for as long as I've been here. Of course, you and I are both aware of what certain people are capable of around this town, based on what's happened in the past. So, at this point, your guess is as good as mine. We'll see what Hutch has to say. I'm headed back to the station right now to talk to him."

But Candy wasn't ready to let the chief go, not just yet. She was still trying to mentally deal with the ramifications of what she'd learned this morning.

"What about the sap?" she asked, thinking back to her encounter yesterday morning with Hutch and Ginny.

"What about it?"

Candy knew her time with the chief was limited, so she spoke quickly. "Well, we know Hutch had a beef with Neil over this stolen sap issue, right? Maybe that's what started this whole thing. Maybe it caused Hutch to attack Neil, drive him over to that boathouse, dump him inside, and lock up Random in a metal shed. Maybe he thought it was a good way to send a message."

"A fairly convoluted message," the chief said, "but we're taking everything into consideration."

Candy held up a finger, her eyes darting back and forth as she thought. "On the other hand, if Hutch *did* kidnap Neil — or kill Mick Rilke with that knife of his — why would he draw attention to it? Why leave the knife right there beside Neil, essentially giving himself away? Who would make a dumb mistake like that? If it really was the murder weapon, why not bury it? Or just throw it into the river? It doesn't make any sense. *And,*" she continued, the look in her eyes growing more intense, "why ask me to get involved like I did, so I could find a trail that leads right back to him? Why not keep a low profile? Why not keep himself out of the whole thing? Why would he bring attention to himself like that? It doesn't seem logical, does it?"

The chief looked slightly agitated as he reached up to scratch his head. "We don't have all the answers right now, Ms. Holliday.

It's an ongoing investigation, as I'm sure you know."

"I do," Candy said agreeably, purposely dialing back her intensity. But she still had a few questions on her mind. "Have you found out who the boathouse belongs to?"

"Again, we're working on that. We have a crime scene van out there right now. I'm not ready to discuss more than that at the moment."

"Have you talked to Ginny Milbright about any of this?" Candy asked.

"About what, specifically?"

"Well, maybe she has answers to some of this. She's probably aware of her husband's whereabouts over the past twenty-four hours or so. From what I've heard, he's just been out at the farm, getting ready for today's maple sugaring operation."

"Your point?"

She shrugged, as if it was obvious. "Maybe Hutch has an alibi. Maybe it's that simple. Maybe he never left Sugar Hill Farm. Maybe he couldn't have traveled to the boathouse, because he was at his own place the entire time."

"We're checking into that, of course."

She changed course again. "What about Mick Rilke?"

As Candy's questioning continued, the

chief's tone had grown more stern, and now he crossed his arms in an exaggerated motion. "What about him?"

Candy noted his defensive posture but plunged ahead anyway. "Could Mick's death be linked somehow to the stolen sap? Or what he was doing at that boathouse?"

The chief sighed visibly. "As I said, this is an ongoing investigation. I'm not at liberty to discuss the details of it right now. But we're working on it, and I guarantee you we'll get to the bottom of it all, sooner rather than later."

The two of them fell into an uneasy silence then as a nurse walked briskly past, her sneakers squeaking on the buffed floor tiles. As they waited for her to walk out of earshot, Officer Molly Prospect of the Cape Willington Police Department rounded the corner and approached them, checking her watch. "He's going to be in there for another half hour or so," she told the chief, after giving Candy a brief nod in greeting. "Then they have a couple of other tests they want to run on him, which should take another hour or two after that. So I'm estimating it could be around noon or even a little later before I get a chance to talk to him."

The chief nodded his acknowledgement.

"Did they say anything about his condition?" Candy asked. She'd known Officer Prospect for a number of years and had been personally interviewed by her a number of times regarding other murder cases in town.

"Nothing specific, Candy, just that he's stable. They'll know more in a couple of hours, but I think he's going to be okay. He got dinged up a little, but they don't think it's anything life threatening."

"Thank goodness," Candy said, holding a hand to her chest and breathing a little easier at this information.

"I'll keep an eye on him, make sure he's doing okay," Officer Prospect continued. "I know he doesn't have any family around here . . . anymore. He's with the doctors and nurses now, and they're taking good care of him. As soon as they tell me more, I'll text you and let you know."

"Thank you," Candy said. She knew she had to get moving, back to Neil's berry farm to help out Finn with the maple sugaring operation, but she also hesitated to leave Neil here by himself. However, she felt a little better knowing Molly Prospect would be keeping an eye on him. She trusted Molly as much as she trusted anyone in town. "You'll let me know as soon as you hear something?"

"As soon as I know." Molly nodded to confirm her statement.

"I think that's my cue," the chief said, swiveling back toward Candy. "But before I go, Ms. Holliday, let me make one thing perfectly clear: While I certainly appreciate all of your contributions up to this point, I want to assure you that the CWPD can take over from here. I'm certain you have other things to do around town today, right?"

"Right, Chief."

He gave her a long, hard stare before he nodded. "Good. Now, if you'll excuse me, I have work to do. Officer Prospect, would you walk out with me? I have a few things I need to go over with you."

He tipped his hat, turned on his heels, and started away. His footsteps echoed down the corridor at a quick pace, with Molly Prospect hurrying to keep up with him.

Moments later, Candy stood by herself with her back literally against the wall. She let out a slow, deep breath. It had been a long day so far. And she was just getting started.

With some effort, she launched herself away from the wall and followed the chief and Officer Prospect down the corridor and out of the building, her mind working as she went.

Everything that had happened over the past twenty-four hours was connected, she thought. It *must* be. It *had* to be. The unexpected call yesterday morning, the stolen sap, the disappearance of Neil and Random, the discovery of Mick Rilke's body in the river near the new community center, the attack of the old purple van with license plates that read RIP DIG, the call from Jean, the map, and the boathouse where she'd found Neil and his dog — it was all too much to be unrelated, to be coincidental. There *had* to be pattern here, a thread that linked all of these seemingly random pieces. She just had to find that thread, and figure out how to unravel it all.

And she would do that, as soon as she could. For the moment, however, other places and duties called to her.

Random was waiting anxiously for her in the Jeep. She'd tried to dissuade him from coming along with her to the hospital, but it had been no use. When she'd opened the driver's side door back at the farm, he had leaped into the vehicle, where he'd parked himself in the passenger seat and refused to budge. The expression on his face was priceless. He was worried, and he knew where she was going. He had no intention of letting her drive away without him. She'd finally relented and let him ride along.

Now, as she approached the Jeep, she could see his nose poking out of the top of the driver's side window, sniffing at the air as he watched her. When she stopped beside the door to greet him, he was standing on the driver's seat, his big tail wagging vigorously back and forth, making his whole body move.

"Hey there," she said, petting him on his protruding nose and muzzle. "How are you doing? You okay? Neil's going to be just fine, I promise. Now back up a little bit there, buddy, so I can get in."

Once she'd settled into the driver's seat and closed the door behind her, he practically attacked her, sniffing her frantically all over. "I know, you smell Neil on me, don't you?" she said, and she let him snuffle at her hands, then ruffled his fur behind his neck and shoulders to get him to settle down. "He's just going to need a little longer to get better. But don't you worry about a thing. Dad and I will take good care of you until Neil's back home, okay?"

She pulled a set of keys from her pocket and started up the engine. "Speaking of home, why don't we pay a visit to your farm and see what's going on, shall we?"

THIRTY-ONE

Three hours later, at a little past one in the afternoon, Candy finally had a chance to sit down, catch her breath, and give her legs and her back a break.

She'd been on her feet from the moment she stepped out of the Jeep at Crawford's Berry Farm. The place was busy — and a bit chaotic. Certainly disorganized. Cars were scattered everywhere on the property, parked randomly at different angles, blocking one another in some spots. Visitors milled around aimlessly in the parking area and up through the still-dormant strawberry fields, uncertain of where to go or what to do. Some were circling the farm's two hoophouses or wandering through the barn, while others were idly sitting on Neil's porch, as if his private home, empty at the moment, were a bed-and-breakfast, or a restaurant about to open. She wondered if they were expecting pancakes to be delivered to them. Or maybe they just wanted to use the bathroom. No one had put out any signs to guide visitors to the sugar shack, or set out the folding tables, or the jars of maple syrup Neil had put aside for sale this weekend, hoping to goose the farm's revenue stream a little. Candy herself had helped Neil box up those bottles in early March, in anticipation of this event. The syrup was from one of the earlier batches of sap Neil had boiled. The dozens of eight- and twelve-ounce bottles sported a new label, which Candy had helped Neil design over the winter. The boxes of bottles were still sitting in the corner of the barn, right where she'd left them.

At least the sugar shack was up and running, which seemed to make everything else bearable. Just catching the sweet scent of the sap in the air was enough to adjust her attitude in a positive direction.

Given his own limited knowledge of boiling sap, Finn had called in a buddy of his, a person known only as Hawthorne, to help out in the sugar shack. Hawthorne sported a long gray ponytail, extensive facial hair, and arm tattoos, and showed off yellow teeth when he smiled. But despite his somewhat ragged appearance, he was a quick, efficient worker and seemed to know what he was doing.

"He's an engineer," Finn had told her as he'd introduced the two of them that morning, soon after Candy's arrival at the farm. "Well, he used to be an engineer. I guess he's a sort of backwoodsman now, right, Hawthorne?"

In reply, their resident engineer and backwoodsman had simply said, "Sure."

"Hawthorne was at the rescheduled community center grand-opening ceremony this morning," Finn noted, as if he were a proud parent. "You were impressed with the festivities, weren't you, Hawthorne?"

"Sure was."

"Sorry I missed it," Candy said, genuinely interested to hear Hawthorne's impression of the event. "So tell me what happened. Lots of people there? What was the general mood like? I suppose you heard from the regular speakers, like Carol McKaskie and Mason Flint and Tillie Shaw, people like that?"

"Yup."

"Anything interesting stick out in your mind?" Candy pressed. "Anything I missed that you think I should know about? Maybe something one of the speakers said, or something you heard from someone in the crowd?"

"Nope."

Candy had shielded her eyes against the southern sun, studying this newcomer. "A man of few words," she said. "I like that. So, Hawthorne, is that your first name or your last?"

"It sure is," he said.

"No, I mean, is Hawthorne your first or last name?"

"It's both," said Finn, "as far as anyone knows. Right, Hawthorne?"

"Sure is."

"Hawthorne used to help out Neil's dad, years ago when they were expanding the berry farm," Finn informed Candy. "I think he helped put in that grove of cherry trees over there, didn't you, Hawthorne?"

"I guess so."

And so it went. Hawthorne was apparently a poet who didn't know much poetry, and a world traveler who couldn't remember where he'd been. But he knew his sap, and he knew his way around the boiling equipment, and he didn't seem to mind hauling buckets of raw sap and arms of firewood back and forth, so Candy had no complaints. In fact, she was grateful for his help, because she had other things to do.

The first half hour had been a little rough, as she'd tried to get all the cars reparked in a roped-off area along the edge of the trees, get signs posted, and get the growing crowds of visitors organized into groups for ten-minute tours of the sugar shack. She ran those herself, serving as the hostess, walking quickly, motioning a lot with her hands, and talking until her voice started to go hoarse. She also, with the voluntary help of one of their visitors named George from Michigan, got the folding tables set up, and located a metal box she could use as a till. The handmade signs she and Neil had created together, with pricing and payment information, were still in a large manila envelope on a wooden shelf in the barn, along with a few office supplies she thought she might need, and she was off and running with maple syrup sales, to which the visitors responded happily. The bottles sold fast, and the till box filled steadily, which would be good news to Neil.

In the absence of his master, Random played a willing host. He greeted the guests as they came and said good-bye to them as they went off to their cars or tour buses. He wagged his tail a lot. He went trouncing off through the berry fields with the kids. He took breaks in the shade near the sugar shack and drank copious amounts of water from his big bowl in the barn. He dutifully did his part to keep things running smoothly.

By Candy's guess, they'd had several hundred visitors come through the place that morning, and they'd sold more than three hundred dollars' worth of syrup — a good day, she thought, and it was still going on.

But around midday the crowds began to thin, as the tourists headed back into town for lunch, and as they continued to clear out into the early afternoon, she finally had time to take a few minutes' rest, settle into a lawn chair in front of the barn, and pull out her phone.

There were quite a few e-mails, texts, and phone messages for her to go through. Apparently she was a person in demand. Everyone from Maggie to Wanda Boyle to Tillie Shaw to her father had contacted her, checking up on her, wondering how she was doing, and asking if there was any news about Neil.

There was also a short message from Officer Molly Prospect at the hospital, who told her that Neil was finally back in his room, resting comfortably, and that Candy was welcome to visit him as soon as she had a chance.

So, good news, she thought as she leaned

back in the chair. She let out a slow breath, feeling deeply relieved. Now she just had to find the time to make the trip back to the hospital to see Neil, since the journey there and back would take several hours.

She lowered her phone and shielded her eyes against the sun as she looked around. The wind had picked up again, scattering the smoke that drifted up from the sugar shack. Leftover fall leaves blew across the fields. The visitors who remained clutched at their hats and coats. Though the crowds had thinned, there were still quite a few people around. Finn and Hawthorne were still boiling sap, so they couldn't keep an eye on the bottles of maple syrup for her. There were tours to give, questions to answer, traffic to manage.

Even though the pace had slowed, she didn't want to abandon her post. She felt she was still needed here. Of course, she was probably needed at the community center as well. She wanted to run by Town Park and see how preparations for the marshmallow roast were going. She'd promised Maggie she'd help in the booth later on. And, in the back of her mind, she still wanted to try to run down that elusive purple van, and the red snowplow truck.

She had much to do, and felt as if she

were being pulled in a dozen different directions. She was about to go talk over her dilemma with Finn — and possibly get one of Hawthorne's succinct responses as well — when she spotted a maroon Chevy Suburban cruising up the lane, churning up the damp earth.

Candy knew right away who it was. For better or worse, Wanda Boyle, managing editor of the *Cape Crier,* had arrived on the scene.

THIRTY-TWO

Candy watched the Suburban approach with mixed feelings of curiosity and unease.

Why would Wanda drive all the way out here at this time of day, Candy wondered, especially when there was so much going on in town right now? She should be covering the preparations taking place in Town Park, or mingling with contented pancake munchers at the community center. Or she should be at the police station, trying to find out what she could about Mick Rilke's murder and Hutch Milbright's knife. Or out on the village's streets and byways, interviewing tourists for a newspaper article.

Maybe Wanda's sudden appearance here was innocent enough. Maybe she'd just driven out to the strawberry farm to see how things were going at the sugar shack, how the crowds had been that morning, and how the bottles of maple syrup were selling. Maybe she'd come to talk about Neil and find out how he was doing. Offer her sympathies for what he'd been through. Maybe she just wanted to lend a little moral support — a thought that made Candy chuckle the moment it crossed her mind.

Or maybe Wanda had a different reason for driving out here.

Whatever it was, Candy knew she would soon find out.

Unfortunately, she thought with a sigh, it appeared her short break was over.

Rather than follow the posted signs and angle off toward the designated parking area back along the trees, where all the other visitors' vehicles were corralled, Wanda plunged straight ahead, toward the farm buildings in front of her. It was typical of her nature, Candy thought. Wanda wasn't one for following the crowd.

Seeing no one in her direct path, she gunned the engine a little as she made a beeline for the barn, steering with one hand for a short distance before she stomped down hard on the brake pedal. Candy, still seated in the lawn chair in front of the open barn doors, with the tables of maple syrup just to her left, watched the whole maneuver with a certain amount of concern. As the Suburban zeroed in on her, she briefly considered abandoning her post, leaping from her chair, and jumping back behind the barn doors for some protection. But she held her ground, as she'd learned to do with Wanda over the years, and simply stared her down as the vehicle approached.

With a certain amount of finesse, Wanda brought the Suburban to an abrupt yet smooth stop right up against the front of the barn, the vehicle's prominent nose just a few feet from the tables of maple syrup. As the SUV idled, its engine pinging and clicking, the big vehicle rocked on its suspension a little, accompanied by a few high-pitched squeaks and creaks.

Candy remained where she was, deciding to let Wanda come to her.

Of course, it didn't happen quite like that — at least, not right away. In fact, Wanda seemed to barely notice her. She remained in the driver's seat with a cell phone pressed tightly to her left ear and was apparently deep in a conversation with the person at the other end. Not missing a beat, Wanda pulled at the emergency brake with her other hand, switched off the engine, flipped down the visor to check her lipstick in the mirror, dabbed with a pinky at one corner of her mouth, flipped the visor back up, pushed open the driver's side door, and hopped out, slamming the door shut with her hip.

She stood for a few moments by the side of the SUV, talking loudly into the phone as she casually surveyed her surroundings.

"We need to get on top of this situation, right away," she said, her eyes moving but not really seeing anything as she focused her thoughts on the call. "We need someone out there. Maybe you should go yourself. Do some digging around. Ask a few questions. See what you can find out." She listened briefly before continuing. "I understand that, but don't worry about the police. Trust me, they have other things on their minds. Just poke around innocently, stay off their radar, see if you can talk to her." Another pause, and Wanda distinctly frowned, her mouth turning down sharply and her plucked eyebrows falling together. "Where did you hear that? Are you sure that's what she said?" As she listened again, her gaze shifted, searching, before eventually coming to rest on Candy.

The two locked eyes.

"Okay, I'll see what I can do," Wanda continued into the phone. "I'm out at the berry farm now. She's right here in front of me." Wanda's eyes flicked up and down Candy, from her face to her feet and back again, as if assessing her. "I'll send her over there right away. Maybe she can get the woman to talk. After all, she still writes for the paper. Maybe we can get an exclusive on this. I'll keep you posted. Oh, and before I forget, tell Lizzie I need that bonfire story by tomorrow A.M. for the website. Can't keep the readers waiting. She's been missing her deadlines a lot lately, and we have to tighten up this ship if we want to keep our readers happy and keep page views up. And tell her to take plenty of pictures. And make sure they're in focus this time. Her last batch was pretty fuzzy." A final pause. "Okay, keep me posted. I'll let you know what happens here."

The moment she pulled the phone away from her ear, her frown disappeared, replaced by a carefully arranged smile, one that Wanda had perfected over the years.

When they'd first encountered each other nearly a decade ago, Wanda had been sharper edged, prickly and defensive, slow to listen and quick to attack. But over time she'd evolved a little, especially after she'd inherited the position of managing editor, her dream job, from Candy. She'd learned to smooth out some of her sharper edges and had developed a new approach, preferring to use honey rather than browbeating to get what she wanted.

She nodded politely at Candy as she slipped the phone into a back pocket. "So here you are!" she said pleasantly as she started in Candy's direction. "We missed you downtown this morning, you know. Your absence was noticed. I kept saying to everyone, 'Where's Candy? Is she doing all right?' But, of course, I heard you'd been up to the hospital to see Neil, and that you were helping out here at the berry farm. How nice of you to do that! You always seem to know exactly where you're needed, don't you?"

Candy could think of several different responses to that last inquiry, not all of them polite, but decided to be pleasant herself. She wasn't ready to get into a tussle with Wanda, not after what she'd been through over the past day or two. "It's nice to hear I was missed," she said, "but I knew you and the others would have everything under control. So, yes, I thought I'd help out here for a few hours, just to make sure the sugar shack tours were running smoothly."

"And everyone in town appreciates your efforts," Wanda said magnanimously. "Especially the tourists. I've heard several of them talking about how impressed they were with the tours and the sugar shack operation out here. And it looks like you've sold plenty of bottles of syrup."

"We've gone through almost three boxes so far, a dozen bottles in each box," Candy said, "and still have a bunch of boxes left for the rest of today and tomorrow. So, how's everything going at the community center? And at Town Park?"

Wanda stopped a few feet in front of her, shielding her eyes with the flat of her hand as the wind tossed about her red hair. Candy finally felt compelled to rise to greet the newcomer, pushing herself to her feet as one of her knees cracked audibly. Random appeared out of nowhere and gave Wanda a quick sniff and hand nuzzle before heading off again.

"Such a delightful dog," Wanda said, watching him go. "Lots of personality. Just like his master."

"He was pretty upset last night," Candy said, "but he's calmed down a lot today. The visitors are helping. They're giving him lots of attention, which is what he needs. It keeps him distracted while Neil's recovering."

"So what's his prognosis?" Wanda asked, and they chatted briefly about Candy's visit to the hospital that morning, and the latest report from Officer Molly Prospect, and

286

Candy's intent to head back to the hospital as soon as possible. "But I don't feel right leaving Finn and Hawthorne here on their own." She paused. "Especially Hawthorne. Have you met him?"

"Our elbows have brushed against each other a time or two. The silent type."

"That's him."

"So how can I help?"

The question was so unexpected, and seemed so out of character for Wanda, that it caught Candy off guard. "With what?"

Wanda turned and waved a hand around the property. "Here. At the berry farm."

Candy wasn't sure what to make of this. "You want to help out here? At the farm? Today? But I thought you'd have more important things to do this afternoon."

"I have lots of important things to do," Wanda said, her suddenly steely gaze swinging back toward Candy, "but I need a favor."

"Ahh." Candy had wondered when that was coming. "So you'll keep an eye on things here at the farm if I run a little errand for you, or something like that?"

"Something like that," Wanda admitted, with a cunning expression on her face, "but I think it might prove beneficial for the both of us."

Intrigued, Candy crossed her arms. "How so?"

"Well," Wanda said, and she leaned in conspiratorially, a single eyebrow raised, "here's what I have in mind."

THIRTY-THREE

Everything came together surprisingly quickly. Wanda called in the troops, or at least a couple of troops — apparently she had no intention of personally staying around the berry farm any longer than she had to — and they arrived with alacrity, as if they'd been hovering nearby, waiting for her summons.

After a few quick hellos, they pitched right in. None other than Carol McKaskie, the vice chair of the town council and longtime member of Wanda's inner circle of friends, took over the sales of maple syrup with a cheery smile and a good eye for marketing and display. She promptly rearranged the offerings on the tables to make them more aesthetically pleasing, and sold three bottles right off. Wanda's son, Bryan, now in his early twenties and sporting a black beard and a dark blue bandanna wrapped around his longish unwashed hair, arrived shortly after to help out in the sugar shack, giving Finn and Hawthorne a little relief. "He's had some experience with this sort of thing," Wanda explained. "He helped with the boiling demonstration down at the community center this morning, but he called in some of the old vets to take over for a while so he could come out here."

It was almost as if Wanda had the whole thing planned from the start, Candy thought, though she doubted that was the case. Instead, Wanda simply had a knack for pulling in the right people for the right project, and she had a big network of friends, family, collaborators, and acquaintances from which to draw. As always, she had her finger on the pulse of the town and knew how to effectively move people around to the places where they were most needed, according to her sole determination.

"That should take care of the situation around here for a while," Wanda said twenty minutes later, with a certain sense of satisfaction, "and I can bring in a couple more folks this afternoon if needed, so you can go off for that little meeting we talked about. And then, of course, you can head over to see Neil."

Candy almost felt grateful to the other woman — something she wasn't used to.

"You're sure you're okay with this?"

Wanda nodded. "I insist. It's all for the good of the village, of course. And tell Ginny I said hi."

"When do you need the story by?"

"I can guarantee you the front page of next Friday's edition," she said, "so Monday afternoon would be ideal, but no later than Tuesday morning. Agreed?"

"Agreed. As long as there's a story there."

Wanda gave her a hard look. "Of course there's a story there, if what I've heard is true. Trust me. Hutch didn't do it. The police are focusing on the wrong man."

This particular bit of information had come to Wanda through the village grapevine, and a quick conference with Finn in the sugar shack, verified with an equally brief phone call by Finn to an unnamed source within the Cape Willington Police Department, seemed to confirm what she'd heard:

Hutch Milbright had an alibi.

What's more, Ginny Milbright was apparently claiming that Hutch's knife — the alleged murder weapon — had been stolen from their home a few weeks earlier. Whether or not either of the Milbrights had contacted the police about the alleged theft of the collectible weapon was unverified, but it threw enough of a doubt about Hutch's involvement with the murder to cause a lot of concern around town.

"You know what this means," Wanda said, more a statement than a question. "Everyone thought this thing was wrapped up and the culprit identified, but this newest development means we could still have a murderer running around, possibly ready to strike again. The whole town is on pins and needles about it."

"It could also just be a smoke screen," Candy said, playing devil's advocate, "something Hutch and Ginny made up to get him off the hook."

Wanda squinted at her. "It could be. But do you really believe that?"

Candy pushed a hand with fingers splayed back through her disheveled hair. "I don't know. I admit the whole thing sounds fishy to me, but where the truth lies, I'm just not sure yet."

"That's why you need to get over to the Milbrights' place ASAP and talk to Ginny," Wanda said. "You're going over there to verify her story and get the details. And you're the only person she'll talk to, for some reason. She's made that clear."

"But why me? She can talk to the police. She can talk to a lawyer. I'm a blueberry farmer."

At that comment, Wanda rolled her eyes. "Who knows what she's thinking? I offered to go myself, but she won't see me. For whatever reason, she wants to talk to you, and you alone. That's why we're relieving you here, so you can go off and do what you do best." She paused, and though the next few words appeared hard for her to get out, she nevertheless managed to do so. "Somehow, once again, it seems you're in the center of all this. I don't know why it keeps happening, but there it is. And, honestly, you're the town's best bet for figuring this out quickly, so we can identify who's behind Mick's murder, put that person behind bars, and get on with our lives."

It was bluntly put, but Candy had heard similar statements before. Wanda was right. Somehow she always managed to get herself stuck in the middle of these cases, and here she was again.

Only this time there was more at stake. This time Neil was involved. What had he stumbled into? she wondered. How had he gotten himself knocked out and dumped in that boathouse? More important, how was he involved in all this? Was there a link between Neil and the stolen sap? Or between Neil and Mick Rilke?

Questions bubbled in Candy's mind as her gaze drifted.

Wanda had turned away for the moment. She was back on her cell phone, again talking loudly about something or other, gesticulating wildly with her hands, a twisted expression on her face. *She certainly has a lot going on,* Candy thought, watching her. And in that moment, she didn't regret giving up her position as the paper's managing editor — or interim managing editor, as it were — for a less complicated, and definitely less stressful, job back on the farm.

But her life had become more complicated again — and more stressful, considering all that was at stake for many of the villagers, including Neil. Once again, she was faced with a dangerous tangle of events.

Candy watched Wanda for a few moments with a hazy vagueness, then shifted her gaze, past Wanda, across the driveway to the red splotch nearby that had caught her eye.

Neil's red Saab wagon, now parked under the trees on the far side of the farmhouse.

When she'd arrived out here earlier in the day, the faded old wagon had been in its usual parking spot in front of the barn. But she'd found the keys on a hook inside the front door, where Neil always kept them, and moved the Saab out of the way, to make room for the tables and clear a path for visitors.

As she'd done so, she'd realized its presence here was a fairly important clue, because if it was *here,* that meant Neil hadn't driven himself to the boathouse. He couldn't have. He had no other way to get there. It only strengthened her suspicion that he'd been abducted somehow, perhaps while he'd been out in the woods collecting sap, and transported to the boathouse by an alternative means.

In a purple van, perhaps?

It was certainly an intriguing thought, and if true, it would begin to weave some of the disparate threads together into a tapestry that finally might reveal some answers.

With her eyes still locked on the Saab, Candy half listened to Wanda and began to spin out scenarios in her head.

Since the car keys were hanging inside, she could conclude that Neil hadn't had them on him when he'd gone out into the woods to collect sap. It meant he had no intention of going anywhere in the Saab. The tractor's keys were always left in its ignition, so he didn't need his key ring to collect sap. And the tractor was gone from its spot in the barn.

So the red station wagon was still here, but the tractor wasn't.

That led her to the most logical and likely explanation: He'd gone out into the woods to collect sap, and never returned. It also meant the tractor was probably still somewhere in the woods.

What time would he have gone out there? She started ticking off the events on her fingers to try to mentally establish some sort of timeline.

This was early Saturday afternoon. She'd found Neil in the boathouse late yesterday afternoon between five thirty and six P.M. She'd come out here to his berry farm earlier yesterday, at around ten thirty A.M., looking for him after she left the Milbrights' place, but he'd been nowhere around. The tractor had been missing at that time, she recalled, and the car had been in its usual spot. She knew that, because she'd visually inspected it.

So, she concluded, Neil had disappeared sometime yesterday afternoon or morning, most likely, or anytime earlier, really, even as far back as Thursday, or even Wednesday. She tried to recall the last time she'd been in contact with him. It had been Tuesday night, four days ago, she remembered, when they'd talked on the phone about their plans for the week. He wouldn't have gone out into the woods that night after they'd talked, but logically it could have been anytime from Wednesday morning to Friday afternoon.

A fairly big window of time. A span of more than forty-eight hours.

Her gaze shifted to the woods at the distant edge of the strawberry fields.

Where was the tractor? she wondered. What had happened to him, whenever he'd gone out there?

Again, she played out a scenario in her head. He'd been out in the woods, sometime in the past couple of days, collecting sap. Something had happened to him along his route. He'd found something, or saw someone doing something. There had been an unexpected encounter of some sort, perhaps resulting in his abduction. Or his coercion to accompany someone someplace. Either way, he'd been assaulted at some point, knocked unconscious, transported to the boathouse, and left there in a canoe with a murder weapon beside him, and Random locked in a nearby shed.

How long had Neil been in that boathouse before she'd found him? Did he remember anything about what had happened to him out in those woods?

She would ask him herself shortly.

Her gaze shifted across the strawberry fields and back toward the buildings. A few visitors were still milling around, some of them wandering into the sugar shack, barn, and hoophouses. A few kids were playing, laughing, and shouting at the edge of the fields. She noted the serenity of the early-spring landscape, the sharp freshening of the breeze, the ever-present cloud of steam and smoke spiraling from the sugar shack, before her gaze shifted back to the distant line of trees at the edge of the gray woods.

Whatever had happened to Neil, it must have started back in those woods, back where his maple sugar trees were located.

She was still staring at the woods when Wanda finally finished her call, tapped at the screen, and lowered her phone. She frowned as she looked over at Candy. "You still here? I thought you'd be gone by now."

"I'm thinking," Candy said, arms crossed and eyebrows knit together.

"About what?"

Candy answered as honestly as she could. "A lot of things."

Wanda caught her drift. "Something bugging you?"

"Lots of things are bugging me. Lots of questions without answers."

"Anything I can answer for you?"

Candy's gaze sharpened as she turned toward Wanda. "Possibly. Have you ever seen a purple van with a license plate that reads RIP DIG?"

"RIP? As in *rest in peace*?" Wanda thought a few moments before she shook her head. "Don't think so. Why?"

"Is there any way you could find out? Maybe put out an alert on one of your social media accounts? I'd ask the police, but I don't think they'd tell me."

"They know about this?"

"I told them everything last night — at least, as much as I could remember."

"This for your little personal investigation?"

"Let's just say I'm curious."

Wanda nodded and lifted her phone again. "Consider it done."

"Let me know what you find out."

"You headed over to Ginny's?"

"I am," Candy said, "but I think I'm going to make a detour first."

"To where?"

Candy didn't respond right away. Instead, as if a sudden thought had occurred to her, she turned her head first one direction, then the other, her eyes suddenly searching with increasing alarm. "Say, have you seen Random around anywhere lately?"

THIRTY-FOUR

He was gone.

She searched the entire farm, the barn and hoophouses and sugar shack, inside the farmhouse and the Saab, back in the groves of cherry trees and over in the pumpkin patch, anywhere and everywhere she thought he might be. But despite all her efforts, her calls and whistles, she couldn't find him. So she searched again, enlisting the help of some of the visitors, who gladly joined in, excited by the quest. But, again, they came up empty.

Random was nowhere to be found. He'd simply disappeared.

Where had he gone?

Candy could think of several possibilities. He'd simply nodded off under an out-of-the-way tree somewhere, or crawled under the porch, or maybe even jumped into the wrong car and was having lunch right at this moment downtown at the inn with some welcoming tourists. But she doubted that's where he was.

And then, Candy realized, she already knew.

He'd gone back into the woods.

It was the most likely explanation. And it was confirmed when she talked to a trio of kids playing at the edge of the woods. Random had been here a little while ago, they told her, and they pointed toward the trees.

"He ran off in that direction," said a young dark-haired girl, dressed in a dark green cotton sweater and white leggings. "I think he was chasing something."

A rabbit, probably, Candy thought. Random loved chasing rabbits.

She called to him some more, but heard no response.

Then, from somewhere back in the woods, she thought she heard what sounded like frantic barking.

She hesitated, uncertain of what to do. This was Random's home. He knew his way around those woods. He probably disappeared back in there all the time. She doubted Neil would worry much if his dog was digging around in the woods. But Neil wasn't here. Random was in her care. And given all that had happened over the past couple of days, she couldn't help but feel a slight uneasiness at his sudden interest in something back among the trees.

She looked toward the sugar shack and thought again about Neil's missing tractor. Probably abandoned somewhere back in the woods, she'd concluded. Is that where Random had gone? Was he possibly looking for Neil, thinking he might still be somewhere in the woods?

She considered walking back among the trees, following some of the trails left by the tractor's passage, to see what she could find. But she had a better idea.

She didn't have to walk. She had her own transportation.

Five minutes later she was behind the wheel of the Jeep. Starting up its engine, she steered it away from the house and barn, headed up around the strawberry fields at a slow pace, and followed a well-worn trail into the woods.

THIRTY-FIVE

As the trees closed in around the Jeep, the farm disappeared behind her, replaced in the rearview mirror by gray trunks, dark crooked branches, and thick brown vegetation matted down from the heavy winter snows.

A short distance along, the trees closed in overhead as well. She drove through an arch of low-slung limbs into an even lower tunnel, where the twisting branches were entangled just above the Jeep's roof. But the trees soon cleared as the trail dipped and bent around with the landscape into a series of tight turns, which switched back and forth.

In some places, other trails angled off in either direction, but these looked less traveled, so despite Robert Frost's advice, she stayed on the main track. As she drove along, she was on the constant lookout for Random and Neil's tractor, but so far she'd seen no evidence of either.

For the most part, the Jeep's four-wheel drive system had little problem negotiating the soggy twin-rutted tracks left behind by the tractor's passage. She encountered some places where the ground turned fairly firm, and she could traverse these areas fairly easily, but she also came across some rougher patches, usually in low, muddy spots, where the trail bottomed out. The ruts in these areas were dug deep, creating high-walled trenches of damp, unstable ground. In a few weeks the trenches would dry and harden, making the trail easier to navigate, but for now these areas had to be crossed with caution. She skirted the muckier spots when she could, but there were a few tense moments when the Jeep's tires became mired in deep mud, and they jittered and jerked as the four-wheel drive took over, working to finally free the vehicle. And she was off again, making good time. That's why she'd decided to take the Jeep into the woods today. It was certainly quicker than walking, as she'd done the day before at the Milbrights' place. Still, she didn't push it too hard. She kept a steady yet cautious pace, not moving too fast, mostly to avoid damage to the Jeep's undercarriage, but also to give herself time to scan the woods as she passed through them.

She saw numerous tapped maple trees. In places, plastic tubing lines creating a gravity-fed collection network were strung between the trunks like silky strands of a giant spiderweb. She passed one large, pill-shaped collection tank, made of opaque polyethylene. It sat on a well-constructed bed of medium-sized branches in a cleared space near the trail. She saw another one a little farther along. Both were more than three-quarters full — which meant Neil probably hadn't emptied the tanks in a while. The sap was still running, obviously, but how fast? How long did it take for the tanks to fill? Twelve hours? Eighteen? A day, or more?

They could hold a lot of sap — fifty or sixty gallons, she estimated. They would take some time to fill, a day or two, probably, even with multiple trees feeding them. That was the point. Neil didn't have to make this trip daily. He could do it every other day, or every third day, depending on the time of the season.

So when was the last time he'd been through here? Her best guess was that the sap in the tanks hadn't been collected since at least sometime the day before, twenty-four hours earlier, and more than likely sometime before that, possibly yesterday morning, or even the previous morning or afternoon.

She looked around but, again, saw no signs of the tractor, nor of Random, so she moved on, slow but steady.

At one point, after skirting a boggy area, she drove up a short rise into a boulder-strewn clearing, from which she could view the surroundings. She stopped and let the engine idle, studying the landscape 360 degrees, before moving on, plunging back down into the woods.

She stopped frequently as she went, keeping the windows rolled down and the radio off, switching off the engine at times so she could listen. Occasionally she'd hear a few distant, echoing barks. They sounded as if they were coming from somewhere up ahead, so she kept going.

The woods thinned, and then, as she came over the crest of another rise and began to descend on the other side, she stopped.

There was the tractor. Or at least part of it. The trail angled to the left, around a bend. The front end of the tractor was hidden by some vegetation. It sat smack-dab in the center of the trail, wheels deep in the ruts, the engine shut off. The large sap-gathering tank on the cart behind it was half-full. There was no one in sight.

Scanning the area, she started off again, continuing on down the slope toward the tractor. She stopped the Jeep about ten feet away from it and shut off the engine. She climbed out and stood hesitantly by the Jeep, still scrutinizing the landscape, looking for any signs of movement or anything out of the ordinary. She thought of calling out to Random but held back. She wasn't sure she was ready to give herself away just yet — in case she wasn't alone out here.

Then again, the sounds made by the Jeep as she drove along the trail would surely have alerted anyone nearby of her approach.

She finally whistled a little and called out softly, "Random? Random, are you around? It's Candy."

Surprisingly, she got a response. She heard him whimper nearby. And movement, a rustling sound of disturbed leaves and soil.

Following a quick search, she found him pulled into a tight ball under the tractor. He occupied the center island between the ruts and the big rubber tires. The island was flat and covered with a thin bed of leaves, dead ferns, and pine needles. Random had made himself a little nest of sorts under there.

She spoke to him softly as she approached, and leaned over to look him in those big wet eyes. "Hey there, Random. What are you doing down there?"

His thumping tail was his only response.

In a soothing voice, she said, "I bet you're looking for Neil, aren't you? But here's not here. He's at the hospital. That's where I was headed. I came to see if you wanted to ride along with me."

At the sounds of the words *Neil* and *ride,* Random rose to his feet. He shook himself, making his collar tags jingle, then kept this head down and body lowered as he crawled out from under the tractor. He came up to her and nuzzled her hand.

"Hi, there," she said as she patted him gently on the neck and shoulder. "How are you doing, buddy?"

She gave him some attention, scratching him and ruffling his fur, then straightened again, and studied the woods around her.

"I wonder why Neil stopped the tractor here," she said to the dog, after a few moments. "It seems an odd place, doesn't it? There's no collection tank here — or anything else."

Except there were some tapped trees, she observed. Quite a few of them, all relatively close together. A sugar bush, Hutch had called it. There was no plastic tubing here, or collection buckets hanging from the

309

trees, as she'd seen on some of the other trees along the way. But they had definitely been tapped. She could see dark spots on the trees, large holes where the spiles had once been hammered into the trees. Multiple taps, it looked like.

She felt a jolt. These trees looked just like the ones she'd seen over at the Milbrights' place yesterday — the illegally tapped trees.

She instantly knew what had happened, and what Neil must have found when he'd been out here collecting sap: He must have caught the sap thief in the act.

Her brow lowered as she squinted into the woods. "Something fishy happened here," she said, and she looked down at Random. "Should we go investigate?" She leaned over to scratch him behind the ears, studying the trees for a few moments. "Yes, I think we should, don't you?"

She straightened and took a couple steps in the direction of the tapped trees, then leaned down to pat the dog one more time, for reassurance. "Stay close by me, okay?" she told him in a low voice, "just in case I run into a little trouble and need some backup."

THIRTY-SIX

Random did as she asked. He stayed right by her side, trotting alertly along as she walked toward the tapped trees at a cautious pace. She said nothing as they went, preferring to listen and observe. Her boots and his paws crunched on the leaves and twigs scattered on the forest floor. The only other sounds were the rising wind, the call of the birds, and the clattering of bare branches overhead.

It didn't take long for her to verify that she was correct in her initial assessment. These trees were not tapped in the normal manner. The holes were larger, almost an inch across, and there were multiple taps — four or five — in most of the trees. Some still had short lengths of PVC piping jammed into the holes, instead of typical spiles. In other trees, the holes were ragged and clogged with congealed sap.

Just as she'd seen over at the Milbrights' place.

She took a few steps back, thinking, as Random sniffed around her feet.

So that's why Neil had stopped his tractor here. His trees, like the Milbrights', had been illegally tapped by . . . someone.

The alleged sap thief had struck again, and was apparently targeting multiple farms.

Maybe, she thought, even hers. There were some clusters of sugar maples toward the back section of Blueberry Acres. They weren't usually tapped, but who knew? She hadn't been back there in a while — she'd had no reason to. Maybe she should.

But that didn't matter right now. What mattered was, who was doing this? And why? Why tap Neil's trees, as well as Hutch's?

She thought back to what Ginny had told her yesterday, out at Sugar Hill Farm: *It must be for the money, is all we can think of.*

Money. Was that really the answer? Or was there more to it?

Glancing around, she noticed that Random had wandered away. She spotted him heading off through the trees, his nose to the ground, shifting first one direction, then the other.

Apparently, he'd picked up a scent.

She thought of calling him back, but quickly realized it would be better to follow him. He might be onto something. Perhaps it was just the scent left by a passing squirrel. Or maybe it was something else.

She'd taken only a few steps when she noticed the footprints. Of course! She should have looked for those right away.

That's what Random was following. He must have caught Neil's scent. Without further hesitation, she continued after the dog.

As she'd done the previous day, when following a similar trail leading away from a grove of tapped trees, she kept her distance from the footprints, since she didn't want to add hers to the older ones.

Again, she saw two distinct sets of prints, but then she stopped. There was a third set, she noticed, and actually a fourth — Random's paw prints. But she discounted those for the moment. Instead, she focused in on an area where all three sets of prints were fairly distinct.

Two of them were fairly close together. The third set — the set Random was following — was apart from the others, though paralleling them. Just as she was doing.

She realized almost immediately what had happened. While driving past collecting sap,

Neil must have spotted the tapped trees and stopped the tractor out here. When he investigated, he'd noticed the footprints, just as she had. He'd followed them, just as she was doing, at some distance, skirting them as she was now, trying to figure out what was going on.

She looked down again at the two sets of footprints that were closer together. Who were these two people, walking side by side in these out-of-the-way woods? Why were they stealing sap from trees? What purpose could they have? And why these trees?

She bent down to get a closer look. Two sets of prints, two different patterns. One pair of boots showed a pattern of ringed circles on the bottoms, around the heels and balls of the feet, while the other had a blockier design made up of geometric shapes, like trapezoids and parallelograms.

She tilted her head. She'd seen both those patterns before.

She reached into her back pocket and took out her phone. In moments, she pulled up the photos of the footprints she'd taken yesterday, out in the woods at Sugar Hill Farm. She focused in on the patterns, the ones shown on the phone and the ones on the ground before her.

It didn't take long for her to realize that

the prints she saw here matched those she'd spotted yesterday. There was no doubt. She even noticed a prominent nick in the heel of one of the boots, one with the geometric pattern, which seemed to confirm that the same person had been in both places.

She also noticed that one set of prints she'd seen yesterday was missing here. The ones with the wavy pattern on the bottoms didn't appear to be in these woods. She'd seen them only at Sugar Hill Farm.

So what did it all mean?

She rose, her gaze following the footprints until they disappeared into the trees.

Yesterday, when she'd seen the footprints in the woods at the Milbrights' place, she'd assumed they'd been made by Hutch and Ginny. She'd also assumed the larger boots with the blocky patterns on the bottoms belonged to Hutch, and the smaller ones with the wavy design belonged to Ginny. If those assumptions held true, then Hutch had been in these woods, on Neil's property, sometime over the past few days. Tapping Neil's trees. The evidence certainly seemed to point to that conclusion.

But why would he have done such a thing? One possibility struck her right away: It could have been an act of retaliation. Maybe Hutch had tapped Neil's trees because he thought Neil had tapped his.

An interesting theory, and it might explain a lot. But did it fit the time frame? In her head she ran back over the events of the past few days. Hutch had discovered the tapped trees on his property yesterday morning — or so he said. She put the timing of his discovery at around eight or nine. Ginny had called her at nine thirty. Her conversation with them at Sugar Hill Farm had taken place at around ten A.M., she recalled. After leaving Sugar Hill Farm yesterday morning, she'd come right over here, to Neil's place, but he'd been gone.

So if Hutch had tapped Neil's trees, he must have done it before she'd talked to him and Ginny yesterday at their place, right? But was that possible? The timeline was murky, she thought, but yes, he could have done it. The Milbright and Crawford farms weren't that far apart. Assuming that's what had happened, had he been discovered by Neil? And who had been out here in the woods with him? Who wore the boots with the circles on the bottoms? They weren't Neil's. His were a short distance away. So if Hutch had been out here, tapping trees, who had been helping him?

She shook her head. It was a tangled knot she had yet to unravel.

While she considered the questions rolling around her mind, she again took photos of both sets of prints using her phone. Then she slipped it back into her pocket and looked around for Random.

Not surprisingly, he was nowhere to be seen. But she knew which direction he'd been headed. He was following the boot-prints toward the back of Neil's property.

She looked off in that direction, studying the landscape, and then turned to look back the way she'd come. Where she'd left the Jeep, near Neil's tractor.

She debated for only a few moments before she made a decision. It was easier, and quicker, to ride than to walk.

THIRTY-SEVEN

She had a tricky time guiding the Jeep through the trees and across the woodsy landscape. She had to go off-trail, navigating carefully, making her own way, which she knew was risky. The land was uneven, broken in places, crisscrossed by creeks and spotted with boulders and rock outcroppings. There were still some snowy patches in the more shadowed places under the trees, and plenty of boggy or muddy spots to avoid. But the Jeep's four-wheel drive, aided by relatively new tires with good tread, had proven itself so far on this rugged terrain, and she had no reason to doubt it now. Besides, she was concerned that if she walked, she'd never catch up to Random. And driving was easier on the knees and ankles than walking. It was, she reasoned, her best option.

At least her route was a relatively direct one. She just had to follow the trail of footprints, which led in a generally north-westward direction. But that wasn't always as easy as it sounded. Sometimes she had difficulty seeing the footprints from the driver's seat, even with the windows rolled down and her head leaned out over the side of the vehicle, so she could scan the ground. And in some places the prints became faint, even disappearing at times. But if she lost the trail for a while, she always managed to pick it up again a little farther on.

She had to twist and turn the steering wheel a lot, finding her way through the trees, seeking out the higher, firmer patches of land. With the windows rolled down she could listen for any out-of-the-ordinary sounds. But she heard nothing uncommon, not even the sounds of Random barking. If he was out here somewhere, he was staying quiet. She wasn't sure if that was a good or a bad thing.

She drove for several minutes, until the woods opened up and the trail of footprints ended. At first she thought she was entering a clearing, but then she realized it was a road that cut through the woods. A narrow dirt road — somewhat muddy now, and seldom traveled, by the looks of it.

And that's where she found Random.

He was plunked down in the middle of

the road on a fairly dry spot, about thirty feet to her right. His tongue was hanging out and he was panting a bit. His watchful eyes flicked back and forth, though not in a suspicious or wary manner. He was just being observant while he took a break.

She drove slowly out of the woods, down a short embankment — probably left behind by winter snowplows as they pushed aside the dirt and gravel, along with snow and ice — and turned onto the road in Random's direction. At her approach, the dog rose to his feet, yawned, stretched in a casual way, and then started toward her, as if he didn't have a care in the world.

She drove another fifteen feet or so before she pulled over to the side of the road, where she came to a stop. She put the Jeep into park and yanked on the emergency brake. With the engine still running, she opened the door and climbed out. She stood for a moment beside the vehicle with her hands in her back pockets, making a quick surveillance of the area as Random approached her. "What are you doing out here?" she asked him. "Something catch your eye? Or your nose?"

As he reached her, he bent his head to sniff at her feet and circled her once, twice, before angling off again, back the way he'd come, jogging along the side of the road, his nose to the ground, shifting back and forth.

Apparently, he was still tracking a scent.

Curious, Candy followed.

The dog stopped a little farther along, in an area by the side of the road. He again circled a few times before he sat down, facing her. His grayish eyebrows twitched a little, giving him an almost quizzical expression.

"So what have you found?" she asked. Her gaze dropped and swept the ground around and in front of her. She could see it now — the lines of tire tracks in the softer dirt at the side of the road. Some appeared to have been made by vehicles whose drivers were simply trying to avoid some of the soggier spots on the road. But at least two sets of the tire tracks went up and over the short embankment a little, as if the drivers had pulled their vehicles over to the side of the road to park, just as she had.

She stopped for a few moments, examining the tracks, then started forward slowly, stepping carefully as she moved out toward the middle of the road. She followed the tire tracks in a parallel line, giving them a wide berth so as not to disturb them, as she'd done previously when coming across potential evidence. Random, who had seated himself near the far end of the tires' impressions, watched her expectantly as she approached, angling back toward him.

As she reached him, she scratched him behind the ears and crouched down. "Tire tracks, huh? Two sets of them. And they look fairly fresh, don't they? A few days old, maybe? Or maybe just a day or two?"

Both sets of tracks were made by nondescript tires — nothing familiar, nothing she recognized. The treads on one set of tires were fairly worn. They wouldn't provide much traction. Probably wouldn't be very good in the winter. The vehicle would tend to slide around a lot. The other set of tires had more tread on them. In fact, they looked like commercial-grade tires, designed for use in mud and snow.

Like something you might find on a snow-plow truck, for instance.

So, she thought as she rose, what did it mean? Had Mick Rilke been out here in his truck sometime in the past few days? Or was she looking at the tire tracks of a completely unrelated vehicle?

The other set of tire tracks, she thought, could have been left by any of a hundred or more vehicles. There were a lot of old cars and trucks around the cape, and around the state. There was no way to tell which vehicles had left these tracks.

The police forensics lab in Augusta could probably figure it out, she thought, by making molds or taking photos of the tracks and running them through some sort of database. But the lab was a long way away, and that would take time — and she was right here.

"Let's look around," she said.

At her words, Random was back on his feet, tail wagging, and as she started off, examining the ground again in a general search pattern, he trotted along right beside her.

It didn't take long to find what she was looking for. The two sets of bootprints she'd followed from the illegally tapped trees emerged from the woods about ten or twelve feet away, to her right, back toward where she'd parked the Jeep. Once they reached the road, the prints separated, one set going one direction, one the other, both paralleling the dirt road. She followed one set that circled back into the woods, and soon came upon an area where some sort of scuffle appeared to have taken place. From there, she saw drag marks leading back toward the road, to the spot Random had found, where the parked vehicles had left their tracks.

Looking around at the evidence before her, she could guess what might have happened here. Neil had spotted someone — two people, maybe — tapping his trees. The alleged sap thief, or thieves. So he'd followed them. But one of the thieves must have noticed Neil was following them. The sound of the tractor in the woods would have been a dead giveaway. So one of them had circled around and ambushed him in the trees near the road — possibly knocked him out, and dragged him back to one of the vehicles they'd parked by the roadside.

But then what? Drove him away? To where? The boathouse?

And what about the second vehicle that had parked here?

As she'd done before, she took a few photos, just in case she wanted to refer to them later. And before she left the area, she swept it a final time, on the lookout for anything that might have been used as a weapon against Neil, a blunt object like a tree limb or a rock, or something else, perhaps a long steel pipe or rod, or a particular piece of sturdy lumber properly sized. Even an old baseball bat. She spotted a few possible items, just limbs and rocks, but none seemed like an obvious weapon.

With a final look around, she headed back to the Jeep, where she rummaged around in the backseat for a few moments before she pulled out an old hand towel she kept there for times just like these. She used it to quickly wipe Random's paws, then laid it flat out on the front passenger seat and motioned him inside. "Come on," she said, coaxing him. "Up you go."

He glanced at her before he looked back up at the seat. After taking a moment to consider his route, he agilely leaped up into the footwell and then onto the seat. He turned in several tight circles, apparently trying to figure out how and where to sit, but he finally plopped himself down.

She closed the door behind him, leaned in the open side window, and patted him reassuringly on the head. "One more stop," she said, "and then we'll go to the hospital to see Neil, okay?"

THIRTY-EIGHT

Even though she'd never driven on this particular road before, something about it seemed familiar — and it didn't take her long to figure out why.

She'd had her suspicions the moment she stepped onto it, following Random out of the woods. It was little more than a single lane wide, narrow and muddy, running in a general direction of southwest to northeast. There was no one else on the road with her. She saw no other vehicles. No villagers, no farmers, no tractors, no tourists. Just a forgotten back lane running through undeveloped land.

She wondered how many people in town even knew about this backwoods road. She was surprised they even bothered to plow it in the winter. But perhaps it was used occasionally as an access road by the town's maintenance crew, allowing them to get from one point on the cape to another fairly quickly.

As she drove along with a fair amount of speed, to avoid getting stuck in the muddier spots, her gaze kept shifting back and forth, from side to side, to the exterior mirrors and the inside rearview mirror, on the lookout for anything unusual. She noticed that some of the woods and open spaces on her left were fenced off, and she suspected it was conservation land. This was confirmed a little farther on, when she passed a small, rustic brown sign with plain white lettering stating the land's designation.

Neil's property, she knew, was bordered on its back end by conservation land.

So was the Milbrights' farm.

A little farther along, as she came around one particular bend, she had a strong feeling of déjà vu. The sense of familiarity overwhelmed her. The fence on her left was gone, the open spaces had filled back in with trees and vegetation, and the woods had again closed in on either side. She slowed the Jeep as she looked around. This stretch of the road was about two hundred feet or so in length, with bends in the road at either end, heading in opposite directions. There were mud ruts all along the way. She recognized some of the trees and landmarks.

And she thought she could spot the place where she'd come out of the woods the day before, and on the other side, where she'd fallen when she'd almost been run over by the purple van.

This was, she knew, the service road behind the Milbrights' property — the same one where she'd encountered the out-of-control van yesterday; the same one Hutch had mentioned, when he'd told her about the red vehicle he'd spotted through the woods a couple of days ago.

So, two vehicles had been through here recently. And Random had found two sets of tire tracks over by Neil's place. Could the tire tracks have been made the same vehicles? An old van with bald tires, perhaps? And an old red snowplow truck with relatively new mud and snow tires?

If so, where had those vehicles been going? And where were they now?

She didn't see them along here — or anything else of interest. She was tempted to stop and snoop around a little, but she was concerned that if she slowed down too much, her tires would sink into the muck, and she'd have a hard time getting them unstuck. So, instead, she gently tapped the gas pedal, urging the Jeep forward a little faster without making the tires dig in too much. Soon she was back up to an appropriate speed for this type of road, following its twists and turns. As she went, she kept her eyes on the road ahead. Random stayed alert as well. He was sitting up now, watching out the windshield and side window as the landscape rolled past. It was almost as if he could sense what was going on.

She thought the road must terminate soon, since the peninsula wasn't that wide, only a few miles from coastline to coastline. And, as she expected, it ended not too far ahead.

As she came around the final curve, she knew why she'd never been aware of this particular dirt service road before. It came to an end on the back side of a parking lot for a maintenance shed belonging to the town's public works department, as indicated by a black-and-white municipal sign out front. The shed was located in an open field on a short spur of a road just thirty feet or so from the Coastal Loop. Ahead of her, she saw cars whizzing back and forth along the main drag, headed into and out of town.

She remembered the shed now. It was a low, one-story white cinder block structure with small windows, a metal roof, and a trio of industrial-sized garage doors at one end, now closed. Back behind the building were several low piles of gravel, sand, and salt. A front-end loader sat idly nearby.

It all looked so familiar. She drove past here all the time. She stopped in at the maintenance shed herself at the beginning of every winter to fill up buckets of sand for use on the lane out at Blueberry Acres. She just never knew there was a dirt road leading from the back of the parking lot and meandering out behind the properties of Neil Crawford and Hutch and Ginny Milbright.

She drove past the maintenance shed without slowing, and finally stepped on the brake when she reached the stop sign at the intersection with the Coastal Loop.

She was back at the river, she realized. It was right there in front of her again, a hundred feet or so away, down a gently sloping embankment with a few riverside houses spotted here and there along the way.

If the purple van and red truck had come through here, which way would they have gone? She knew the van had been traveling northeast when it had passed by her, but didn't know which direction it might have turned once it reached this intersection. Same for the red snowplow truck, if it had come this way.

She looked to her left, northward. In that direction was a long, heavily traveled stretch of road that led up to Route 1. It ran past Judicious F. P. Bosworth's place, just a little farther up the road, and eventually to the bridge, riverside cabins, and boathouse where she'd found Neil and Random.

Her head turned in the other direction. That way led past a number of just-out-of-town properties, including those belonging to the Milbrights and the Gumms, and the police station, as well as a couple of auto repair garages, a small fire station, and a few old warehouses and storage facilities, before reaching the edge of the village.

She thought only a few moments before she turned the steering wheel to the right and gunned the engine.

It was time to find out what Ginny Milbright wanted.

THIRTY-NINE

For the third time in two days, Candy drove up the lane at Sugar Hill Farm, headed toward the house, barn, and sugar shack at the Milbrights' place.

She was surprised to find the lane wasn't as bad as she'd anticipated, and instantly knew why. It appeared some members of the town's maintenance crew had been out here since her last visit, probably first thing this morning. They'd laid down a new top layer of dirt and gravel, and smoothed it down nicely, filling in the ruts and puddles, making it passable for the expected heavy traffic during Maple Madness Weekend.

And when she got to the barn, where the sign welcoming visitors to the "world-famous sugar shack" still hung, she saw a decent crowd. One of the tour buses was just pulling out, headed back to town, about half filled with tourists. Visitors were milling around the place, though the vibe was more subdued than it had been over at Crawford's Berry Farm that morning.

She parked in a spot near the barn and spent some time encouraging Random to wait for her inside the vehicle, which caused him no small amount of consternation. But she was finally able to convince him to settle, and managed to escape from the Jeep without the shaggy dog beating her out the door.

She didn't see Ginny initially, so she checked inside the barn first. The Milbrights had set up their small retail operation in here, consisting of two old, unadorned folding tables, pushed together and topped with two dozen bottles or so of Sugar Hill Farm's maple syrup. They appeared to have sold a decent number so far, but at the moment, the tables were abandoned, with no one to keep an eye on them.

Candy bypassed the house for the moment and next headed up toward the sugar shack on the right. It was still in operation, the sweet-smelling smoke rising in spiraling streams from its cupola. A few visitors hovered around the door or just inside, and there, talking in the midst of them, was Ginny.

Despite everything that had happened today, the woman looked composed, all business, though a little tired. Her eyes seemed to droop, her hair was disheveled, and her clothes were rumpled, which seemed natural, given the fact that she'd probably been boiling sap all day while managing the crowds and activities on the property. With Hutch gone, hauled off by the police for questioning, she'd no doubt had to take on all the responsibilities of running the place herself. But she seemed to be handling the situation well enough. She spotted Candy approaching and, after a moments' hesitation, acknowledged her with a small, almost indistinct nod.

Candy returned the nod and hovered a discreet distance away, until Ginny finished talking to her guests. As they began to drift away, Ginny turned around, appeared to speak to someone behind her inside the building, and then, with hands thrust deep into the pockets of her worn fleece vest, she stepped out the doorway and headed in Candy's direction.

"I didn't think you were coming," Ginny said in a surprisingly controlled tone as she approached Candy.

"I got delayed." Candy said honestly. In a quieter voice, she added, "Have you heard from Hutch? How's everything going for him?"

Ginny shrugged. "He's having a rough time, naturally," she said, expressionless, her mouth a straight line. "He's been over there all day, ever since they picked him up this morning. He's flabbergasted by this bogus accusation, of course. It's just devastated him, that anyone thinks he could have done something like this. But he's a big man. He can take it. And he's been cooperating fully. We both have, of course."

"Of course," Candy said. "Have you heard any details?"

"Well, they've questioned him extensively, but haven't come to any sort of resolution — at least, not from what I've heard. I was down there myself for a little while, as long as I could spare, trying to talk some sense into them, telling them they need to release him. They know Hutch didn't have anything to do with this, but they said they're just being thorough. *Pee-shaw* on that," Ginny said, and she made a spitting motion. "It's harassment, pure and simple."

Candy could understand the other woman's frustration. Her husband was accused of murder, which must weigh heavily on both of them. Plus, she'd been running the farm without Hutch on one of its busiest days of the year, working mostly in a hot sugar shack and trying to keep the customers happy at a time when she probably felt the complete opposite. It was a lot to deal with.

"How are things going here?" Candy asked, looking around.

Ginny sighed heavily and let her shoulders slump. "Not bad, but not as good as we'd hoped, given what's happened. It's been hectic, as you can imagine. I had to call in some help. It was too much for me to do myself, and I probably ticked off a few people and missed some sales."

"Who's helping out?"

"Hutch's nephews — his sister's boys. Nice young men. They're just teenagers but they've helped out around here before. They're old pros at this. And it gives me a break when I need it."

Candy glanced at the sky. The sun was past its peak as they headed into mid-afternoon. Events at Town Park would be starting up soon. "How much longer are you going to stay open?"

"I think we have a couple more tour buses left," Ginny said, checking her watch, "and then that's it. We'll start shutting down the boiling operation in another hour or so. The boys' folks are picking them up at four, and then they're going to the marshmallow roast. It should be quite a bonfire, from what I've heard."

"Yes, it should be," Candy said. "I'm headed over there myself later on, after I make a stop at the hospital to see Neil."

"Right, Neil." Ginny said the words flatly, as if they were distasteful in her mouth. "Speaking of which."

Candy caught the shift in the other woman's demeanor. "Something wrong?" she asked.

Ginny looked around, assessing the current situation. "Well, that's why I asked you out here," she said, "and why I agreed to talk only to you." She nodded toward the house and crooked a finger. "I think it'll be better if we talk inside. I can afford to step away for a few minutes. Come on, I want to show you something."

337

FORTY

The Milbrights' house was in need of a little TLC, Candy thought as she followed Ginny into the kitchen. Unwashed dishes were stacked high in the sink. The counters were cluttered with cereal boxes, empty coffee cups, mixing bowls, pot holders, cutting boards, plastic storage containers, and other items that had not been put away. Trash was overflowing in a bin beside the door. The floor needed sweeping — and a good scrubbing. A floor mat in the entryway was caked with dried mud. And nearby sat a line of mud-encrusted boots, as well as sneakers and other types of shoes.

Candy had an urge to check the bottoms of some of those boots, to see if the patterns matched the footprints she'd seen out in the woods. But she didn't feel comfortable doing it right in front of Ginny. It would be too obvious. Besides, the other woman was moving quickly through the house.

"It's this way," Ginny said, heading into a hallway on the other side of the kitchen and pulling open a beat-up wooden door. She reached inside the doorframe and flicked on a light switch.

Candy followed hesitantly, craning her head around as she looked at the door, and what lay beyond. She saw a set of rickety stairs, leading down into shadows. "What's down there?" she asked.

"The basement," Ginny said, with an odd look in her eyes.

"And what's in the basement?"

"That's what I wanted to show you." Ginny waved a hand toward the stairs. "After you."

Again, Candy hesitated. For some reason, alarm bells were going off in her head. "Um, okay."

Against her better judgment, she brushed past Ginny and stood for a moment at the top of the stairs, looking into the basement. The lights were indeed on down there, though they were somewhat dim. She could see a cement floor at the bottom, and some well-worn area rugs. And a bunch of junk littering the floor.

"Go ahead," Ginny said encouragingly.

"There's nothing down there that can harm you — much."

That didn't help ease Candy's wariness. She had a strange feeling the other woman was enjoying this. But she wasn't about to back away. As cautiously as possible, and keeping an eye out in both directions, ahead and behind her, Candy started downward.

In the back of her mind, she absently wondered whether she'd ever walk back up those stairs again. But she shook it away as a ridiculous thought, and concentrated on not tripping, falling down the stairs, and breaking her neck.

A few of the steps creaked as she put her weight on them, but they all held, despite their dilapidated appearance, and she made her way to the bottom without incident. Ginny came down quickly behind her, noisily trouncing down the steps in her heavy boots.

At the bottom, Candy moved aside to let Ginny pass by. The ceiling was low, with open beams for the floor above, so Candy kept her head bent over a little, though it wasn't really necessary. The beams were a good half-dozen inches above her head. But she bet it was a tight fit for Hutch, who was tall and bulky.

It was a typical basement in a New England home. Chilly and damp. Shadowy and a little creepy. Spiderwebs in the corners, many of them abandoned years ago, now wispy and gray. At a quick glance, Candy saw stacks of old boxes, discarded pieces of furniture, and shelves packed with items no one would ever use again, like old pots and pans, flowerpots, and last year's Christmas wrapping paper. An old red wagon with faded paint and a homemade wooden rocking horse kept each other company off to one side. An abandoned loom sat nearby. It looked like it might have been an antique, possibly of some value, left here to rot. In one corner was a workbench with a few tools scattered on it. In another, a washer and dryer, old and rusting, were pushed together under a naked lightbulb.

"We're going this way." Ginny pointed, and she started off on a path through the clutter, paying it no attention and making no apologies.

A little farther along, Candy saw a pool table that looked playable. Just beyond that, the far side of the basement had been partitioned off with thin brown paneling, now slightly warped. A flimsy door in the paneling on the right side led into a room beyond.

Ginny walked to the door and turned the

knob. Again, she pointed. "Hutch's man cave," she explained as she pushed open the door and entered. Candy followed her in.

This part of the basement, surprisingly, was fairly neat, not at all like the carnage on the other side of the door and paneling. There were decent rugs covering the cement floor in here. All the walls were decorated with posters and paintings, as she'd seen in Mick Rilke's workshop, but while those had been mostly historical in nature, these were more oriented toward hunting, wild animals, and the outdoors. A fairly uncluttered desk sat across the room, facing them, with an oak desk chair pushed up to it. Along the wall to their left, an old tube-style TV and a similarly old stereo system perched on a long, low table near a couple of worn easy chairs. A trio of hunting rifles rested on pegs tapped into the wall to their right. And, under the hunting rifles, were a number of long wood-and-glass display cases, in relatively good shape. A gray boxy machine near the display cases gave off a low humming sound.

"A dehumidifier," Ginny said, noticing Candy's gaze. "Hutch likes to keep it dry down here. To protect the collection, you know."

"The collection?"

Candy finally had an inkling of what this was all about.

"You've already seen one of his pieces, of course. I thought you might like to see the rest of them. Hutch is quite the knife collector, you know."

Candy gulped. "No, I . . . I didn't know that," she said, then clarified, "Well, yes, I did, but I just found out a little while ago."

Ginny nodded, as if she'd expected this. "Word getting around town, is it?"

When Candy didn't respond, Ginny pointed to the display cases. "This is what I wanted to show you."

There were three cases in all, each about four feet wide, well made with good wood, sitting side by side along the wall. The tops of the cases were glass, and each had its own light bar along its entire width, with separate switches, to illuminate the items on display inside. Ginny moved to the case the farthest away first.

"This is his early-history collection," she said, clicking on the interior light and pointing through the glass. "Not a whole lot here, since relics from that era are hard to come by, and expensive. But he has an old Roman dagger that's been authenticated, and some pieces of helmets, a spear tip, and an old belt buckle. He's pretty proud of that one," she said with a shake of her head. "Says it belonged to someone famous, Tacitus or Romulus or someone like that." She waved a hand in the air and moved on, flicking one light switch off and two more on.

"The one on that side," she said, pointing to the case on the right, while stopping in front of the one in the center, "has his more contemporary items, including some pretty expensive collectible hunting knives, many of them from around the world. He has a particular love of Russian knives, for some reason. Guess it makes him feel like a Russkie, though his family is from Scotland and Germany. And in this one," she said, tapping on the glass top in front of her, "are his most prized items, and the largest part of the collection. Historical items from the eighteenth and nineteenth centuries, including a number of pieces from the Civil War era. Here, let me show you."

She grasped the edge of the glass top and lifted. It was hinged in the back end and swung open smoothly and easily, without any creaks or squeals — obviously well-oiled hinges, Candy thought. Ginny pushed the top the whole way to the back wall and latched it in place with a convenient hook. "Easy access," she told Candy. "Hutch likes to handle his weapons a lot. Make small talk to them, clean and shine them, that sort of thing. He's neater than I am, as you might have noticed. He loves these things more than me. He takes pride in them. Here, this is one of his nicer pieces."

She took a thin, dark blue cloth lying in a corner of the case and used it to lift out an old dagger with a dark metal handle and a long, thin steel blade. "This is a woman's knife," Ginny explained as she held it up for Candy to see, "said to belong to a barmaid who worked in a saloon in Devil's Half Acre back during the state's early logging days. That's in modern-day Bangor, you know, right along the Penobscot River. Very notorious place. Of course" — and she winked — "I use the term *barmaid* loosely. Women like that had to protect themselves in those days — just like they do now. Here, hold it."

She handed it to Candy as if it were a newborn baby in swaddling clothes.

Candy hesitated a few moments, but had no choice. She reached out to take hold of the knife with both hands. "Use the cloth," Ginny advised. "Hutch doesn't like fingerprints on them. He's fussy that way. Says it musses them up. Damages and disfigures the metal somehow. Personally, I think a weapon like that needs to be felt in the hand, to understand its true heritage." She shrugged. "But that's just me."

It was heavier than Candy expected. Even through the cloth, she noticed right away how balanced it was, how right it felt in the hand, as Ginny had noted. She could imagine some "barmaid" sliding this into the top of her stockings before she went to work. It had a dull sheen, and its edges and tip were pockmarked and unsharpened. It no longer looked quite as lethal as she imagined it must once have. But it obviously was well taken care of, and cherished.

She handed it back to Ginny. "Very nice," she said.

Ginny took the knife and returned it to its spot, then pointed to another, an ivory-handled folding knife. "This here," she said, "once belonged to a security agent who worked for one of the steamship lines that ran side-wheelers up and down the rivers and bays around here. And, of course" — she pointed to an empty spot in the case — "you know about this one."

She looked over at Candy. "It's the one that's missing, of course. The knife that once belonged to Silas Sykes. I'm sure you've heard a lot about *him* over the years." Her gaze hardened. "I hear you dug up a treasure chest belonging to Silas Sykes a few years back, you and your father and

Neil Crawford, right?"

Candy had to admit the other woman was correct. "Yes, that's true."

"So your boyfriend must have had an interest in items belonging to Silas, right?"

"My boyfriend?" Candy gave her a confused look. "He's not my boyfriend, but . . . I'm not quite sure —" She paused, her brow wrinkling, and she felt a twitching on her spine. "I'm not quite sure what you're saying."

"I'm saying," Ginny said, as she reached up to unlatch the glass top and gently lower it back into place, "that Neil was over here a few weeks ago. Hutch brought him down here, to see his collection. We haven't had much contact with Neil over the years, you know, despite the fact that we're sort of in the same business. Not sure why. He just likes to keep to himself, we figured. But he stopped by every once in a while. He came over here a few weeks ago to talk about the Maple Madness Weekend and the sugar shack operations and how we were going to coordinate everything and things like that. We were all cordial enough. As we were talking, Hutch offered to show Neil his collection, like I said. As you can imagine, Neil was fairly attracted to that knife belonging to Silas Sykes."

"Attracted to it?" Candy asked. That didn't quite sound like the Neil she knew.

"He paid it a lot of attention, sure," Ginny continued. "And it makes sense. He's got a connection of sorts to Silas. That property of his once belonged to the Sykes family — or, at least, Silas used to squat on it. Got burned out at one time, so I've heard. Anyway, that knife held a lot of interest for Neil. That's why, when it went missing, we thought we knew right away who took it."

"Neil?" Candy was caught by surprise. "You think *he* stole it? From Hutch? I'd heard it was missing but —" She paused, thinking. "So when did this happen?"

"Like I said, a few weeks ago."

"Did you report it to the police?"

"We did not," Ginny said. "We wanted to keep it between ourselves. We didn't want to bring the police into it — at least not right away. But, well, of course, the whole thing has escalated now, hasn't it?"

Candy felt her chest tightening. "What do you mean?"

"Well, it's clear enough what happened, isn't it?" said Ginny, almost impatiently. "Neil Crawford stole that blade from Hutch's case and used it to kill Mick Rilke."

Candy was shocked by this accusation. "But why would he do that?" she asked, her

348

voice squeaking a little as she spoke.

Ginny's eyes drilled into her. "I don't know. You're the one going up there, aren't you, to the hospital, to see him, right? Why don't you ask him yourself?"

FORTY-ONE

Half an hour later, as Candy drove westward on Route 1, those words still echoed in her mind.

"Why don't you ask him yourself?"

How exactly would she do that? she wondered. How could she possibly frame such a question? *Neil, did you murder Mick Rilke with an antique knife you stole from Hutch Milbright's display case in the basement?* The very idea seemed ludicrous, inconceivable. And yet, it made sense in a certain way. The knife had been found next to Neil in the boathouse. He certainly could have handled it at some point, and left his fingerprints on it. Allegedly it was the murder weapon. But had he stabbed Mick Rilke in the back with it?

Candy couldn't imagine such a scenario.

But she also couldn't completely rule it out, which bothered her more than she cared to admit.

After Ginny's bombshell, the two of them had walked back up the basement stairs, across the kitchen, and outside. Candy didn't speak much; she barely knew what to say. But Ginny continued to support her husband, and pressed her accusations of Neil.

"So you see," she'd said as they walked down off the porch and started across the driveway toward the Jeep, "Hutch couldn't have done it. He didn't have the knife in his possession. Neil had it."

"Do you have any real evidence of that?" Candy had asked, finally finding her voice. "Did you see Neil take it from the case?"

Ginny admitted she had not. "I wasn't down there with them at the time, and Hutch didn't see him take it. That's why we didn't go to the police right away. But no one else has been down there since — just Hutch and me, of course. Neil's the only one who could have taken it. And it seems obvious, given his connection to Silas Sykes, doesn't it? And the fact that the knife was found right beside him in that boathouse, where you came across him?"

Candy had to admit it did make sense, at least on the surface, but she had a hard time hiding the distress she felt. "Did you talk to Neil about this?"

"Of course we did. Hutch called him and asked him if he knew anything about it. Your boyfriend played dumb, of course. Said he didn't know what we were talking about. That's what caused some of the bad blood between him and Hutch over the past few weeks. You know what happened then."

"You think this has something to do with the stolen sap?"

Ginny had never answered, and the question had hung in the air as the final tour bus arrived, jouncing up the lane and chugging to a stop near the barn. As the passengers began to disembark, Ginny had a few final words for Candy, before she went off to greet her newest visitors. "You'd better find out what he's up to," she'd said, "and then you'd better contact the police with what you know." And with a final nod of her head, Ginny had set off toward the newest arrivals.

Candy had barely said good-bye, her mind deep in thought as she absently made her way toward the Jeep. She'd been looking down as she walked, her gaze unfocused, but she'd suddenly had the presence of mind to notice that Ginny had left behind a fairly clean set of bootprints as she walked away. Candy had stopped dead in her tracks, staring down at the prints, studying them. But she quickly knew the patterns left by Ginny's boots didn't match any of those she'd seen out in the woods over the past couple of days. No blocky designs in geometric shapes, no wavy patterns, no concentric circles.

It left her even more confused. If not Ginny, then who had been back in those woods with Hutch? Who left the other sets of bootprints?

Now, as she drove westward along Route 1 toward the hospital, Candy looked over at Random, who was sitting up in the seat next to her, keeping a watchful eye on her as well as on the road ahead. He seemed to sense her mood, and gave her a series of apprehensive looks. She reached over to rub him behind the ears and pat his neck. "Don't you worry," she said in a comforting tone. "We'll figure out what's going on. I promise."

Her words seemed to reassure him as they hurtled down the road, following the sun west.

But his good mood didn't last long. Once again, when they reached the hospital, she had to leave him behind in the Jeep, a difficult task. Being so cooped up was becoming uncomfortable for him, she knew, and she felt his eagerness to see Neil, as well as the simple need to stretch his legs. She considered talking to the nurses, or even asking one of them to watch him, but knew he wouldn't be welcome inside. "I promise I'll be as quick as I can," she told him, "and I'll bring you something to eat. And then we'll find a place where you can run around a little."

She made a mental note to check in the back to see if she had a leash with her, then hurried into the building.

She found Neil resting comfortably in his room. His head of usually untamed brown hair, which could grow curly as the humidity increased, remained corralled by the bandages he wore, but his familiar bearded face had some of its color back, especially in his high cheekbones and broad forehead. His lips were a little dry and swollen, and his eyelids were still darkened by the blow he'd received, but overall he looked like he'd improved since she'd seen him earlier in the day.

His eyes were closed and his hands folded flat on his stomach, but as she breezed into his room and came to a stop at his bedside, breathing a little quickly due to her brisk walk into the place, he winked open an eye and smiled weakly.

"There you are," he said, reaching out a

long-fingered hand in greeting. "I heard your sneakers coming down the hallway. It's really good to see you."

Candy took his hand in hers. It felt rough, warm, and reassuring. With her other hand she rearranged the sheets around him. "It's good to see you too, stranger. You're looking better."

"I'm feeling better," he said, raising his other hand to probe the bandages a little, "though my head still throbs. But they've been taking good care of me. They gave me something that put me out for a while. Speaking of which, I heard you sat up with me half the night."

"I was here for a few hours," she admitted, "until they kicked me out."

That drew a chuckle from him. "Well, thank you for doing that. And for watching Random. How's he doing?"

"Just fine. Being brave like the rest of us. He's waiting out in the Jeep. I wish I could bring him inside to see you. He's terribly worried, you know."

"I'm sure he is," Neil said, with a catch in his throat, "and I've been worried about him. But I know he's in good hands, if you and Doc are taking care of him. He hasn't been too much trouble, has he?"

"Actually, quite the opposite. Believe it or

not, he's been helping out with the investigation. That nose of his has been pretty useful lately."

Neil seemed amused by the thought. "He's a good tracker, that's for sure. But usually he's out chasing squirrels."

"Oh, he's been doing that, too," Candy said, smiling, "and greeting visitors at the berry farm all day, playing the perfect host. But he's also been chasing down suspicious footprints in the woods, and tire tracks out behind your property."

Neil's expression changed, becoming more serious. "You've been doing some detective work, haven't you?" he said, sitting up a little in bed. "What have you found out?"

Candy hesitated only a moment, wondering if this was the right time to discuss these things, but decided it was as good a time as any, and plunged on. "Well, a lot," she said, and quickly she told him all that had happened since the previous morning, starting with her meeting with Hutch and Ginny, her encounter with the purple van, and her trip to the boathouse, and continuing to this afternoon, including Wanda Boyle's impromptu visit to the berry farm, and the disappearance of Random, and how she'd gone looking for him in the woods and found the tractor, the tapped trees, and the trail of footprints. And how Random had discovered the dual sets of tire tracks on the dirt road behind the farm.

"It looks like there were two vehicles parked back there," Candy said, and Neil nodded, his gaze becoming more focused as she went on. He listened with growing interest as she told him about her visit to Sugar Hill Farm just a little while ago, and her conversation with Ginny Milbright, and her uneasy trip into the basement, where she'd viewed Hutch's collection, which was missing an antique knife that once belonged to Silas Sykes — the same one found beside Neil in the boathouse.

"Ah, yes, the knife," Neil said, his voice a bit hoarse due to his injury and some of the procedures he'd endured during the day. "The police asked me about that. I told them I did see it a few weeks ago, down in Hutch's basement, when he took me down there to show me his collection. And, as Ginny said, I was pretty fascinated by it, to be honest, since it once belonged to Silas Sykes — because, as you know, my family has some history with that guy. But I didn't take the knife. She's wrong about that part. Hutch said it went missing after my visit. He called me a few days later and asked if I

knew what happened to it. I told him no —
same thing I told the police, though I don't
know if they believe me. But I never saw
that knife again after that day in their basement. I still haven't, since I was, you know,
unconscious when you found me."

As he spoke these last few words, a look
of gratitude flashed through his eyes. His
gaze shifted to her, and she saw something
in them she hadn't seen before. "By the way,
I want to thank you for doing that — finding me like that. It was very, well, Nancy
Drew of you."

"Nancy Drew?" Candy gave him an
amused look, and Neil smiled.

"As you can imagine," he continued, turning serious again, "I'm pretty glad you came
along when you did. I'm not sure what
would have happened if you hadn't found
me."

She squeezed his hand. "It was just dumb
luck, really."

But he wouldn't accept that explanation.
"No, it wasn't," he said earnestly. "You,
well, you rescued me. You might have saved
my life."

Candy attempted to brush aside the comment. "I'm just glad I found you when I
did, and that we got you to the hospital,
and that you're okay."

"Me too," he said softly.

They were silent for a few moments after that, looking into each other's eyes, exchanging unspoken feelings they both felt but weren't quite ready to address just yet.

The period of silence stretched longer than both of them expected, and they could almost hear each other's hearts beating, until the myriad hospital sounds intruded in the background. Candy finally pressed her lips together. Her whole mouth felt dry for some reason. "Well," she said, "if it's any consolation, *I* believe you. About the knife, I mean. I know you didn't take it."

"That makes one," Neil said, and he smiled again, though he looked weary. "Now I just have to convince the police, the Milbrights, and the rest of the town."

She put her other hand on top of his reassuringly. "I'll tell you the same thing I just told Random on the way here. Don't worry. We'll figure it out," she said with true determination. "Somehow that knife got from Hutch's basement to that boathouse. We just have to figure out who put it there — and who used it to kill Mick."

"Mick," Neil echoed, his voice suddenly sounding distant. "So what everyone's been saying about him is true? He's really dead?"

Candy nodded. "Yes, it's true. I'm sorry."

"But it doesn't make any sense," Neil said, sounding confused and a little angry. "It just doesn't seem real."

"No, it doesn't. I think I stumbled upon the exact spot where it happened. The strange part is, it was right outside the boathouse where I found you. Someone bound him up and dragged him into the river. His body was found floating downstream, near the docks and warehouses, yesterday morning, right before the grand opening of the community center was supposed to take place."

"Right, the grand opening," Neil said, as if suddenly remembering. "I was supposed to go to that thing, I think, but I never made it. I got waylaid in the woods." He rubbed the back of his head again, though this time more for show than because of the injury itself.

Candy hesitated a moment before she asked curiously, "Do you remember what happened to you? In those woods?"

"Some of it," he admitted, though he looked uncertain.

"What's the last thing you remember?"

"Well, again, the police asked me that," he said, "and it took me a little while to put it all together in my head. I don't recall all of it, and a lot of it is still fuzzy, but I do remember driving the tractor out into the woods with Random. I remember the time of day, and how the sky looked, and what the weather was like. And how the trees looked. We're nearing the end of the season. We should have bud break in another few weeks. But the trees are still producing okay. I checked them all out and emptied the tanks along the way. But when I got beyond the ridge, something started to feel strange in the woods. It wasn't hard to figure out what it was."

"You noticed the tapped trees," Candy said.

His nod was subtle. "I spotted them right away. There was just something different about them. I knew they'd been tampered with. So I stopped the tractor and went to check them out. I found those footprints you mentioned. There were two sets, just like you said. So I followed them, just like you did. And that's when I realized Random had disappeared."

"He tends to do that."

Neil nodded. "He does. He's sort of a free spirit, like me. I guess I need to have a talk with him about that. Anyway, I followed the footprints through the woods for a while. And then . . . I saw one of them."

"Who? One of the sap thieves?"

"I think so, yeah. He was headed toward the back of the property, carrying a couple of buckets with him. I wondered what he was doing in my woods."

"Do you know who it was?"

"I do," Neil said, surprisingly. "I followed him for a while without being seen, and circled around to his right. I finally caught up close enough to get a good look at this face."

The strawberry farmer took a deep breath and gave her an almost apologetic look as he continued. "I know this won't help my case, and I'm probably incriminating myself in some way by saying this — giving myself a motivation for his murder, to be specific — but it was Mick Rilke."

FORTY-TWO

Candy could barely prevent herself from gasping. "You mean *he's* the one who's been doing all this?"

"At least part of it, yes." Neil let out a breath of air and shook his head. "Much as it pains me to say this, I believe he's the one who tapped my trees and stole my sap."

"And Hutch's too?"

"Hutch?" Neil shook his head. "I don't know. Do you think the same person tapped the trees in both places?"

"That's what we have to find out. When I talked to the Milbrights about it yesterday, they thought you were doing it."

"Me?" Neil looked aghast. "Why would they think I did it?"

"It has something to do with that knife," Candy said, "and I think there's also some jealously on their part because of what you've been doing at your farm."

"Hmm, yes, I've heard that before," Neil

said. "I've tried to build a few bridges with them but sometimes people rub each other the wrong way. I had the same situation with Mick."

"You did?"

Neil nodded. "Apparently it goes back years, decades, to events that happened when my dad was still around, running the place. I don't know the whole story, but there were some bad feelings. But again, I mostly just tried to stay out of it." He sighed and tossed his head a little. "But I guess I couldn't stay out of it forever. Somehow they dragged me into it, and now I guess I'm a suspect in Mick's murder."

Candy saw the problem then, the reason for his reluctance in identifying the sap thief. "If you saw Mick stealing from you, and you've had conflicts with him in the past, then that means you have probable cause," she pointed out.

"Bingo." The regret was heavy in his voice. "It gives me a motivation for murder."

"And you've told the police all this — about seeing him in the woods?"

"I have."

"And what did they say?"

"What do they ever say? *We'll get back to you.* Oh, and I shouldn't leave town — although, technically, I'm not in town at the

364

moment. But I got the gist of it. They want me to stay around for more questioning."

"Right," Candy said, and she turned to look behind her, back to the hallway and the direction from which she'd come. "They don't appear to have a guard on your door."

"Not yet," Neil said, "but it's probably only a matter of time."

Candy could see the evidence against him, and it didn't look good. "You had the knife by your side, essentially in your possession. Ginny is claiming you stole it from Hutch, though she hasn't reported that to the police — yet. You saw Mick stealing sap from your trees. It's an easy one-two-three link."

"Easy," Neil glumly agreed with her. "That about wraps it up, doesn't it?"

"With a neat little bow," Candy agreed. She had a sudden thought. "Did you handle that knife when Hutch showed it to you a few weeks ago? Are your fingerprints on it?"

Neil shook his head. "I had to use this dumb little cloth he had in the case. He didn't want my fingerprints anywhere on the thing."

"Well, at least that's one point in our favor," Candy said, "and thank goodness for that dumb little cloth, although I'm sure they're still going to check the knife for prints at the lab. That could seal the case, if they find anything."

"Hopefully they won't," Neil said.

"Hopefully." Candy was silent as she thought. "So," she said after a few moments, returning to his narrative, "what happened after you saw Mick in the woods? You spotted him, but did you confront him? Did he see you? What did he say?"

Neil shook his head, and his eyes became shaded. "None of those things happened. I saw him, and that's honestly all I remember. The next thing I knew, I was waking up in that boathouse, with you staring down at me and Random barking."

"You don't remember anything in between?"

"Nothing. Nada. Whatever happened to me, I went out pretty fast."

Again, Candy's mind whirred. "I think we can probably figure out what happened. Right after you spotted Mick, someone hit you in the back of the head with some sort of weapon — a tree branch, maybe, or a rock or something like that. I came across that spot too, where I think it happened, when I was following those tracks in the woods. I saw two sets of prints out there, in addition to yours. And two sets of tire tracks. That means there were at least two other people back there, and two vehicles.

My guess is that the two vehicles were Mick's red truck and a purple . . ."

But she was interrupted by her phone, which pinged in her back pocket. That particular sound meant she'd received a text. Thinking it might be important, she reached back and pulled out the phone. "Hang on a minute," she said as she quickly checked the screen.

It was a text from Wanda Boyle. Candy read it quickly:

Found out about that purple van with license plate RIP DIG. NOT rest in peace.

A follow-up text added, *Belongs to someone named Russ Pooley. Middle initial I. Asking around about the family name. Will contact you when I know more.*

"Pooley," Candy said as she stared at the texts, her brow wrinkling in thought.

"What's that?"

Candy looked up, and then read the texts back to Neil. "I was just talking about it," she said. "This purple van on the road behind the Milbrights' place that almost ran me over yesterday. It belongs to someone named Russ Pooley." She paused, and then she remembered.

"I've seen that name before," she said, the light going on in her eyes. "Just recently, in fact."

FORTY-THREE

Quickly she told Neil what she intended to do, but he didn't want to let her go. "You don't know what you're walking into," he said, sounding worried. "It could be anything."

But Candy would not be deterred. "All those places looked like they were deserted when I was out there yesterday. Maybe there's some sort of connection," she said, recalling the names on the signs by the small cabins and cottages she'd passed along the river. Bell was one of the names she'd seen. And Cook, and Kimball, and Robinson.

And Pooley.

She couldn't recall that place in particular. It hadn't jumped out at her in any way. There had been six or eight of the small riverside cabins she'd passed that had been nondescript. Nothing to distinguish them — just low wooden structures, most looking run-down, painted muted colors, some with chimneys, some with screened porches, all dark and locked up.

Could that be where the purple van had been headed? To one of those cabins by the river?

And who was Russ Pooley, the apparent owner of the purple van? Was there a connection between him, whoever he was, and the riverside cabin with the same name on it?

"Anyway," she said, with a glint of anticipation in her eyes, "I doubt there's anyone at any of those places today, with everything going on in town. I'll just run over there real quick and check it out. Maybe do a little snooping around, see what I can find out. I should be okay, if I keep my head low and my nose clean."

She glanced around at the clock on the wall. It was just after four in the afternoon. "And after that I have to head over to Town Park. I haven't been there all day, and I feel like I've been shirking my duties. I promised Maggie I'd help out in the booth."

Neil understood. They'd been friends and neighbors long enough for him to know how she operated. He knew he couldn't talk her out of it, or make her change her mind. It was simply her nature in cases like this. And over the years, she'd had a lot of success in solving them — though often at her own peril.

"Take Random with you," Neil said, still uncertain he should let her go off on her own. It was clear he wanted to go with her himself, and felt frustrated that he couldn't. "He'll help you keep an eye on things. And if you see anything suspicious, anything at all, promise me you won't get yourself tangled up in it. Just back away and call the police. Better yet," he added, swinging his head around to look out the door, "they might still be hanging around the building. You should say something to them on the way out, just to let them know what's going on."

"If I see someone, I'll say something," Candy agreed, slipping the phone back into her pocket and looking suddenly distracted.

"Promise me," he said, and he took her hand again, before she could walk away. "Because I don't know what I'd do if anything happened to you."

That made her stop, and shift her head, and refocus on him. For a moment, everything else was forgotten. She grasped his hand tightly and felt a sudden glow inside. "Really?"

"Really," he said honestly as he looked

into her eyes. "I mean, I've been lying here all day, thinking a lot, and I've decided there's something I want you to know — something I've been meaning to tell you for a while, though I didn't really know how to say it until now. But, well, I've started wondering why I've been doing all this."

"All what?"

"All this," he said, and he waved a hand in the general direction of Cape Willington. "The farm. The maple sugaring. The strawberries. The cherry trees and the hoophouses and all the sweat and effort. And, to be honest, when I asked myself that question, I wasn't sure of the answer. I've been doing it all by myself for so long that I've lost touch with the purpose of it. The reason behind it. But then, after I thought about it for a really long time" — and here he paused to allow himself a brief smile — "I realized why I've been doing it. I've been doing it for us."

Candy wasn't quite sure what he meant. "For us?"

Neil suddenly looked hesitant. "Of course, I don't mean to presume anything," he said hastily.

"No, no." Candy squeezed his hand again. "It's okay, go ahead and presume."

Again, he smiled. "Okay, well, since you

insist — but really, it's why I came here in the first place. For the property, sure. For my family's legacy, okay. But it has to be more than that. And I realized I was doing it to be close to you."

"Really?" she said again.

"Really. Look, I know I'm not the most outspoken, outgoing person in the world. I know I keep to myself a lot, that I can be a loner. But I don't think — no, let me rephrase that — I'm *sure* that's not the way I want to spend the rest of my life. I have to be doing this *for* someone, other than just for me. I guess it's just taken me a while to figure this out, but part of the reason I moved back here from Vermont, and sold the place there, was that I wanted to run a farm close to yours. I wanted to spend time with you. I wanted to work with you. I wanted to, well, be next to you."

He stopped. He had the look of someone who'd realized he'd probably said too much.

Still holding his hand, Candy brushed aside a few stray strands of her honey-colored hair, leaned over, and kissed him on his cheek just above the beard. Staying close to him, looking into his eyes, she said, "I feel the same way, Neil. I always have. And, well, I guess I'm sort of just like you. I live with my dad, of course, but I've been by myself for a long time, since I got divorced years ago. And, like you, it's taken me a while to admit . . . well, I guess that's why I've been spending more and more time at the berry farm with you and Random."

Suddenly, at the mention of the dog's name, her eyes went wide and she straightened, slapping her forehead with her palm. "Random!"

Neil looked suddenly worried. "What about him?"

"I left him in the Jeep," Candy said, "and he's probably famished. I have to take him something to eat and drink, otherwise he'll be in a panic."

Again, Neil understood. He squeezed her hand a final time, reassuringly, and then let her go. "We'll talk, okay?"

"Okay," she said, and she gave him another quick kiss on the cheek. "I'll be back," she said, "as soon as I can. And then you and I are going to have to spend some time together."

He beamed. "I'll look forward to every moment. And, hey, you be careful out there."

"And you get better, as soon as you can. We need you back at the farm."

Their good-byes were rushed and a little awkward, if only because neither of them quite knew how to separate from each other. But Candy finally made her way back into the hallway and down the stairs to the first floor, her thoughts like a swarm of butterflies in flight on a sunny afternoon.

But she didn't forget Random. On the way out of the hospital, she stopped at a vending machine and bought a packaged ham sandwich and a bottle of water. And, just for fun, some peanut butter crackers. He'd enjoy those, she thought. He loved peanut butter. A nice treat for all his patience today.

She made a quick scan of the place, looking for Molly Prospect, but the officer was nowhere to be seen. No doubt she was back in town already, as was Chief Durr. Candy decided she'd simply stop by the police station on her way into town and talk to them there.

Then she was out the door, into the waning day, headed back to the river.

FORTY-FOUR

As she drove eastward from the hospital along Route 1, Candy went over Neil's words again and again in her head, reliving their conversation, remembering the look in his eyes and the touch of his hands, wondering what his words might mean for the both of them, and what kind of a future the two of them might have together. It gave her a lot to think about.

But as she approached the intersection with the Coastal Loop and the bridge over the English River, her thoughts became more focused. At the traffic light, she made a left-hand turn off the main road onto the quiet side street that ran north along the river, where the boathouse and waterfront cabins were located. She parked in the same general area she had the day before, and again she had to tussle with Random. "I don't have a leash," she told him, "and I'm not sure this is a good place for you to be running around."

Before she left the hospital, she'd given him a few minutes outside to stretch his legs, but he was antsy again after the long drive, his eyes flashing. She managed to calm him a little by giving him a couple of peanut butter crackers, which she'd kept in reserve for just this occasion. And she left the side window rolled partially down for him, so he could sniff at the moist air while he kept an eye on her. Feeling it was the best she could do for now, she closed up the Jeep and headed down toward the river-bank.

She stopped at the water's edge near a small eddy, created by a trio of boulders just upstream, and surveyed the landscape as she gauged her next move. She knew where she was headed, but Neil's words echoed in her mind:

"You don't know what you're walking into."

He was right. She'd have to be cautious. There was still a murderer around some-where. She felt she was close to flushing the culprit out, but this was always the trickiest part.

Slowly, quietly, and with a great sense of vigilance, she started off, hoping she was doing the right thing. *Just a few minutes,* she told herself, *a quick reconnoiter.* And then she'd head back to the Jeep and drive to the police station to report what she'd found — if indeed she found anything of interest.

She headed downstream, careful of her footing on the uneven bank. The river rushed and gurgled on her left, and on her right were the cabins, tucked backed among the foliage, shadow-striped by the slanting sun and surrounding trees. Just as they had the day before, they all looked deserted. Their doors appeared to be padlocked, the windows were dark, and the parking spots beside the cabins were universally empty, except for an occasional abandoned car or off-road utility vehicle.

As she passed by each cabin, she looked for an identifying sign or plaque. Again, she saw cabins belonging to the Bells and the Donovans and the Cooks. A little farther along, the Robinsons' place, identified by a hand-painted sign, perched on a low rise above the river. The shades were drawn and the place looked quiet. Again, no one home, from what she could tell.

As she silently walked past, she knew what was coming next, so she slowed and instinctively took a few steps sideways, into the vegetation on her right. It was, she thought, an attempt to camouflage herself as she hovered for a few moments, so she could scan the area ahead, looking for any signs of movement.

Her gaze swept back and forth several times, but she saw no one. She could see the cabin ahead, though, through the trees.

The Pooley place.

It was painted a faded bluish gray, she saw now, looking much like the color of river water, which might be why she hadn't noticed it much her last time through here. It was a low-roofed affair with a stone chimney at one end and a small bay window out front. Other than that it was just a box, really, nothing fancy. A rickety-looking double-car garage, also painted bluish gray, stood next to it on the south side.

She looked downriver. How much farther away was Gully's Boathouse? she wondered. Not far. She thought she could see traces of yellow police tape through the trees. Maybe three or four houses farther downstream. The two places were close together.

She pondered that for a moment, wondering what it might mean — if anything.

Seeing no one around, she left her cover and crept forward a few steps — and began to wonder why she'd worried so much about the place, or even thought there might be something here. Because there wasn't much, other than a few fishing poles in a rack on one side of the building, and a battered black barbeque grill nearby that looked as if it had been left out in the elements for too many years. A few empty beer cans and a couple of discarded bottles of charcoal lighter fluid had been tossed to the ground nearby. Nothing threatening in the least about the place.

With her hands stuck deep in her pockets, she started across the open space in front of the cabin. Her gaze shifted back and forth, keeping an eye out for anything unusual, but as before, she saw nothing to give her concern. She approached the building from the side, and then, deciding to be proactive, she walked to the front door and rapped lightly on it several times. She waited and knocked again. Not surprisingly, no one answered.

She circled the cabin, holding her hands to the sides of her face as she peered into a few windows. From what she could see, it was a typical setup. Wood floors covered with area rugs, rustic furniture, a well-used fireplace, a small kitchen with equally small appliances. A couple of bedrooms, each furnished with a set of twin beds covered with bedspreads that looked decades old. Nothing that stood out.

She turned to face the garage, which looked like it was on its last leg, barely able to stand on its own. Perhaps she'd find something in there.

She'd just started toward it when she heard a sound that made her jump. A low, steady rumbling echoed through the woods. A few moments later, she realized it was the sound of an engine of some sort. A vehicle, approaching from the west — from the direction of the river road, probably coming along one of the lanes that led to the cabins.

By the sound of it, the vehicle was coming in her direction.

Apparently, the owners had arrived. And here she was, standing right out in the open, trespassing on their property.

She cursed her timing as her head shot back and forth, looking for a place to hide while also watching for the oncoming vehicle. She could see the flash of a chrome grille and a glint of light off the windshield. She had only a few moments to figure out what to do.

She spotted the old garage nearby. Without further hesitation, she darted toward it. There were two bays, two garage doors, both closed. Neither had windows, so she couldn't see inside. She thought of trying to open one of the garage doors but decided against it. Not enough time. But she saw a side door on the wall facing her, so she angled toward that. There was a big stainless steel hasp across the door and frame, and a padlock hanging from the metal eye. But it looked like the padlock was open. The door appeared to be unlocked.

She hurried to it. Indeed, the padlock was not closed. She could get in.

With a quick glance back over her shoulder, she flipped the hasp to one side, turned the knob, pushed open the door with her shoulder, and slipped inside, just as the vehicle emerged from the dense riverside vegetation and pulled up beside the cabin.

She closed the door behind her and stood just on the other side, her ear right up against the wood. There was no window in this door either, so she couldn't see what was going on outside, but she could hear the vehicle's engine sputter and shut down. It ticked a little as it cooled. Then, silence.

She kept her back against the door. She could hear only her own breathing in her ears. It sounded too loud, so she tried to slow her breaths. She wondered if she'd been spotted. But in her next thought, she wondered if it mattered. Was she overreacting? For a moment, she considered just opening the door and showing herself, making up some excuse for her presence here. But, instead, she waited.

And, as she turned her head, she looked. Straight ahead of her, into the garage.

Two vehicles sat in front of her, close enough for her to touch them.

It took her a moment to realize what she was seeing, what they were. Their colors were muted in the dim, filtered light, but she could make them out well enough.

A red truck, and a purple van.

FORTY-FIVE

For a moment she didn't quite believe what she was seeing. It was almost like a mirage, an illusion, something conjured up out of her dreams by a magician. Real, but at the same time, not real. In fact, totally unreal.

These were the vehicles she'd been searching for over the past two days. And now here they were, right in front of her, in this broken-down building. She knew it instantly. There was no mistake.

Both vehicles had been backed into the garage and were parked so their headlights faced the garage doors. The red truck was closest to her, about an arm's length away. It was beat up, its wheel wells encrusted with dried mud, but it looked drivable. The snowplow attachment was hooked up to the front end, its curved steel blade topped by two square spotlights on black stalks. There were no markings on the sides of the truck; Mick had never bothered with that for the plow truck, though his summer landscaping truck displayed his name and number. The driver's side window was rolled down; the cab looked empty.

The van was parked on the other side of the red truck. As if drawn by a magnet, Candy moved away from the door and angled around the front of the red truck, steering as far from the eight-foot-wide blade as possible. She crossed in front of the twin garage doors and stopped before the van, directly in the center, with the old grille right in front of her.

She looked down. RIP DIG, the license plate read.

There it was, plain as day. This was the van that had tried to run her down yesterday on the back road behind the Milbrights' place.

Candy froze as she heard footsteps nearby, on the other side of the garage doors. She could hear the crunch of heavy boots on the gravel, twigs, and scattered leaves.

She also heard a few barks in the distance.

Random.

Whoever was outside must have heard them too, for the person paused, as if listening.

Candy held her breath.

Almost immediately, the footsteps started

off again, headed back the way they'd come, by the sound of it. They were soon out of earshot.

The barks stopped as well.

Candy let out a breath and decided to take the opportunity to shift her position. She felt vulnerable here, in the front, right by the garage doors. It would be better on the other side, behind the vehicles.

As quickly as possible, she moved away from the garage doors and slinked back between the truck and van, to the shadows at the rear of the building, where she thought she might have a better chance of going undetected. Maybe the owner was leaving. Maybe it had just been a quick trip to pick up something, or to check and make sure the place was locked up.

Her heartbeat quickened again as she heard the footsteps returning. They were approaching the garage again. This time, it sounded as if they were headed toward the side door. They reached it and stopped there.

Candy waited, holding her breath. As quietly as possible, she crouched down, so if someone should open the door, she'd be hidden behind the van's tall back end.

Just then her phone dinged in her pocket, once, twice, breaking the silence.

Candy scrunched up her face in disbelief. She'd just received a couple of texts — and possibly given herself away.

Again she waited, ignoring the phone for now, afraid to move a muscle. She was sure she'd been found out. She expected the door to swing open at any moment.

But that didn't happen. Instead, she heard a scrape of metal on metal, as if someone had moved the hasp, and a distinctive deep clunk that sounded like the padlock being snapped together.

She knew what had happened. She'd been locked in.

Maybe the owner was just making sure the place was locked up properly, as she'd thought earlier. Maybe it was just simple security. Or maybe not. Maybe it was something more deliberate — to trap her inside.

For a few moments nothing happened. Then she heard a strange sound, like water splashing on the door, as if someone had turned a hose on it. The splattering continued, around the corner of the building and along the bottoms of the garage doors.

What was going on? Was the owner hosing the place down?

No, it was something else, she thought. She smelled it now, the noxious yet weirdly aromatic fumes. They made her nose twitch and her blood rush faster through her.

Fuel. Raw fuel. Like gasoline.

Or charcoal lighter fluid. Being sprayed around the foundations of the building and around all the doors. The exits.

The realization rushed through her. In that moment her flight instinct kicked in. She knew she had to get out of here, fast.

She looked around, head turning back and forth, seeking some alternative avenue of escape — maybe a back door, a window she hadn't noticed, even a pet door. She searched the walls, her gaze jumping around frantically, lowering and rising. She rose to her feet as well and shifted to her right a few steps, moving along the back of the garage, scanning its rear wall, looking for anything — even a crowbar or an ax she could use to break her way out.

The black-and-white photo popped into her field of vision out of nowhere. As she swung her gaze along the back wall, it was just there, right before her eyes. It took her a few moments to focus on it and realize what it was — one of a number of old photos attached to the garage's back wall with small black nails. She looked up and around at the collection, stuck up here as if it were some sort of memory wall. The photos were mostly groups shots, all black-and-white, most eight by ten inches in size, heavily creased and faded, several decades old. Her eyes skipped around the images. Typical scenes you'd see at a riverfront cabin. Kids in shorts playing in the water, or swinging from tire swings, or sitting on a midstream boulder, shirtless, with fishing poles and big smiles.

Family scenes, she realized. Probably the Pooleys, decades ago.

She turned her attention back to the one photo directly in front of her, the one she'd first noticed. She knew right away what it was, because she'd seen it before — just yesterday, in fact.

It was a photo of a high school graduating class. Cape Willington High School, the Class of 1981.

The exact same photo she'd seen in Jean Rilke's living room yesterday.

Once again, she could easily spot Mick in the photo. He stood toward the end of the top riser, young, husky, and mop-topped. And on this photo there were two initials above his head, written with an old ballpoint pen.

MR.

That wasn't the only set of initials on the photo. There were others. Two in particular

388

caught her attention.

HM.

VIP.

The first one she knew. Hutch Milbright, standing next to a young Jean Rilke — though she'd obviously used a maiden name then, which Candy didn't know.

But it was the last set of initials that drew her interest. *VIP.* The letters floated above the head of a young woman standing next to Mick Rilke on the top riser. She wasn't as tall as he was, but she was taller than most of the other females in the class. She had wispy brown hair and a natural look, probably because she wasn't wearing any makeup.

The more Candy looked at that young face, the more familiar it became.

It all clicked in then, in a shocking second. Her eyes swung between the young man and woman standing next to each other on the top riser, with the initials *MR* and *VIP* over their heads. Someone had drawn a small heart between the two of them, at about shoulder height. Obviously they'd been an item in high school. And she recognized the young woman now.

Ginny Milbright.

Ginny, short for Virginia.

Identified in the photo as *VIP.* Her maiden

name, at her high school graduation, before she was married.

Virginia Pooley.

That had to be it.

And it fit. Candy remembered the message on the antique map she'd seen in Mick Rilke's workshop: *VIP 5 DIG.*

VIP — Virginia I. Pooley, now known around town as Ginny Milbright. Candy thought she knew what the message on the map might have meant, or at least part of it. It was a reminder Mick wrote to himself, to meet *VIP,* probably at five, at the place marked with the *X* on the map.

Here. Right here, where she was standing. This garage, this cabin. This is where they'd met — either here, or right downstream at the boathouse, where Mick had died.

Her head jerked around. She smelled smoke. Whoever was outside must have lit the lighter fluid.

Moments later, she watched in horror as both garage doors, as well as the side door through which she'd entered, burst into flames with a great *whump!* and a rush of hot air.

FORTY-SIX

Candy panicked as a feeling of claustrophobia washed over her. The flames seemed to have momentarily sucked all the air out of the garage, followed by a backlash of heat and smoke. She started coughing almost instantly, and held the back of her hand to her mouth as she looked around frantically for a way to escape. But she was trapped. She couldn't go out the way she'd come, through the side door, or through the garage doors at the front. She'd never make it through that wall of flames. It was only a matter of moments — seconds — until the flames made their way across the garage to her. The place would probably go up like a matchbox. No doubt the floor was a sea of oil stains, left behind by all the vehicles parked here over the decades. That would accelerate the flames. She had to find a way out, and fast. But at first glance, there were no options.

She thought she could hear a vehicle starting up outside. The owner must be leaving, she thought. Leaving her here, to burn with this building, with the truck and van.

It was an intentional act, she realized in shock. Someone was trying to murder her — and obviously get rid of some of the evidence at the same time. Evidence, and a pesky amateur sleuth, both extinguished in a tragic fire at a deserted cabin along the English River. Very convenient.

How many secrets would the charred remains of the red truck and purple van give up? Certainly their license plates would still be decipherable. The snowplow would identify Mick Rilke's truck. But the photos would be gone, along with any fingerprints and hair follicles and other evidence, which might provide clues to the murderer's identity.

As for her, nothing much would remain in five minutes or so, unless she could find a way out.

She crouched down again, to get below the toxic smoke given off by the rapidly burning wood. The flames were licking at the ceiling, probing crosswise like red-hot fingers, almost living things that slithered above, seeking to consume all around her.

She shouted then, a series of long, loud

screams, the pitch as high as she could get it. She kicked madly at the wood panels along the back wall, looking for a weak spot, an opening of any sort. But despite the garage's rickety nature, the wall appeared solid.

There was no way out. She couldn't escape. She was going to die here in this run-down garage by the river, in the company of two worthless old vehicles.

She turned and pounded at the wall with renewed vigor, using both fists, then turned and attacked the wall with her shoulder as the flames lapped over her head and crept toward her along the side walls. The hot air and smoke stung her eyes and lungs, until she finally sank down to her knees, leaning back against the wall, still striking at it with one of her fists, though the energy was going out of her.

She thought of making a last-ditch effort, running toward the front of the garage, looking to see if either of the vehicles had keys in them. Maybe she could drive her way out, like something from a Hollywood movie. Straight through the burning doors, maybe in the snowplow truck. She was assessing her chances of survival when she heard scraping sounds low on the other side of the wall. And barks. Loud barks outside, but close by.

"Random!" she shouted, hope springing back up in her. "Random, I'm in here!" He must have squeezed his way out of the Jeep somehow through the partially opened window and followed her scent to the garage.

The shaggy dog barked frantically in response, and the scraping and scratching sounds grew more frenzied.

She realized what he was doing. He was trying to dig his way into the building from the other side. She looked down. The garage had been built on a concrete slab, but over the years the slab had cracked and broken near the back edge. She could see a wedge of dirt where a triangular section of the concrete had broken away. There was a small space, perhaps only a couple of inches tall, between the bottom of the wood panels and the ground, a space once filled by the concrete slab. And she could see thick-taloned paws clawing at the dirt there now.

It might work, she thought as she watched Random trying to dig his way in, but he needed help.

She couldn't do it with her bare hands. She needed something else. Something sharp, like a shovel or an ax.

A moment later, she knew where she

might find one.

Keeping low to the ground, shielding her face against the heat, she twisted around and crab-walked her way back between the two vehicles, until she reached the passenger-side door of Mick's red truck. She reached up and pulled at the handle, which felt warm to the touch. She yanked opened the door and peered inside. She checked the ignition first, on just the slightest chance, but no key. Next, she looked behind the passenger seat, and found exactly what she was searching for. No self-respecting landscaper and snowplow driver would go out without an ax or hatchet to break up ice and clear out brush. And in that, Mick was not unique.

She thanked him mentally as she wrapped her fingers around the handle of the hatchet and made a fast retreat. She'd hoped for something a little larger, but this would do in a pinch. And she was definitely in a pinch.

She tried not to inhale the smoke as she scrambled back between the vehicles. She made one quick detour, back along the wall to the cluster of black-and-white photos. She reached up and swiped the graduation photo from the wall, folded it together as best she could with one hand, slid it into her back pocket, and crab-walked back to the spot where Random was still digging.

"Stay back!" she shouted to him through the wall. "I'm coming out!"

And she rose, gripped the hatchet with two hands, drew it back like she was winding up to hit a baseball, and swung as hard as she could.

FORTY-SEVEN

It took her a dozen solid strikes with the honed blade, using all her strength, to break through. The wood splintered slowly at first, but it was old and weathered, and upon repeated hits it finally gave way. She managed to open up a wedge of space about a foot and a half high, roughly triangular in shape. She kicked away a few remaining shards with the toe of her boot and dropped to her hands and knees so she could peer through.

The first thing she saw was Random's dirtied paws and muzzle on the other side. He backed away and ruffed low in his throat as he saw her. "Hi, there," she said, and stuck her own nose out, so she could take in a few deep breaths of untainted air before she drew back and studied the opening she'd made.

It was admittedly a small space, but Random had loosened up some of the ground underneath, which she was able to scrape away with her hands, and she thought if she could get her head and shoulders through, she might be able to wiggle her way out.

As she ducked her head low and turned it slightly so it would fit through the opening, which was wider at the bottom, she felt a wave of heat hit her body. Her eyes flicked around, just before her head slipped under the wood panels, and she caught a glimpse of the garage behind her. It was almost totally consumed by the flames. She hesitated no more, needing no further encouragement. She went headfirst, and she had to contort her shoulders to the point she nearly wrenched them out of their sockets, but she got them through. The hips were almost as tough, but again, she wiggled around until she managed to free herself. She pulled her legs out quickly behind her just in time, as the flames were literally licking at her boots.

She scooted backward on her hands and feet until she was half a dozen yards away, back in the shelter of the trees, some distance from the garage, which was now fully engulfed in flames. Random was all over her, sniffing and nudging and licking her. She tried to acknowledge him but she was mesmerized by the fire. The flames were out of control, licking and stretching upward. Black smoke roiled into the air. The heat was intense. She'd made it out just as the place was about to come down.

As if in response to her thought, part of the garage's roof collapsed with a great crunch of timbers and metal. That triggered an instability in the building, and one of the side walls fell inward, crashing on top of the two vehicles inside. And the back wall — the one she'd just come through — looked as if it was about to fall also, but in her direction. She didn't think she was far enough away, and realized she still could get caught in the flames, if not struck down by waves of heat.

She heard a bark behind her then, and a brief scuffle, and felt a hand clamp down on her shoulder. Another hand wrapped around her waist and pulled her backward involuntarily. She let out a yelp of surprise as she struggled to twist around, to see who had such a tight grip on her. She saw a black sleeve and black pants. "We need to get you away from here!" a familiar voice shouted in her ear.

She wheeled her head around. "Judicious?"

She allowed herself to be pulled back

then, and in fact she helped, pushing at the
ground with her feet to propel the both of
them farther backward and away from the
fire. The building had gone up quickly, as
she'd expected, but she hadn't expected
how intense it would be, and how close
she'd come to being consumed by those
flames, along with everything else.

"Are you okay?" asked Judicious F. P.
Bosworth, who had appeared out of nowhere to help get her to safety. "I was walking along the river and I . . ."

But there was too much confusion to
answer. The flames were still roaring, rapidly
destroying the building. It had folded into
itself, three of the four walls, as well as the
roof, curling inward and downward like the
fingers of a claw. But the back wall had not
yet come down; it still leaned at a ninety-
degree angle as it burned. She and Judicious and Random were a safe distance
away, though, and all they could do was
watch.

Judicious spoke up again. "Do you need
an ambulance? Are you hurt? Did you get
burned anywhere?" He was breathing heavily, sitting down, spread-eagle, with her lying between his legs, leaning up against his
chest. His hand was still wrapped around
her waist. It felt almost comforting. Random

was hovering nearby, turning back and forth, not quite sure what to do.

"No, no," she said, sitting up. "I . . . I think I'm okay." She looked around. They were back in the relative shelter of the woods, though she had no doubt the flames could spread quickly into this area, leaping from tree to tree. Behind them, shadows were gathering. She hadn't realized how quickly the light was fading — perhaps because the area in front of them was lit up like high noon. But even as she turned back toward the building, she realized the fire was beginning to die down, its fuel consumed, the garage's charred skeleton all that remained, though she could still hear several loud snaps and pops, and the crackle of the flames.

She turned again, and finally got a good look at the person who had helped rescue her. She saw the familiar straight nose, the intense eyes, the unshaven face framed by long dark hair, which was covered in part by a wide-brimmed floppy hat made of grayish-green felt. "Judicious, what are you doing here?" she asked.

He didn't answer right away, but his hand around her waist loosened. They separated a bit as she rubbed at her shoulders and legs.

"I was . . . I was passing by," he said finally. He sounded a little stunned, though he recovered quickly. "It was just a whim. I've been trying to figure out what's been going on around here, same as you, and thought I'd take a look. Then I noticed the smoke, and heard the barking, and thought I should check it out."

"I'm glad you did, but how did you —" She broke off as a sudden thought rose over all the others going through her mind. Frantically her head shifted back and forth, her eyes searching. "Did you see her?" she asked Judicious.

"See who?"

"Ginny. Just now. Where's Ginny?"

"Ginny?"

"Ginny Milbright. She —" But Candy halted again. She didn't know for sure Ginny Milbright had locked her inside the garage and lit the place ablaze. It could have been someone else — someone who had driven away just moments ago.

"Did you see a vehicle parked around here?" she asked Judicious. "Anything at all? It left here moments ago."

Again, Judicious hesitated before he answered, as if trying to focus his thoughts. "A car," he said finally. "There was a car here. I saw it drive away."

"What kind of car? Can you describe it?"

"An old white SUV of some sort. Like a Ford, maybe."

"Ginny Milbright's Ford Explorer," Candy filled in.

Judicious nodded. "I've seen it around here a few times over the past three or four weeks, driving up and down the road."

"You're sure that's what it was? A white Ford?"

When Judicious confirmed that it was, to the best of his recollection, she said, "Did you see which way it went?" As she spoke, she pushed herself to her feet, brushing herself off as she did so.

"Back toward town, I think. I could see its taillights through the trees. It was headed south."

"South," Candy repeated, "toward town."

"That's right," said Judicious, and he rose also. Random was all around their feet then, sniffing and jumping up a little. Candy leaned down and gave him a grateful hug. "You're my best friend right now, you know that?" she told him affectionately. But she kept her praise brief, as her next move filled her thoughts. She made a decision quickly.

As she straightened, she pulled her phone out of her pocket and held it out toward Judicious. "Do you know how to use one of

403

these things?"

As a low-tech person, Judicious didn't own a mobile phone, as far as she knew. Or a landline. Or a TV. Or a car. He was a recluse, a mystic, and a bit of an enigma who lived a simple life. And he was always full of surprises. "Of course," he said, as if it was the most elementary thing in the world.

She handed it to him. "Call the police," she told him. "Ask for Chief Durr, or Molly Prospect, or anyone, really. Tell them what happened here, and have them send a fire truck ASAP. The garage is gone but we don't want the embers spreading to the other cabins, or into the woods. And they need to get a forensics teams out here right away. There's evidence that needs to be collected. Tell them I think Ginny Milbright is behind all this, and perhaps Mick's death as well. And tell them we think she's headed toward town, for whatever reason."

Candy paused, her mind racing, trying to tick off everything she could think of. "Then call my dad. His number's on there. Tell him I'll meet him at the bonfire in Town Park in fifteen minutes. Tell him to keep an eye out for that white Ford Explorer, and to get the word out to all the villagers. And tell him to be careful — Ginny might be armed, and she's certainly dangerous."

"Why?" Judicious asked as he took the phone from her. "What are you going to do?"

Candy gave him a hard look. "I'm going after her."

FORTY-EIGHT

She drove as fast as she dared, her foot to the floor, a madwoman behind the wheel.

She gripped the steering wheel with both hands, because she was worried that if she didn't, they'd start shaking uncontrollably. She kept her gaze focused on the road ahead, on the lookout for a white Ford Explorer. She wasn't quite sure what she'd do if she caught up with it. She still wasn't completely sure Ginny Milbright was the culprit. But she knew she was getting closer to finding out who had murdered Mick — and who had tried to murder her, twice.

She had a hard time wrapping her head around all that had just happened. Questions swirled, with a big one standing out above all the others: Why would Ginny have done any of this, if she was truly the person behind it? What could she hope to gain? Perhaps more accurately, what was she trying to hide? Had she murdered Mick? If so, for what reason? And why set up Neil — or her own husband, for that matter — to take the blame?

As she pondered these questions, her gaze shifted to her right. Random once again sat next to her in the passenger seat, riding shotgun, as he'd done for most of the day. Initially she'd thought of leaving him behind at the Pooley cabin, in the care of Judicious, but decided that would be a foolish decision. For one thing, Random had just rescued her from a burning building. He'd saved her life. At the very least, he had earned the spot next to her. It wouldn't have been fair to leave him behind. He deserved to see this thing through to the end as much as anyone.

And he just might save my life again, she'd told herself. *Or help flush out a killer.*

That last thought was reinforced by what had happened a little earlier, before she'd left the Pooley place. Once she'd made the decision to take Random with her into town, she'd had a difficult time getting him back into the Jeep. He'd hovered around the cabin, his nose down, sniffing at the ground, angling back and forth in a pre-occupied manner.

He'd found something familiar, she realized, a scent he recognized. But he discovered more than that. He'd come across a large bootprint with a blocky pattern on the bottom, made up of geometric shapes. She quickly scanned the area and saw a number of similar bootprints in the soft earth. They all looked freshly made.

That was the final clue she needed. It had all clicked into place in a matter of seconds. She thought she knew, finally, what must have happened, though she still didn't know the reasons behind it. But that would come soon enough.

And Random, with that sensitive nose of his, just might be her secret weapon.

After some calling and hand clapping, she'd finally managed to get the shaggy dog to respond. Again, before he climbed into the Jeep, she'd cleaned him up a little, but now, as she looked over at him, she noticed there were still traces of mud and dirt on his paws and muzzle. She reached over to brush off his fur, and he looked at her gratefully, his soulful eyes full of expression. She wondered what he might say if he could speak. She thought she knew. It was as if he understood what was at stake. And he was anxious to get on with it.

So was she.

At that moment, she couldn't imagine anyone else she'd rather have in the seat beside her.

Traffic was dodgy, especially once they crossed back over Route 1 and were headed south on the Coastal Loop with the rest of the weekend and tourist traffic. The road was busier than usual, approaching levels seen only during the summer months. It appeared, Candy thought with a small bit of satisfaction, that the village's attempt at an early spring festival was a success. There would be a good crowd in Town Park this evening for the bonfire and marshmallow roast. Good for the town, good for the local merchants, vendors, and shop owners, and good for the villagers themselves. But more difficult for her, since the crowds could complicate her search for Ginny. It would make it easier for the other woman to blend in with the rest of the tourists, if that was her goal.

What was she after? Candy wondered. What did she intend to do? Candy hoped, by putting out the word through her father, that multiple pairs of eyes were on the lookout right now, and that whatever Ginny intended, they could stop her in time.

Candy had never hesitated in handing her phone over to Judicious. He needed it to communicate with the authorities from the Pooley cabin, and by sending word ahead, she could easily meet up with her father and use his phone if she had to. Only when they were halfway to town did she realize she'd forgotten to check the text messages that had arrived when she'd been hiding in the garage. Fleetingly she wondered who they'd been from, and what they'd been about, but she'd have to find out later. There was no point in worrying about it now.

They were nearing town when a fire truck, lights blaring and sirens screaming, zoomed past in the opposite lane, headed northward up the cape — to the smoldering garage by the river, no doubt. It was followed in quick succession by two police cars, also with their light bars aglow and sirens blaring. Minutes later she passed the police station on her right. She wanted to slow, wanted to turn in, walk through the double glass doors, and tell whoever was behind the front desk that she needed to see Chief Durr right away.

But she didn't do any of that. He probably wasn't there anyway, she rationalized, not with the call that had just come in from Judicious, and not with all the activity in Town Park. More than likely he was at the park right now, and not at the station anyway. She was sure she'd find at least a few police officers in the village. She'd rather talk to them there, since she didn't want to get bogged down at the station, answering endless questions and getting nowhere.

So onward she drove, into town.

FORTY-NINE

As she expected, the line of cars heading
into the downtown area was backed up
north of Edgewood Road, which marked
the village's northern boundary. After that,
it was stop-and-go into the village center.

Her foot rode the brake pedal as she
peered ahead as best she could. She knew,
from previous events, that most of the cars
would get directed, either by signs or
volunteer traffic controllers, into the high
school's parking lot, which was one of a
number of designated parking areas around
the village. Parking was also available at the
elementary school, which was several blocks
away, and in various smaller lots around
town, between and behind the buildings.
Briefly she considered pulling into the high
school lot and walking the rest of the way,
but she decided to take her chances and see
if she could find something closer in.

She avoided the small parking area at the

community center on her left, as she thought it would probably be jammed, and a quick glance in that direction as she passed by confirmed her guess. It reminded her of the parking lot at the Lobster Shack on Fourth of July weekend — a chaos of cars.

She decided, instead, to try Main Street, and ran into a bit of luck when she spotted a car in front of her, halfway down the street, backing out of its spot just as she turned the corner. An old Mercedes challenged her for the spot but she would not be deterred. She'd driven in Boston. She had some skill at these sorts of maneuvers. She claimed the space for her own with a smile and a wave.

Random had been on his feet the moment they'd hit the edge of town, perhaps spurred by all the activity. He knew something was up. She had no intention of leaving him behind this time; she wanted him at her side. Her only concern was how to control him. She strongly wished for a leash, but she checked the back again and found none in the Jeep. Not even a length of rope she could use. Instead, after digging under the seats and in the cargo space in back, all she came up with was a couple of old scarves, which she'd tossed into the backseat at

413

some point during the winter. Might as well put them to good use, she decided.

She considered tying the ends of the scarves together to form one long scarf she could use as a leash, but knew that would pull apart too easily, considering how big and strong Random was, so she decided to use only one of the scarves. She chose the longest one and looped it halfway through the dog's collar, while he waited dutifully for her to fiddle with him. Then she took both ends of the scarf together in her fist, wrapping them around her palm several times. It was admittedly a short leash, but it would work for now. She had the dog exit on the driver's side with her, locked up the Jeep, and they were off.

The sun was falling toward the tops of the trees to the west, and the village's antique-style streetlights were just starting to come on. The storefronts were all lit up, decked out with festive displays and colorful decorations, warm and welcoming as the cool evening approached. The streets were filled with buzzing couples and families, seniors and teens, all enjoying the activities, few aware of the danger that lurked in their midst.

As she walked briskly down Main Street, Random practically glued up against her

414

side — more from his own preference than from the short makeshift leash — she kept her gaze in a continual roving pattern, on the lookout for any signs of a white Ford Explorer driven by Ginny Milbright. She saw a few vehicles that were similar in appearance, but none was the one she sought.

She passed by the Black Forest Bakery on her left, dark now with a CLOSED sign hanging in its window, and just past that she crossed the street and headed down Ocean Avenue toward Town Park, the Lightkeeper's Inn, and the oceanfront.

Down along the street, vendors were selling food and trinkets, balloons and T-shirts. She could hear music drifting up from Town Park. People were everywhere. She and Random wove in and out of the crowd in unison, as if they'd done this for decades, never slowing, always watchful. Half a dozen storefronts past the opera house, which stood about halfway down the block, they rounded a corner, and the park opened up in front of them.

It was lit up like Christmas Eve. Trees were strung with lights, colorful signs welcomed visitors, and the booths that had been set up throughout the park, all with individual lighting of their own, offered food and wares of all sorts. But naturally the scene was dominated by the big bonfire at its center, which was already lit, its flames reaching upward. The town's maintenance crew had been collecting branches, brush, and logs for weeks, and had set up a tepee-like structure six feet tall inside a ring of cinder blocks. A group of volunteers in matching yellow T-shirts manned the fire and kept an eye on it, to make certain it stayed contained and didn't get out of hand. The fire truck had been here as well, for safety reasons, but it had just been called north to tend to another fire.

Around the bonfire, at a safe distance, villagers and visitors had gathered to roast marshmallows and wieners on long sticks provided for just such a purpose by some of the vendors in the park. Not too far away, on a short stage under a ring of colored lights, a folk trio played. Everyone was chattering and munching on marshmallows and hot dogs, cotton candy and caramel apples. Others sipped Moxie, a popular local soft drink, or ate ice cream cones. And she saw more than a few people nibbling on Chocolate Maple Brownies from the Black Forest Bakery's booth, which she spotted off toward her left, on the north side of the park.

It was a festive scene.

With Random at her side, Candy headed down the walkway toward the bonfire, looking for her father. She'd taken barely a dozen steps when she heard someone behind her call her name. She slowed and turned toward the sound of the voice. It was Wanda Boyle, hurrying down the sidewalk after her.

"There you are," Wanda said breathlessly as she approached. "I just heard what happened. It's all over town. Sounds like you took some heat, but at least you didn't get fried." She smiled briefly at her own humor. "Really, it's a good thing you got out of there alive. Your father's been raising the hue and cry."

"You've talked to him?" Candy asked, looking around. "Have you seen him?"

Wanda pointed. "He's down near the bonfire, waiting for you, I think. So, did you get my texts?"

"Your texts?" It took Candy only a moment to make the connection. "So *you're* the one who texted me when I was in that garage? You almost got me *killed*!"

Wanda looked slightly affronted, uncertain how to take that reaction. "What are you talking about?"

Candy shook her head and waved a dismissive hand. "I'll explain later. And no, I haven't had a chance to read them. What did they say?"

"Well, it was that license plate you asked me about. RIP DIG, remember?"

"I remember." Candy was growing impatient. "But you already told me about that. It belongs to someone named Russ Pooley, right?"

"That's part of it, yes. Russ was the RIP. His middle name was Ike, by the way. Like the president. Not Eisenhower, just Ike. I guess he was born sometime in the fifties, and his parents liked the nickname. Anyway, it was the other set of initials that I texted you about — DIG."

Candy's impatience disappeared, and Wanda now had her full attention. "And what did you find out?"

Wanda pulled herself up a little as she spoke, taking advance credit for the information she'd uncovered. "Well, it appears they were best friends. Russ Pooley and this DIG guy. His last name is Gulliver. Doug Gulliver, who apparently also had a middle name that started with an *I*."

"Gulliver?" Candy's brow furrowed for a moment as she puzzled it out. After a few moments, her eyes brightened. "Irving," she said. "His middle name is Irving."

Wanda gave her an odd look. "Now how

the heck would you know something like that?"

"Because," Candy said, "I saw it on a boathouse. Gully's Boathouse, to be exact. Irving Gulliver must have been Doug's father. And it all fits. It makes perfect sense. The families were friends. Their boathouse and cabin were close to each other, just a few buildings apart. She probably would have known the boathouse was deserted. That's why she and Mick dumped him there, rather than at the Pooley cabin. She must have hoped it would be some sort of diversion, a misdirection. To throw the police off the scent. But they must have had an argument about something. . . ."

Her voice trailed off, and she realized the other woman was watching her strangely, shaking her head.

"I have no idea what you're talking about," Wanda said, "but if it makes sense to you, that's all that matters."

Candy refocused. "So what about those two — Russ and Doug? Are either of them still around?"

Wanda shook her head. "Both are gone. They were good friends, from what I've heard. Shared just about everything. Doug passed away a decade or so ago. He was killed in a freak boating accident. And Russ died just a few years back."

"And his family would have inherited the cabin — and the purple van that went with it."

Wanda nodded vaguely. "Sure, I suppose so, if that's relevant to the current situation."

"It just might be," Candy said, and she reached out and patted Wanda on the shoulder. "Good job. Thanks for your help," she said, and turned to go, but Wanda called after her again.

"So how did everything go with Ginny? At the Milbrights' place?" She raised her voice just a notch as Candy kept moving. "I'm still getting a story out of this for the paper, right?"

Candy nodded and waved. "Oh, you're definitely getting a story," she called into the air as she and Random continued down the walkway toward the bonfire. "It just needs an ending."

FIFTY

She and her father spotted each other at about the same time. Henry Holliday was on the far side of the bonfire, standing with a small group of people, his head down, listening intently to whatever they all were discussing. He wore a soft, tan, wide-brimmed hat that had seen better days, a faded green cotton jacket, and chinos that needed a good washing. He looked up at a break in the conversation, spotted Candy on the sidewalk, and waved in her direction. "Candy!" he called to her, and he motioned for her to join them. "Over here! We have some news!"

He was standing with three other people, she noticed as she drew closer to the group. Artie Groves was there, although Doc's other two buddies, Finn Woodbury and Bumpy Brigham, were absent. Mason Flint was in the circle, looking impatient as his gaze seemed to be everywhere at once, keeping a close eye on all the activities taking place in the park. Tillie Shaw, chair of the town's events committee, completed the group. She looked drained, like she'd been up for two days straight without respite. She held a clipboard in one hand and a walkie-talkie in the other. Her hair was windblown and her cheeks were flushed, but there was also a focus in her gaze that told Candy she was on top of things.

As Candy joined the group, Tillie told her, "We've been in contact with the police. They've got an APB out. State troopers are combing Route 1 and points east and west, and, of course, the CWPD is patrolling this area. If Ginny's around here, they'll find her."

"We've been in touch with Hutch," Doc added, and when his daughter gave him a questioning look, he continued. "The police have released him for the moment. He's back at the farm. Been there an hour or so. I just got off the phone with him. He says he hasn't seen Ginny anywhere. She's not at their place."

"And I've talked to Bumpy," Artie added. "He's still at the community center, wrapping up everything there. I've been trying to get hold of Finn too. Far as I know, he's still over at the Crawford place, shutting down the sugaring operation and keeping an eye on everything. He'll let us know if anyone unexpected shows up there."

That had been one of Candy's concerns on the drive down — that she'd been wrong about Ginny's destination. Ginny could have gone anywhere — back to Sugar Hill Farm, or to Crawford's Berry Farm, or even to Blueberry Acres. She could be on her way down to Portland now, or Boston, or halfway to New Hampshire. She could even be trying to cross the border into Canada. She could be anywhere.

But Candy didn't believe she'd gone to any of those places. Ginny was here somewhere, she thought, still in Cape Willington, probably here in the village. She had no evidence to prove that; she was simply following her instincts at this point. And for some reason, she thought Ginny wasn't finished with this town yet.

"What about her Explorer? Has anyone seen it?"

"They're still looking," her father said. "No sign so far."

But even as he spoke, Tillie's walkie-talkie started to squawk, and she turned away briefly as she held it up so she could listen to the incoming message. Moments later she turned back to the group.

"They've found it," she told them.

"The Explorer?" Candy asked.

Tillie nodded. "At least, it matches the description. They think it's the right one. They found it parked up along the river, just south of the bridge to Fowler's Corner. No one's in it. They say it looks like it's been abandoned. The police are checking it out now."

Candy turned, her eyes scanning the crowd. "Then she's here somewhere," she said ominously.

As she looked around, she noticed how crowded the place had become. Town Park was jammed with activity. The bonfire was roaring nicely. People were milling around casually, roasting marshmallows, listening to music, chatting and enjoying themselves.

How would they ever find Ginny Milbright in a crowd this big? She could blend in easily, making herself almost impossible to spot.

But Candy had a secret weapon.

She looked down at Random, who had been straining and snuffling at the air as she held him. She bent down and gave him a brisk scratch behind his collar. "So, buddy, you ready to go to work?"

FIFTY-ONE

They wouldn't let her go off on her own — and, honestly, after what had happened at the Pooley cabin, she was glad for the company. The more eyes, she thought, the better.

Besides, Tillie had access to a golf cart, which someone had loaned the town for the weekend's events. After a quick discussion, they decided it would be easier to ride than to walk, and the cart would get them to where they needed to be quicker. Mason decided to stay behind, to keep an eye on the activities in the park, so Tillie drove, with Candy and Random up front on the narrow bench seat beside her. Doc and Artie climbed on the backward-facing second-row seat.

With everyone on board, they started off.

"I think Random has Ginny's scent," Candy said, talking over her shoulder to her father and Artie as Tillie steered the cart up a wide walkway, out of the park, and to the busy sidewalk that ran along the Coastal Loop. They were headed up along the river, past the docks, warehouses, and community center, toward the bridge across the English River, just a little farther upstream.

"He must have picked it up somewhere — my guess is back in the woods. I found bootprints in the woods, around two sets of illegally tapped trees, one at the Milbrights' place and the other on Neil's property. My guess is someone's been trying to force a feud between the two of them, for whatever reason. I'm certain that one set of those prints belonged to Ginny. Random picked up her scent again at the Pooley cabin, and I spotted a bootprint that matched the ones I saw out in the woods."

"And you think he can pick up her scent now," her father asked, "and lead us to Ginny?"

"That's the plan," Candy said, and as they drove through the well-lit town, she told them all she had discovered over the past two days, including details about the missing knife, and what she believed were misleading accusations by Ginny. "It must have all been for a reason," she said as they angled down an asphalt driveway past the community center and weaved through a series of old riverside buildings toward the waterfront.

"And what do you think that reason is?" Artie called to her, as the wind took some of his words away.

Candy could only shake her head as they drove on.

They soon reached the undeveloped land at the north end of the dock and warehouse complex. From here, it was just open land up along the river to the bridge. As the cart pulled to a stop, Random was eager to get out and start working. Candy did her best to control him, but he would have none of it. She finally stopped fighting him and let the scarf slip away from his collar. Suddenly freed, he dashed off with a series of quick barks and rapidly disappeared into the lengthening shadows along the river. It was dusk. Though there was still some light, a grayness was falling over the landscape.

"Anyone bring a flashlight?" Doc asked as he stepped down off the golf cart, looking up at the sky.

"Mine's at home," Artie admitted.

"I got one in the Jeep," Candy said, finding herself ill equipped for the first time in a while.

"I've got one!" Tillie said, and she pulled

a small LED flashlight out of her back pocket.

Candy pointed the way. "Then you lead," she said.

"How far are we going?" Artie asked, looking hesitantly over at the black river.

Candy pointed to the bridge. "Not far."

They started off, but it turned out she was right in her last statement. They'd walked only a short distance before they saw flashes of light around a vehicle up ahead, and Random was already headed back in their direction. "Flashlights up ahead. The police are checking out the Explorer," Tillie said as she listened to some squawking on her walkie-talkie.

"And here comes Random," said Artie, turning and pointing.

The dog passed them by, about twenty feet away, going the opposite direction. He was headed back toward the riverside warehouses, his nose still to the ground. But he looked over at them briefly as he passed by, his eyes glowing in the beam of Tillie's flashlight. She called out to him, but Candy put a hand on the other woman's shoulder, quieting her.

"Let him go," she said. "Let's see where he leads us."

Traveling as a pack, the four of them

shadowed Random as he weaved his way back toward the dock and warehouse complex. They moved quietly, not wanting to disturb him at his work. He seemed to have found a scent, but after a few minutes, he looked distracted, and Candy wasn't sure he was on the right one. His movements became erratic. A number of times he stopped, shifted direction, and started again. She got the feeling, as she watched him, that he was searching, rather than on the actual trail of Ginny's scent.

They followed him between a number of buildings, past the community center, and up to the sidewalk along the main road. There, he became overwhelmed by all the scents he was encountering, and soon started wandering idly in a circle.

"If she came this way," Candy said, "she must have crossed the street and gone over toward the bonfire. But she could be anywhere. Maybe we should fan out and look for her."

So they did. Her father started off toward the bonfire and the central part of the park, Artie headed toward the upper part of the park, around the food booths, and Tillie dashed back for the golf cart, telling them she'd check the warehouse area.

Candy reattached the scarf to Random's

collar, so she wouldn't lose him in the crowd, and together they started off down the sidewalk along the Coastal Loop toward the lighthouse and museum. They passed by the back end of the community center, still all lit up inside, though the pancake operation had closed down a while ago. But she could still smell the lingering scents of pancakes and syrup, as well as the smells of roasting marshmallows and wieners, carried on the wind. It appeared Random had caught the scents as well, for he had his nose up in the air now, not on the ground.

They were halfway down the street when Tillie flagged them down. She came up behind them in the golf cart, the walkie-talkie in her hand. "I just heard from the police," she said. "It's not the right vehicle."

Candy stopped in her tracks, surprised. "It's not?"

Tillie shook her head. "Not the right license plate."

"Are you sure?" That couldn't be right, she thought. It *had* to be Ginny's vehicle.

But it appeared it wasn't. "It belongs to someone from down around Portland. Cape Elizabeth, I think they said. Another cape, way to the south. Anyway, I thought you should know." She pointed over toward the docks. "I'll check down this way." And she was off again, deftly spinning the golf cart around and pointing it down the slope.

Candy stood in the center of the sidewalk with Random waiting patiently at her side, allowing the crowds to flow around them as she tried to figure out the meaning of what she'd just learned.

It wasn't Ginny's vehicle. They still didn't know if she was here. This could all be a waste of time, a wild-goose chase. They could be looking for her in completely the wrong place.

She felt a growing sense of dread in her chest, as she sensed the whole thing slipping away from her.

That's when she spotted Finn Woodbury.

He was coming up the sidewalk toward her, hands in his pockets, attention focused across the street, at the bonfire and the activities in the park.

At first she wasn't certain it was Finn. Hadn't Artie just said he was still out at the Crawford farm, shutting down the maple sugaring operation and keeping an eye on the place?

What was he doing *here*? And if he was here, then who was keeping an eye on the farm?

Confused, she started forward and called to him. At the sound of her voice, he turned his head, spotted her, and waved, with a big smile on his face.

"Hey, how's it going?" he said as she approached, and looking down, he added, "Hey, Random, how are you, buddy?" He looked back up at Candy. "So how's Neil doing? You see him at the hospital?"

"Yes, I did. He's doing fine, but . . . Finn, what are you doing here? I thought you were out at the Crawford farm. Didn't Artie call you?"

"He might have," Finn said, and he reached into his pocket and pulled out his phone. "Battery ran out this afternoon. Haven't had a chance to recharge it yet."

"But we thought you were going to stay out at the farm and keep an eye on the place."

"I was going to," he said, and his smile wavered as he heard the edge of concern in her tone, "but somebody relieved me. Is everything okay?"

"You haven't heard?"

"Heard what?"

"About Ginny?"

"Ginny Milbright? Oh, sure, I heard. She's over there now, keeping an eye on the place. Tell you the truth, Hawthorne and I appreciated the break. We've both been out there all day, you know, in that hot sugar shack. That Boyle kid was there for a while but had to leave early, so we lost his help, but we got the whole thing shut down okay, and the crowds cleared out. There were still a few stragglers hanging around the place, but Ginny stopped by and said she'd keep an eye on everything if we wanted to take a break and check out the festivities in town." His smile returned. "Even said she might fire up the boiling operation and run one more batch through. Just to help us out, you know."

Candy gave him a look of disbelief. "You mean she's not *here*?"

"Where?"

"Here!" Candy squeaked, losing control of her voice. "At Town Park?"

Finn looked around and shrugged. "No, like I just said, she's over at the Crawford farm, firing up the place. That's what she said. She was going to fire up the place."

"Oh my God," Candy said.

And when Finn turned back toward her, his smile was suddenly gone.

FIFTY-TWO

She looked around desperately. "Where are you parked?"

Confused by this sudden change in the conversation, Finn pointed behind him, toward the lighthouse. "Over by the museum. I . . . Why, what's going on? Is everything all right?"

She looked back over her shoulder, at the early-evening sky toward the southwest, and thought she detected a faint glow there. She hoped it was just her imagination — and that she wasn't too late.

"Find my father," she said, turning back to Finn, talking with urgency now. "Or Tillie Shaw. Tell them what you just told me. Tell them to send the police and a fire truck over to Crawford's Berry Farm, right away."

Finn looked shocked. "You don't mean —"

"I hope I'm wrong," Candy said. "Find

434

them, and tell them. There's no time to lose."

"And what about you? Where are you going?"

She didn't answer him. She and Random were already moving.

As they started back up the street, Candy suddenly regretted the fact that she'd left her phone with Judicious, though it had seemed like a good idea at the time. And she regretted even more the fact that Finn's phone had died. She was out of touch now, at the most critical moment, with no way to contact anyone. She considered stopping one of the pedestrians she passed and asking if she could borrow their phone, but ultimately decided she had no time even for that. They had to move. They had to get out to Neil's place as fast as possible.

So they quickened their pace, half running the rest of the way up the sidewalk, to the intersection with Main Street. There they jogged to their left, crossed the street, and headed down the town's main thoroughfare, past Duffy's Main Street Diner and Zeke's General Store and the Black Forest Bakery, until they reached the Jeep parked down near the Pine Cone Bookstore. She already had her keys out of her pocket and unlocked the passenger-side door first, letting Random leap up inside before she closed the door, ran around the front end, and jumped into the driver's seat.

Minutes later, they were once again barreling along the road, this time on the southern leg of the Coastal Loop, which ran past a residential area and the elementary school before it took them out of town.

This road wasn't as busy as the Loop's northern leg, since it ran in a more westerly direction, out along the cape's southern and western coastlines, past loosely spaced homes and garages, and woods, fields, and agricultural land beyond that. They quickly passed the turnoff to Blueberry Acres on their right, but she kept driving straight ahead. Crawford's Berry Farm was another mile or so farther on, along a northwesterly curve of the coastline.

Minutes later, they were pulling into the dirt lane at the berry farm. After all the traffic it had received during the day, the lane was a bit of a mess, as Candy expected. Ruts were deep and the mud was treacherous in places. It would need work in the morning, another layer of soil and gravel to make it passable. They'd have to call the town's maintenance crew and ask for some assistance. But there wasn't time to worry about that now. Her only thought was that she had to save Neil's farm, so she gunned the engine and plowed on through.

But as they came around a bend and she could see beyond the trees, her heart sank, for she knew they were already too late.

The darkening sky was all lit up. It looked like the place was ablaze.

In the beams of the Jeep's headlights, she saw the old white Ford Explorer now. It was pulled up beside Neil's barn, parked askew, its nose toward the barn and its tail out in the driveway. Ginny had made no attempt to hide it. Maybe she knew the end was near, and she just wanted to take something with her before she was hauled off to jail.

Apparently that "something" was Neil's farm.

As they drew closer and Candy finally could make out what was happening up ahead, she had a brief sense of relief. The fire, she realized, hadn't taken Neil's house, or the barn. It seemed to be concentrated farther back on his property, back in the darkness of the fields and woods.

"The sugar shack," she breathed, saying the words out loud.

Ginny had set fire to Neil's maple sugar shack — the one he had helped build when he was a teenager living here with his family.

Her eyes never left the blaze in front of her as she pulled the Jeep to an abrupt stop near the white Explorer and shut off the engine. Even before she had a chance to pull the keys out of the ignition and unbelt herself, Random was in her lap, pushing at the driver's side door with his head, looking for a way out. She had no choice but to open the door for him. The moment she pulled the handle, he shoved the door open farther and leaped out, making a quick escape.

"Random!" she called after him, but he was already gone, racing up through the strawberry fields toward the burning sugar shack. He was quickly lost in the darkness, beyond the reach of the headlights and spotlights. She could hear him barking frantically as he went.

She always kept two flashlights in the Jeep, a larger one in the glove box and a smaller one in the center console bin. She took both with her. She had no weapon, though, not even a golf club or a baseball bat. The best she could manage was a long-handled plastic ice scraper she found behind the front seats. But it was better than nothing, so she took that in one hand, the larger flashlight in the other, and tucked the small flashlight into a back pocket.

As she stepped out of the vehicle, she saw several people standing around, watching the fire. Looking right, she noticed there were a few cars still sitting in the designated parking area. Visitors, she thought. Stragglers who hadn't left the farm yet, still milling around, enjoying the bucolic setting.

Time to get them out of here.

"The farm is closed down for the night," she told the first couple she came to. "Pass the word, would you please? It's not safe. We need to get everyone out of here and back to town."

While the visitors began to head to their cars, some reluctantly, Candy flicked on the flashlight and started off between the house and barn at a half jog, up through the strawberry fields toward the burning sugar shack.

As she drew closer she saw that, like the garage earlier, it was nearly consumed in flames. They crackled and popped as they reached into the sky, wriggling like whips, throwing fiery sparks and dark smoke into the night air. The roof was engulfed, the sides of the building near collapse. The flames had spread to several trees close to the shack, and had ignited a nearby pile of firewood as well. Fortunately, Neil's tractor wasn't parked in its usual spot next to the shack — it was still out in the woods, where it had been abandoned a couple of days earlier. But most of the sap collection buckets, which had been piled up along one wall, were gone, as were all the other tools and equipment Neil had gathered over the years for the boiling operation.

Candy stood in the middle of the fields in shock, watching the place burn down. She only hoped no one had been inside.

For a few moments, she didn't know what to do. There was no way to save it. She had no hose out here, no water. No way to douse the flames. Besides, the heat was too intense. She couldn't get close to the building if she wanted to. Her only hope now was that the fire didn't spread to the other buildings.

She heard barks then, quick and urgent. She twisted around, trying to locate the source.

They were coming from the barn, she realized.

Leaving the sugar shack to burn out on its own, she took off at a brisk pace, back the way she'd come, careful of her footing as she headed down through the dark strawberry fields. She held the flashlight in front of her, aimed down, as she walked between the rows, feeling the soft, boggy earth under her feet. Ahead, the barn was lit up by spotlights at its four corners, but there was only limited lighting inside, she knew, just a few lightbulbs hanging from an open wire strung through the beams. Most of the visitors had left. The parking area was almost empty. She saw no one around the barn.

She wasn't sure who or what she'd find inside, so she slowed as she approached. She'd have to be careful, she knew, so she hoisted the plastic ice scraper in a menacing fashion as she angled cautiously to the right side, coming around the corner of the building and entering through the open double doors.

The place was dimly lit, but she'd been in here many times before and knew her way around. Random was barking frantically in the opposite back corner. It sounded as if he had someone cornered there.

She heard a voice then, spoken by a shadow wedged back into the corner, apparently talking to the dog in soothing tones, trying to get him to quiet down. Candy turned her flashlight in that direction, and shined it directly into the face of Ginny Milbright.

FIFTY-THREE

She was dressed all in black, including a black sweatshirt, zipped up tight, with the hood pulled low over her head. But now, caught in the beam of the flashlight, she reached up and brushed the hood back from her head.

Her hair was a mess, stringy and unwashed. Her face was pale and drawn, streaked with sweat despite the coolness of the evening. She held in one black-gloved hand a long tree limb that she'd obviously used as a firebrand. Though it was now extinguished, its tip, singed black, still glowed. She held it out in front of her, ready to use it as a weapon against Random if she had to.

The dog, however, was not attacking her, but rather it appeared he simply was trying to keep her contained, as if she were a goat or sheep. He stood back from her a short distance, his four paws planted widely apart,

442

ready to spring forward if necessary. He held his head and nose still, his eyes zeroed in on her. He was like a hunting dog that had tracked down its prey, and was waiting expectantly to see what it did.

Candy took a few steps closer, and Ginny brandished the firebrand. For a fleeting moment, Candy saw humor in the fact that both of them were similarly equipped, with essentially worthless weapons. At least it would be a fair duel, if it came to that.

"Ginny, what are you doing here?" she asked, keeping her voice low and even, so as not to provoke the other woman.

It didn't work. Ginny responded with a barely controlled sneer. "Call off your dog and we'll talk."

Candy looked from Ginny to Random and back again. "He remembers, doesn't he?" she said after a moment. "What happened to him and Neil?"

"I don't know what you're talking about."

"I think," Candy continued, pointing out into the darkness, "he remembers what happened back in those woods a couple of days ago — how he found you back there stealing sap from Neil's trees, and how you ambushed Neil, and then kidnapped the both of them. He remembers how you locked him in the shed at Gully's Boathouse. And he remembers your scent. He smelled it in those woods today, and he picked it up again over at the Pooley place, just a little while ago."

For the moment, Ginny decided to play dumb. "I don't know where you came up with that story," she said in a defensive tone, "but you're wrong. I was never at any of those places."

"But you were," Candy said. "I can prove it."

"How?"

"Let me take a look at your boots."

Ginny stiffened. "My boots? What about them?"

"You've changed them, haven't you? Since this afternoon, when I was at your place?"

Instinctively, Ginny looked down. "How did you? . . ." But then it dawned on her. "The footprints."

"That's right, the footprints." Candy shined the flashlight down toward Ginny's feet. "You wear big boots," she said, "like those you have on now, with blocky geometric patterns on the bottoms, I'm guessing. I've seen those patterns in a few places recently — in your woods over at Sugar Hill Farm, for instance, and out in Neil's woods. You get around, don't you? At first, I assumed they were Hutch's prints, the bigger

444

ones. But they weren't, were they? They were yours."

Ginny grunted. "Hutch has small feet," she admitted. "It's a sore spot with him."

"And I saw those same prints at the Pooley cabin, where you locked me in the garage. That's when I put it all together. That's your family's place, isn't it?" Candy said, reasoning it out. "You inherited it when your father, Russ, passed away. I'm surprised you were so willing to destroy it like that."

Ginny glared at her. She worked her mouth oddly and squinted her eyes, and started to say something, but then huffed, as if she'd changed her mind. "How did you get out of that garage anyway? I thought I had it all sealed up with you inside."

"I managed to escape, with Random's help. You should be glad I did. Otherwise, you'd be responsible for two murders."

Ginny shrugged stiffly. "It makes no difference at this point. The damage is done."

"And you couldn't help returning to the scene of the crime, could you?" Candy pointed out. "So what made you show up when you did? How did you know I was there?"

"I didn't," Ginny admitted, "but I've been keeping an eye on the place. I figured someone might come snooping around sooner or later. I knew the evidence was parked in that garage, and I was still trying to figure out how and where to move those vehicles. When I spotted your Jeep parked out on the road, I knew you were there. It wasn't hard to figure out you were hiding in the garage. I knew what you'd found. Then I heard your phone beep, so I made my move."

Both women were silent for a moment. Ginny shifted, as if she was thinking of making a dash for it, but Random growled and shifted also, and Ginny pressed farther back into the corner.

"Call him off," she said.

"Not yet." Candy knew she didn't have much time, and her mind was working as she tried to put the pieces together. "So how was Mick involved in this?" she asked after a few moments. "Were the two of you working together?"

Ginny rolled her eyes. "Isn't it obvious? I thought you were some sort of great detective."

Candy agreed with the other woman, at least on one of those points. "I guess it is obvious. You two were the ones who tapped Neil's trees, weren't you? You and Mick, working together. Neil spotted the two of you while you were back in his woods and recognized Mick. But before he could do anything about it, you came up behind him and knocked him out, probably with a branch like the one you're holding right now."

"It was a little thicker," Ginny admitted, "with a little more punch. I thought I might have hit him too hard at first. Killed him." She paused, and her tone hardened. "That was my first mistake, I guess. Maybe I just should have ended it right there, and left his body in the woods for someone else to find."

"But you didn't, did you? You loaded Neil and Random into Mick's red truck. What was your plan at that point? What were you going to do with him?"

Apparently resigned to the fact that she'd been found out, Ginny shook her head and hesitated, as if she was struggling to remember all that had happened that day. "We didn't know. It got . . . crazy," she said finally, her voice falling almost to a whisper. "We heard his tractor coming through the trees and thought we could get away in time, but that damned dog came after us." She raised the firebrand and pointed it at Random, who tensed. "He knew me, of course. We were neighbors. We'd run into each other before. But when he found us, I couldn't calm him down. I tried to shoo him away, but he wouldn't go. And then Neil spotted Mick, and I had to do something."

She paused again, and licked her lips before she continued. "When Neil went down, I tried to restrain the dog, but he got wild on me. Mick got a little wild too. He was worried about Neil, wanted to take him to the hospital. But I convinced him to throw Neil in the back of the truck and toss a tarp over him. I told him we should drive to the boathouse, until we figured out what to do. I knew no one would be there. That place has been vacant for years, practically abandoned, ever since Doug Gulliver passed away. Doug and my dad were best friends, you know. They even co-owned that purple van, which was our river van — both families, all of us jammed in there whenever we went canoeing or hiking or exploring."

"The van's license plate," Candy interjected. "RIP DIG. Russ Pooley. Doug Gulliver. Both with middle names that began with *I*. That's where it came from."

Ginny nodded her head slightly in acknowledgement and went on. "We always had a lot of fun with dad's initials — R. I. P. Doug Gulliver especially. He made a lot of jokes about it over the years, and insisted they use both sets of initials for that license plate. We grew up together, the Gullivers and the Pooleys, since our cabins were close together on the river, so I knew all about Gully's Boathouse. I figured it would be a good place to hide out for a while. Mick finally agreed. But he couldn't restrain Random and drive the truck at the same time, so I had to ride in the cab along with him, to keep the dog under control."

"And that's when Hutch spotted you on that back road on Thursday afternoon," Candy said, "and an older couple saw you as well, a little while later, going north on the Coastal Loop in Mick's truck. I talked to them at the community center yesterday. They said you were driving crazy, all over the road."

"They did, huh?" An enigmatic smile crossed Ginny's face. "That's the way it always goes, isn't it? Something always happens that you don't expect. Someone's always where they shouldn't be, or sees something they weren't supposed to see. You can count on it."

"Why draw so much attention to yourself like that? What happened on the way up there?"

Ginny gave her a resigned look. "What you'd expect. Random was going crazy.

Mick was going a little crazy too. We argued the whole way, and he wasn't paying much attention to where he was going. Like I said, he wanted to take Neil right to the hospital. But I told him that if we did that, we'd expose ourselves. Everyone would know what we'd done, and we'd probably wind up in jail."

"It would have been better than murder," Candy said softly.

"Maybe," Ginny allowed, "but that wasn't my intention. Just so you know. Everything happened so fast. It just got out of hand. I don't know how else to explain it. I wasn't even sure what I was doing. There wasn't time to make sense of it. I just did it. I was trying to protect the both of us."

"Then why did you attack him like that?" Candy asked. "What happened between the two of you? Why stab him, wrap him up in the net, and roll him into the river? And why put the knife in the canoe next to Neil?"

Ginny laughed at this list of accusations. "Did I really do all that?" she asked, shaking her head, as if in disbelief. "You never really know what you're capable of doing until you're backed into a corner, do you? I guess I found out. I will say this: My second mistake was tying up Mick's hands and feet. At the time, it seemed like the right thing, to make sure he was restrained, since he was still alive at the time. But I guess it wasn't necessary. If I had just wrapped him in the net and set him adrift in the river, his death might have been passed off as accidental. Of course, the knife wound would have been hard to explain, but they might have missed it, at least until the autopsy. But the tied-up hands and feet were a dead giveaway. I realized it too late."

She shrugged. "My bad," she said, and she smiled again, though it was a different kind of smile, sad and regretful. "Mick used to say that, you know? *'My bad.'* " She sighed, her gaze unfocused. "He was a good man."

"So why did you do it?" Candy pressed.

Ginny's mood changed almost instantly. "Because he was going to ruin everything!" she said in an exasperated tone. "He was worried about Neil. He was going to take him to the hospital. I couldn't let him do that, and I couldn't talk him out of it. I knew Neil had seen Mick and could identify him, and then Mick could identify me. We were illegally tapping trees. So we fought about what to do, and —"

"You stabbed Mick in the back and rolled him into the river."

Ginny looked nearly hysterical now. "I

451

didn't know what else to do! I couldn't go to jail."

"So you took another way out," Candy said. She paused, but when Ginny didn't respond, she continued. "I can guess at the rest. I figure Mick went into the water sometime right around sunset on Thursday night, around seven P.M. After Mick was gone, you tried your best to cover your tracks, and checked in the boathouse to make sure Neil was still unconscious. I imagine you considered taking him out too. It would have been easy at that point. But he saw only Mick in the woods, right? Not you. He couldn't identify you, so there was no real need to kill him — especially when you had another option."

Again, Candy paused, and again Ginny said nothing. But the other woman gave a subtle nod of her head, so Candy went on.

"You realized that if you left the knife in the canoe next to Neil, it would incriminate Hutch in the murder."

Ginny finally spoke up. "No, not him," she corrected. "Neil."

"Neil," Candy said with a nod of her head. She considered that for a moment. "It all would have worked out perfectly, wouldn't it? You'd already accused Neil of stealing the knife from Hutch's collection, so you could make a case that he had it in his possession. But why tell me about it this afternoon? Why not tell the police instead?"

"Oh, we did," Ginny revealed. "Or, rather, Hutch did, when they interrogated him. I told him to make sure he mentioned the stolen knife to the police. But I wanted you to know it too. That's why I asked you over to the place and showed you his collection."

"To throw me off the scent?"

"Something like that."

"So what about the knife?" Candy asked. "Neil didn't steal it from Hutch, did he?"

"No," Ginny acknowledged. "You're right about that. I got mad at Hutch one day, because of . . . something. I don't even remember what it was now. He can be a frustrating man."

"So you retaliated by stealing one of his knives?"

"Like I said, he loved those knives more than me. It was the only way I could get his attention."

"His attention? To tell him what?"

"About Neil! About what he was doing to our place."

"And what was Neil doing to your place?"

"I told you all this yesterday morning," Ginny said, her tone turning accusatory, "when you were out at the farm, but I guess you weren't listening."

"I'm listening now."

And Ginny complied. "We've had a rough time lately," she said. "Hutch spends more time with his knives than he does working on the farm. We can't make ends meet anymore — not since Neil moved into town."

"Is that why you did it? Money?"

"That's part of it," Ginny admitted. "That, and a lot of anger, and frustration, and even revenge."

"And Mick offered to help you teach Neil a lesson?"

"Mick." Ginny mouthed the name almost regretfully, and Candy could see the pain in the other woman's eyes. "We'd been friends since high school," she said. "We always got along well, even after we married other people. I guess we both had sort of a rebellious streak, which is why we stayed close. We understood each other. One day a month or so ago, I ran into him at the garden center, and we got to talking. I told him I was at the end of my rope," Ginny confessed. "I said I had to do something. I had to get Hutch's attention and force him to recognize what was going on."

"Why didn't you just talk to Neil about it?" Candy asked.

"We tried," Ginny said, her exasperation returning. "We wanted to come to some sort of agreement with him about supply and pricing. But he'd have none of it. He said he was too independent."

"Sounds like Neil," Candy admitted. "He does tend to keep to himself."

"And *you* didn't help," Ginny continued, "lending him a hand over there, helping him sell his maple syrup, taking away half of our profits."

Candy could see the other woman's point, and it saddened her. If only she'd known, all this could have been avoided. Instead, the actions of a desperate person had resulted in tragedy.

"So you talked to Mick, and told him your problem, and then what? You started tapping trees?"

"It was Mick's idea, really. He planned a lot of it out," Ginny explained. "We figured we'd get them mad at each other. Hutch and Neil. Start some sort of feud. Make something happen, try to force them to see what was going on. It probably sounds crazy now, but it seemed like a good idea at the time. Part of our rebellious nature, I guess. We began by tapping that sugar bush out toward the end of our property. Hutch loves those trees. We figured it would get him really riled up. And then we headed over to Neil's place."

"Where everything fell apart."

Again, Ginny said nothing, but nodded.

Candy shifted her stance. It was time to end this. There were only a few more threads she needed to unravel before she called the police. "The purple van," she said. "You left it behind when you rode with Mick to the boathouse. So you had to go back and pick it up. I assume it was purely coincidence that you encountered me on that back road when you did?"

Ginny shrugged. "I thought I picked a perfect time to do that. But like I said, something always goes wrong. Someone's always in the wrong place. And there you were, snooping around. I should have known. I thought it was all over then, that you'd spotted me, and could identify me, so of course I had to try to take you out."

"You almost succeeded," Candy said. "That's twice you tried to kill me."

"You're a definite nuisance, that's for sure."

"So why bring me into this whole thing in the first place? Why call me out to your farm yesterday morning? I would think I'd be the last person you'd want to talk to."

Ginny shook her head, and the grim

chuckle returned. "Believe me, that wasn't my idea. It was Hutch's. He was furious when he found those tapped trees, as I thought he might be. I had hoped he'd march right over here to Neil's place and start a ruckus, but instead he wanted to go to the police. Of course, I couldn't let that happen, not right then. Not after what had happened at the boathouse the night before. I tried to talk him out of it, so when he suggested we talk to you instead, I had no choice but to go along."

"And you used the opportunity in the best way possible, to throw me off the track, send me off in a different direction."

"It almost worked."

"Almost," Candy agreed. "And what about the knife? You said you stole it from Hutch yourself. So why didn't you return it to the case, after you made your point? And how did it get to the boathouse that night?"

"The knife," Ginny said, almost whimsically. "Stealing that was more convenient than I realized at the time. It gave me a way to keep the pressure on Neil — and Hutch bought the whole theft thing, hook, line, and sinker. He can be pretty gullible at times. I didn't want to leave it around the house or barn, so I took it to the cabin and hid it there. And then Mick happened to

457

see it one day."

"When you rendezvoused there with him," Candy said. "One afternoon around five P.M., is my guess."

Ginny looked at her quizzically. "And how would you know that?"

"He left a message to himself," Candy said, "written on a map in his workshop. And then I found this, in that garage you burned down." From her back pocket, she pulled out the old photo of the high school graduating class she'd taken from the garage's back wall before her escape. She unfolded it and held it up for the other woman to see. "You were known as VIP in high school."

Ginny looked grim. "Mick still called me that," she said, "even after I was married."

"It sounds like he cared a lot about you."

Ginny shrugged, as if it was all water under the bridge. "I suppose, but he could still be infuriating at times. He took an immediate liking to that knife when he saw it. I told him to keep his hands off it, but he wouldn't listen to me. I should have just tossed it into the river," she said, "and none of this would have happened. But I didn't. I held on to it. Stupid mistake."

"So how did it get into Mick's back?" Candy asked, her tone softening just a bit.

Ginny sighed and shook her head. "It was . . . just there, at the wrong time," she said, and she turned angry again, as if she was still mad at Mick. "We met at the cabin again before we tapped the trees, to co-ordinate our efforts. He insisted on taking two vehicles — said we might need one as a backup, depending on how much sap we got. That's why we took that old van. And then, right before we left the cabin, he must have spotted the knife, and took it with him that day. I didn't notice he had it tucked into his belt until we got out in the woods. I was furious with him about it, so I took it away from him, and slipped it into my coat pocket."

"So you had it with you when you got to the boathouse," Candy said.

"Like I said, it was right there, in my pocket. It slipped right into my hand. What could I do? It's too bad, though. I'm sorry he's gone," she admitted. "I'm sorry for what happened. We had a lot of fun together, back when we were young. And I'll give him this much — he knew what he was doing. He knew how to milk those trees in record time. And he knew those back roads pretty well too."

She was about to say more when they heard a siren nearby. Candy took a few steps back and turned her head. She saw red lights reflected off the trees outside the barn. A few moments later, a fire truck pulled into the driveway and screeched to a halt as a trio of volunteer firemen leaped off and headed up through the strawberry fields toward the burning sugar shack, to assess the damage.

Candy was about to call out to them when she heard Random barking furiously. She turned just in time to see Ginny headed out the far side of the barn. She'd used the distraction to make her escape, and wildly swung the branch she carried to keep Random at bay. Candy tucked the photo back into a pocket and started after her, but quickly realized Ginny was circling around the back of the barn on the outside, trying to get to her white Explorer. So Candy reversed direction and headed out the front of the barn. But she was a few steps too late. Ginny had managed to fight off Random and was climbing into her SUV. Candy sprinted toward it and had just reached its front bumper when it backed away, tires spinning a little in the soggy ground. It shimmied back and forth erratically, until Ginny slammed on the brakes, switched gears, and gunned the engine, bringing the vehicle around, headed toward the exit. As it slipped and slid in the mud, Random barked furiously at the tires.

Candy glanced over toward her Jeep. She was about to run toward it and chase after Ginny. But she didn't have to.

The fire truck had left deep ruts in the lane. The tires of Ginny's big Explorer dropped right down into one of the deepest ruts. The SUV sank fast and quickly became mired in the muck. It must have been a rear-wheel drive edition, not equipped with four-wheel drive, like Candy's Jeep. The front tires popped up a little as the rear wheels spun viciously, digging deeper, unable to get any traction. As Random circled the vehicle, barking at it from every angle, Ginny gunned the engine again and again, but to no avail.

Mud season had claimed its latest victim.

"I've been thinking," said Neil Crawford a few days later as he sat at the kitchen table, "of getting out of the maple sugaring business."

"You are? Really?" Candy flicked her cornflower blue eyes toward him and tilted her head curiously. After taking a moment to consider his statement, she said, "Gee, I'm not sure if that's a good thing or a bad thing."

"Exactly!" said Neil, and he waggled a finger at her. "Once again, you've hit it right on the head."

"I seem to have a knack for doing that."

"You do indeed. It's one of the things I like about you."

"So what brought you to this momentous decision?" she asked, leaning forward so she could pinch off a small piece of his Chocolate Maple Brownie, which she popped into her mouth. It was a few days old, but still delicious. As she chewed, she arched an inquisitive eyebrow at him.

"Well, I'm sure you've heard what kind of week I've had."

"I've heard. It was a rough one."

"It was indeed. And, to be honest, I'm just not sure I'm cut out for it anymore — sugaring, I mean. I didn't realize it could be so, well, competitive."

"I think *cutthroat* is the word you're looking for," piped in Maggie Wolfsburger, who received a questioning look from her husband at her comment. She nudged Herr Georg. "Well, it's true, isn't it?" The German baker could only smile and nod.

"Money can make people do strange things," Candy agreed.

"It's true it got out of hand around here," Doc said. He was leaning back against the kitchen counter, arms crossed thoughtfully. "But it's not just here on the cape. There have been reports of stolen sap around this region for years. Burned-down sugar shacks too."

"Right, burned-down shacks." Neil let out a long, resigned breath. They'd released him from the hospital that morning, and Candy had driven up to Ellsworth to pick him up — taking Random with her, of course. And since it was his first evening back in town, she'd insisted he have dinner with her and Doc. He'd accepted, and been grateful for the invitation, but first he'd wanted to stop by the berry farm to survey the damage and pick up a few things. They hadn't stayed long. There wasn't much left to see of the sugar shack, except a still-smoldering foundation.

Now they were all gathered in the kitchen at Blueberry Acres — and the group had grown as word got around that Neil was back. Finn Woodbury and his wife, Marti, had come over as soon as they'd heard, bringing fried chicken and potato salad with them to help out with dinner. Maggie and Herr Georg ran over as well. She'd saved some brownies for them, and brought a big bowl of salad, homemade dinner rolls, and a peach pie. Artie had stopped by with his own homemade chili, and Bumpy had pulled in as well, bringing beer, wine, and chips. They'd just about finished eating dinner, and were lingering over coffee and dessert.

"So are you going to rebuild?" asked Bumpy, nibbling on a large slice of pie with a dollop of homemade whipped cream on top.

"Well, that's what I've been wondering," Neil said, looking at all the faces around him in the kitchen. His head was still bandaged, though not as heavily as the first day or two after the injury, and he was starting to get some color back in his normally weathered face. He was expected to make a full recovery. "I'm not sure I have the heart for it anymore, after all that's happened."

"That's perfectly understandable," Doc said, nodding his head. "You had a lot wrapped up in that place — a lot of your boyhood. Hard to replace what you've lost."

"Right," Neil said, "so I've been thinking that maybe it's time to start something new."

"What do you have in mind?" Candy asked. She sat at the table across from him, perched on her chair, listening intently.

Neil leaned forward and put his arms on the table, hands clasped in front of him. "Well, this might sound strange," he said, "but I'm thinking sheep."

"Sheep?" echoed Bumpy.

"Yeah, I had a flock in Vermont and, to be honest, I miss having them around. Maybe even a few alpacas too. Their wool would bring in some extra income, which would make up for the loss of maple syrup sales, and they'd give Random some company."

Random's ears perked at the mention of his name.

Candy liked the idea. "We could start

weaving," she said. "I noticed an abandoned loom down in the basement at the Milbrights' place. I might ask Hutch about it — though I think I'll wait a few weeks, give him a little space before I approach him again."

"Smart idea," Neil said. "And there's more. I've been thinking of switching the greenhouses over to herbs and organic plants — lavender, chamomile, basil, echinacea, that sort of thing. Ginseng, which I've heard can be pretty profitable. Maybe even organic peppers and gourmet mushrooms. I have a friend who's starting up a natural tea company. He said he'd buy just about anything I can grow, and I can sell the rest to Chef Colin down at the inn, and to a few other restaurants in town. I've even toyed with the idea of trying African violets and heirloom roses at certain times of the year."

Candy was impressed. "A major makeover then," she said.

Neil nodded. "As far as I can tell, there's not much competition around here for that sort of thing. Hopefully I won't disrupt anyone else's revenue streams or anything crazy like that."

"Well, that's mighty neighborly of you," Doc said with a nod of acknowledgement, "and, of course, you know we'll help out any way we can."

"I'm counting on it," said Neil.

The conversation turned then, and several of the folks in the kitchen moved into the living room as the local news came on the TV, to see if they could catch the latest details about Ginny Milbright. She was currently in the county jail, but was about to be transferred to a women's correctional facility near Augusta.

As a TV reporter standing in front of the prison began to tell Ginny's story, everyone crowded into the living room to hear what she was saying — except Candy and Neil. They found themselves sitting at the kitchen table, together, just the two of them, as twilight settled quietly over the blueberry fields outside the kitchen window. Random rested under the table at their feet.

"So," Candy said, breaking the silence, "it sounds like you have big plans then."

"I guess I do," Neil said. "I always do. But I'm beginning to think, well, I don't think I can do it alone anymore." He reached across the table and took her hand. "I know this might sound sudden, but like I said in the hospital, I've been thinking about it for a long time. I've been thinking, well, maybe we can do it together. You and I."

"You have?"

He nodded. "There's a lot we can do at the berry farm. And we can do a lot here at Blueberry Acres too. We can build that farm stand you've been talking about, and another hoophouse. Maybe we can join some of our operations together. Share some resources." He paused, then added almost shyly, "Share our lives."

With his other hand, he reached into his shirt pocket and took out a small black velvet jewelry box. "This was my mother's," he said. "I've been saving it for years, waiting for the right person. Well, I think I've found the right person." Releasing her hand for a moment, he opened the case and took out an antique engagement ring, which he held in the fingers of one hand. With the other, he took Candy's hand in his again.

He straightened himself, took a breath, and asked, "Candy Holliday, will you marry me?"

Candy could feel the emotions well up inside her. She looked at Neil's damaged face, into his gray-green eyes, and saw a future there. She saw not only a partner, but a friend, a companion, a lover. Someone to share laughs and memories with. Someone to grow old with.

She'd thought of this possibility, of this

moment, at fleeting times over the years, when her hand had brushed against his, or when she watched him laughing as he played with Random, or when he was simply staring at the stars with her, neither of them saying a word.

It was time, she thought, for her as well as for him. It was time to move on with their lives, to take the next step together. Only a small part of her hesitated, a small uncertainty at leaving behind a life she'd known so long, as a single woman. But she also knew she was ready to try a relationship again.

"Well," said a voice behind her impatiently, "are you going to give him an answer or not?"

Candy turned and saw her father standing behind her in the doorway. And everyone else was peeking around him as well, eavesdropping, expectant looks on their faces, curious to hear the conversation going on in the kitchen, the TV reporter forgotten.

Candy turned back to Neil. He was smiling at her, waiting for an answer as well.

Random jumped up then, sensing something of import was about to happen, and he obviously didn't want to miss it. He crossed to Candy and nuzzled her hand, and she reached down and gave him a quick scratch behind the ears. "Well, Random," she said to him, "what do you think I should do?"

But she already knew. She only had to look into his eyes — and into Neil's.

"The answer," she said, "is yes! Of course!"

And as they both rose, leaned across the table, and kissed, those gathered around crowded in with cheers, applause, backslaps, and congratulations. And Random barked joyfully.

RECIPES

THE BLACK FOREST BAKERY'S CHOCOLATE MAPLE BROWNIES

Serves 12

1/3 cup butter or shortening
2 ounces baking chocolate
1 cup sugar
1 teaspoon pure maple extract
2 eggs
3/4 cups flour
1/4 teaspoon salt

Preheat the oven to 325 degrees.

Grease one 11-inch-by-8-inch rectangular baking pan or 8-inch-by-8-inch square pan.

In a medium saucepan, over low heat, melt 1/3 cup butter or shortening. Stir constantly.

Add the chocolate and stir until melted and blended.

Take the pan off the heat.

Add the sugar and maple extract. Stir well.

Add the eggs one at a time, mixing well after each addition.

Add the flour and salt, mix until blended.

Pour into the greased pan.

Bake for 30 minutes.

MELODY'S MAPLE BANANA BREAD
Serves 8

3 bananas, mashed
1/2 cup sugar
1/2 to 2/3 cups maple syrup
2 eggs
2 teaspoons maple extract
1/2 cups chopped walnuts (optional)
2 cups flour
1 teaspoon baking soda
1/2 teaspoon baking powder
1/4 teaspoon salt

Preheat the oven to 325 degrees.

Grease a loaf pan with butter or shortening.

In a large bowl, mix the mashed bananas and the sugar.

Add the maple syrup and mix.

Add the eggs one at a time, mixing after each.

Add the maple extract and mix.

Add the walnuts and mix.

Add the flour, baking soda, baking powder, and salt a little at a time, mixing after each addition.

Pour batter into the greased loaf pan.

Bake for 60–70 minutes until a wooden pick inserted in the center comes out clean.

Cool and remove from the pan.

Doc usually devours this bread within minutes! Enjoy!

LIGHTKEEPER'S INN MAPLE GLAZED CARROTS

Serves 4

12 medium carrots
2 tablespoons butter
1/4 cup maple syrup

In a medium-sized saucepan filled with water, bring the water to a boil.

Clean 12 carrots.

Cut the carrots in 2-inch–3-inch lengths.

Put the carrots into the boiling water and cook for 10–12 minutes, or until tender.

While the carrots are cooking, melt the butter in a small saucepan.

Add the maple syrup to the melted butter and cook over low heat for 2–3 minutes.

When the carrots are cooked, drain the water out of the pan.

Add the glaze mixture to the carrots and mix.

Place in a serving dish or on a plate, serve hot.

MELODY'S CAFE'S
MAPLE DROP COOKIES
Makes 8 dozen bite-sized cookies

3/4 cup maple syrup
1/2 cup sugar
2 eggs
1 cup sour cream
2 tablespoons melted butter
2 teaspoons maple extract (vanilla can also be used)
2 1/2 cups flour
1 teaspoon baking soda
1 teaspoon baking powder
1/2 teaspoon salt

Preheat the oven to 375 degrees.

Grease one cookie sheet.

In a large mixing bowl, mix the maple syrup and sugar together.

Add eggs one at a time, beating well after each.

Add the sour cream and mix.

In a small saucepan, melt the butter. When the butter is melted, add it to the bowl and mix well.

Add the maple extract (or vanilla). Mix well.

Add the flour a little at a time, mixing after each addition.

Add the baking soda, baking powder, and salt. Mix well. The dough is a bit sticky, and that is fine.

Drop by small teaspoonfuls onto the greased cookie sheet.

Bake for about 8 minutes or until firm-looking and golden brown on the bottoms.

ABOUT THE AUTHOR

B. B. Haywood is the author of the *New York Times* bestselling Candy Holliday murder mystery series, including *Town in a Cinnamon Toast, Town in a Sweet Pickle, Town in a Strawberry Swirl, Town in a Pumpkin Bash, Town in a Wild Moose Chase, Town in a Lobster Stew,* and *Town in a Blueberry Jam.*

Author Residence: Monterey, MA & Gainesville, FL